Deuces Wild: *Beginners' Luck*

L. S. King

Deuces Wild: *Beginners' Luck*

L. S. King

Loriendil Publishing
Felton, Delaware
www.loriendil.com

Cover designed by MiblArt

ISBN-10: 0692345035
ISBN-13: 978-0692345030

www.loriendil.com

Printed in the United States of America

Second Edition

For Peggie Glanert

Foreword

There is something intriguing about the prospect of throwing two different temperaments together and watching the sparks fly. Especially when one party is a rigorously meticulous death-dealer, and the other is a happy-go-lucky life-giver.

In *Deuces Wild: Beginners' Luck*, we get to see the beginning of a classic, literary friendship. Two diametrically opposed personalities work together to forge their uneasy bond, thrown together by cruelty, circumstance, and sealed by something as old-school as "honor."

The real trick occurs when we realize that while we, ourselves, may not be lethal card sharks or dispossessed ranchers, we find something in their friendship that resonates with us. We observe the genesis of a relationship that will ultimately stand the test of time. However, the friendship is a genuine one, revealed in all its false starts, stubbed toes, and cantankerous reality. No great friendship is formed overnight, nor easily defined. Going in, there are no guarantees, especially when the friendship in question starts on the worst possible footing, as a matter of honor rather than a matter of preference. It is the grudging collusion of dark and light, civility and hickishness, violence and grace, brutality and mercy.

Deuces Wild is ultimately a discussion of the incomprehensible nature of friendship. Author L. S. King gives us a series, which combines the best Western vibe of Butch and Sundance with the space-faring vigor of Joss Whedon's *Firefly*. This is a new series whose elements feel familiar, but whose treatment is entirely fresh.

In the game of life, all limits are removed, the table is cleared, and all bets are open.

And with these two, the deuces *are* wild.

Johne Cook
Overlord (*Managing Editor*)
Ray Gun Revival

www.raygunrevival.com

Acknowledgments

Many thanks to James King for his invaluable help in creating the ships and weapons Slap and Tristan have been up against throughout all of the *Deuces Wild* stories.

Special thanks to Dr. Jonathan Crofts for his patience as he attempts to keep me from breaking too many physics rule outright.

These two men are my heroes.

Anything technically or scientifically NOT right in my stories is due to my own fallibility and misunderstanding.

Deuces Wild is dedicated to the memory of my best friend, Peggie Glanert; my inspiration for an enduring friendship.

< www.loriendil.com/Starsky >

Originally appeared as a monthly serial in
Ray Gun Revival Online Magazine

Deuces Wild: *Beginners' Luck*

L. S. King

Reluctant Allies, *part one*

Raucous laughter, human and alien body odors combining in the heat, and the smell of stale liquor assaulted Slap's senses as he walked through the open door of the Rocket Wash Bar. Paint flaked from the adobe walls. Off-world aliens aside, it wasn't that different from home.

Pack over his shoulder, he picked his way through the crowd, looking for a table. The few empty chairs didn't seem good choices considering the glares from those seated nearby.

Slap muscled through to the bar and after calling twice to get the barkeep's attention, he banged a hand on the counter. Two eyestalks swiveled to stare at him. Slap gaped for a second before saying, "Something to eat. And a drink. Anything."

The bartender turned around, his mouth twisting as he spoke. "Ten quel. Cash. No credchits."

Cash! Slap gulped and fumbled in his vest. If a meal and drink cost that much, what would a room cost? He put the money on the bar and glanced around as the bartender turned to the wall tap. A motion on his right caught his attention but something told him not to move his head or look down. Cutting his eyes, he saw a hand sliding a thin stim-blade out of a sheath sewn cleverly into a black vest.

Brago's Bands, what was this guy up to? A glass thunked the counter in front of Slap, and he wrapped his hand around the handle, while keeping attuned to the man next to him. He felt a slight tug at the pack on his left shoulder—a thief trying to steal? Without thinking, Slap swung around, and his glass impacted with a face. The 'thief' hit the floor, a needlegun clattering out of his hand. *What the—?* He stared at the unconscious man for a split second, but the sounds of a fight behind him made him turn. The man in the black vest thrust his stim-blade into a man's gut. The attacker screamed in agony. Black Vest then kicked a second— right into Slap's chest.

Slap threw an arm around the man's throat and tightened. As he waited for the struggling man to pass out, he watched in awe as Black Vest continued to fight two more men. He looked like a dancer—leaping, spinning, kicking. Before long his opponents all lay on the floor.

1

Slap realized the man in his arms had gone limp and dropped him. Black Vest turned, regarded the two men at Slap's feet, and gazed up with coal black eyes. "Thanks."

"Don't mention it."

People crowded closer, gawking at the bodies and muttering. Black Vest's gaze darted about as he sheathed the deadly knife. "I think we'd better leave."

Slap agreed and followed him outside. The night air felt fresh and cool. "Why were they all fighting you?"

"Quiet. We have to get away from here. Come on."

Slap shrugged his pack higher on his shoulder as he rolled his eyes, then followed Black Vest through the narrow streets. As hot as the days could get, the nights got cold, and Slap found himself shivering in his sleeveless vest as he peered ahead at the dark shape of his companion. Once he stumbled over a body in an alley and got a mumbled snarl as the person woke.

Finally they entered the gate of an inn. Slap blinked at the faux torches glowing at each side of the arch. Wouldn't real fire be cheaper? But then most of the lighting he'd seen hadn't been natural. He shrugged. City ways.

They took a flight of curved stairs to the left of the courtyard, barely illuminated by sconces dimly flickering with—yep, artificial light. Slap's hand ran along the rough-plastered wall to keep his bearings as they ascended. Once inside a small room, the man closed the door and turned the light on low. He faced Slap. "Now we can talk."

"Why were those men trying to kill you?"

"They were assassins." He ran a hand through his hair. "I think."

"Assassins? Who in the world are you that assassins would want to kill you?"

"Never mind." He walked to the bed and grabbed a small satchel from the foot of it. "By jumping in to help me you might have made yourself a target." He straightened and stared at Slap. "I'd advise you to get as far away from here as possible. Jump planet if you can."

"Jump planet? Brago's Bands, I don't even have money for a place to sleep, or food"—he thought with regret of the liquor lost

2

when his glass hit the one assassin's face—"much less enough money to get a ticket off this rock."

The man eyed him for a few moments. "I can help with that. But right now, let's see if we can get something to eat." He rummaged in the bag and pulled out a small item. He pocketed it in his vest, but Slap didn't see what it was. The man headed for the door. "There's a boarding house not far away that has a decent cook."

"What's wrong with this one?"

"It's known I took a room here. Too dangerous. Let's go."

Slap wasn't going to argue at the mention of food.

= = =

His companion ate quietly and neatly. Slap had the chance to really look him over in the flicker of the torchlight—real fire this time. His hair was dark and his skin naturally olive although it had a space-pale tinge. He was average height, which meant Slap's size dwarfed him. His bare arms, although not bulky, boasted defined muscle. But his eyes were unforgettable. They pierced like black ice.

The man had chosen a table at the outside of the courtyard and sat with his back to the wall. Although he remained still, his eyes darted here and there, always alert.

Slap shoveled food in his mouth as fast as he could, wishing he could untangle all the questions he had. But he had the feeling the quiet man across from him wouldn't answer anyway.

He slurped the hot rich drink—whatever it was. "Thanks for the meal."

Black Vest's only reply was to meet his eyes for a moment. Great. A real talkative type.

He thought about leaving the planet. Naw. He wanted to get far away from home, but not that far. As long as he was away from the Mordas, and the ruins of what used to be his homestead. He closed his eyes for a second as images of charred bodies and the smoking shell of his house flittered across his mind. He drank more of the hot brew, dashing the memories away with a large gulp.

The man stood. "I've paid your bill for the room tonight. I think you'll be safe." He tossed a small pouch on the table. "That will take care of getting you away from here—on planet or off. Thanks again for your help."

Black Vest strode out. Slap picked up the pouch and opened it to find more money than he'd ever seen. Well, whaddaya know.

= = =

Tristan wandered in the shadows, listening. Though new to the planet, and this port city, he knew the sorts of places to go to learn what he needed. Relief washed over him to find he merely had a bounty on his head from the leader of a local underworld faction called the Mordas. He smiled. He must have made a good impression when he hijacked both their incoming shipment and its payment.

At least it wasn't Dray's assassins. Yet. But Tristan's luck—and cunning—wouldn't last forever.

He wound his way through the back ways to a place he knew Mordas henchmen gathered to drink and brag. The bar had an old-style ducted heating/cooling system. It even had an outside entrance to the sublevel. Ancient architecture was so accommodating. He was soon inside and listening at one of the vents.

The drunken men vented their anger loudly both at their loss and that their boss blamed them for it. They were helpless and knew it. Tristan allowed himself a silent chuckle. These petty crooks were no worry. He started to rise when he heard a door slam and someone yell, "Get up, you lazy bums! We know where his partner is. Old boarding house near the shipyard gates."

Tristan ground his teeth. Complications irritated him. Granted, he owed that hick for stepping in, but why didn't he mind his own business in the first place? Now he owed that local his life. And Tristan always paid his debts. He had to get back before those men got there.

= = =

4

Slap yawned and stretched. The bed was comfortable and, surprisingly, clean. That off-worlder had good taste, that was certain. But was he crazy? Assassins, danger, having to leave—leave the planet? Yeah, Ol' Black Vest was loco all right.

He rolled up under the covers and tried to sleep. The creaks and groans of the old building kept making him jump awake. This was ridiculous. He rose with a grumble and snatched in the dark for his clothes. What he needed was a few stiff drinks to help him relax. He dressed, slid the sheath for his old-fashioned steel knife into the back of his vest, and donned his hat.

Halfway to the door, it slammed open and three men entered. Slap could see their outlines in the dim light of the hallway but knew they couldn't see him. He drew his knife and aimed—by the thunk and groan, he knew he hit his target. With a growl, he charged the other two and knocked them back. He picked one up by the neck and crotch and threw him across the room, then grabbed the other by the throat and squeezed before tossing him as well.

He felt along the floor with his foot until he found the body and retrieved his knife. Using the man's shirt, he wiped it clean, then straightened. He returned the knife to its sheath with a sigh. Black Vest might have been right.

"I see you did all right without my help."

Slap spun, hand on his knife, to see the slender silhouette in his doorway. Black Vest. He relaxed. "I guess so. These your friends again?"

"The local gangdom doesn't seem to like me. Or you, now that we are known to be acquaintances."

"The Mordas?"

"Yes."

Slap scowled. "I don't like them either. But I can take care of myself."

"So I see. But I think you're mistaken in your assessment. You're vastly outnumbered. Your best bet is to leave with me. My ship is docked on the southeast side of the port. We can be there and off this planet before dawn."

"And then what? I don't want to go anywhere else. This lousy rock is my home." Home—home was ashes, dead and desolate. No laughter, no life. Maybe another planet would be a fresh start.

But what did he know about this man? He had assassins after him, and the Mordas. He had money. And a ship. But—he'd come back to help when he thought Slap was in danger. That was enough. Slap grabbed his pack from the floor by the bed. He took a deep breath and gave a nonchalant shrug. "But who says folks can't leave home for an adventure or two? Let's go."

= = =

"This way," the local said when they got to the bottom of the stairs. Tristan followed him but stopped in the doorway and hissed, "The kitchen?"

"My breakfast is paid for and fighting makes me hungry."

Tristan sighed and leaned against the wall while the hick gulped down food. Young this one was, barely a man. He was very tall—a full head higher than Tristan—and muscular, broad-shouldered, but lean. Physical laborer, definitely. Probably a farmhand from his old-style denim pants and the felt, open crown cowboy hat. He certainly could throw bodies around. What planet could Tristan safely leave him on?

"Are you done yet?" Tristan asked as his unwanted companion wiped the plate with a piece of bread. "The Mordas could send more men."

Mouth full, the man stood. "Ready," he mumbled.

Resisting the urge to roll his eyes, Tristan headed for the back door.

"Hey, wait."

Tristan pivoted back around. "What now?"

"What's your name?"

He peered at the tall man in the glow from the niche-lights. It couldn't hurt to share the alias he used now. "Tristan."

The man nodded and stood, as if waiting for something. Tristan turned to leave and felt a touch on his shoulder. "Folks call me Slap."

Tristan stopped and twisted to look up into his face. "Slap? That's it?"

Slap shrugged. "It's all I need."

Tristan sighed and continued toward the back door. It could be worse. His name could be Lennie.

6

= = =

Slap followed quietly. He didn't try to talk, which relieved Tristan. They wound through the streets toward the space port, past open air markets, but the vendors were closed. Beggars slept in the street.

"Which one is yours?" Slap asked as they neared the gate for private ships.

Tristan pointed through the fence to a small craft at the far side of the dockyard. "Beyond the Falchion, between the two yachts." Not the best he'd ever owned, but it was a good ship.

Slap whistled through his teeth. "Cutlas class? Sweet."

Tristan nodded, but before he could say anything a flash made him close his eyes. An explosion thundered in his ears. A body knocked him to the ground, and he gasped for breath. More explosions shattered the air.

"Get off me, you lug!" Tristan shoved at Slap who rolled over and sat up.

"Just trying to protect you."

"I don't need it." Tristan brushed the dust off his clothes and rose.

"Brago's Bands," Slap said in a hush.

Tristan looked through the fence to where Slap gaped and bit back a groan. He stared at the flaming wreckage that had been his ship. All the supplies he'd stolen from the Mordas, and his way off this planet—gone. "You know,"—Tristan rubbed his forehead—"since I first laid eyes on you, it's been one thing or another."

Slap snorted. "If I hadn't wanted to stop and eat, we'da been aboard her." He turned, his eyes narrowed. "The Mordas really must want you bad."

Tristan gave him a grim smile. "Not as badly as I want them, now."

= = =

"So what are you going to do?" Slap asked as they hurried away from the gate.

"Never mind. Just follow me."

7

Slap hunched his pack higher onto his shoulder. "You know, that's getting irritating."

"What is?"

"You treating me like I'm a kid and don't know nothing. I'm in this with you, like it or not. Why can't you tell me what's going on?"

Tristan stopped and stared with those penetrating black eyes. Slap glared back, not willing to let this man get the best of him.

Finally Tristan turned and continued walking, saying over his shoulder, "When we get there. I want to move fast, and talking would slow us down."

Slap made sure his answering sigh was loud.

They left the spaceport and wove through the streets. The way grew dirtier—if one went by the reek of sewage—and, from what he could tell in the faint light of the nearly full moon, the buildings older.

Finally they arrived at the edge of a property that contained the burned-out remains of a factory. Several outbuildings still stood on the lot. They crept closer and hunkered behind a pile of charred timber.

"What's your plan?" Slap whispered, squinting over at his new friend.

"Since I stole that one shipment, they've gotten paranoid and moved their supplies out here." Tristan nodded toward a structure on their far left as he pulled on gloves and flexed the fingers. "I'm going to take care of the rest of their inventory. That should hamstring them long enough to suit me."

"So what are these supplies that are so all-fired important?"

"Munitions."

"Munitions?" Slap scratched his chin. "The Mordas are thugs, I know, but what would they need to stockpile munitions for?"

"They have buyers off-world. One of them is a nasty group of mercenaries. Makes the Mordas seem like peacemakers."

Slap frowned. "So what are you, some sort of space cop?"

Tristan stared at Slap for a moment with a look of astonishment and gave a silent chuckle. "No. I just don't like the buyers." Tristan rose slightly and peered over the top of the lumber. "Keep on the look-out. I'm going to sneak past the guards."

Slap lifted his eyebrows at the bold-but-insane plan. "That easy? What do you have, some invisibility screen?"

"Don't I wish." Tristan's eyes crinkled in a slight smile. "I have to use a more old-fashioned method. Stealth."

Slap watched in awe as his new buddy faded into the night, his dark clothes and hair making him almost unseen. He held his breath and chewed a ragged nail while waiting.

= = =

The few guards were easy to slip past. The property had enough piles of rubbish to cover much of Tristan's movement. If only that dratted moon would go behind clouds. He glanced up. Clear sky scattered with stars. Not even a wisp of haze. He crept around toward the back of the targeted outbuilding. Broken windows badly boarded up, the grate hanging by one hinge off an exhaust vent—they might be traps instead of easy entrances, but Tristan wasn't going in.

He lifted the vest to reveal the retooled ammo belt around his waist and set the timers for all the detonators. Fifteen minutes should be enough. He crept close to the wall. One through a crack between two boards at one window, another shoved past a broken pane of glass—on Tristan went, crouching and running from place to place, inserting his little devices.

Three to go.

A scrape—a boot on gravel. Tristan froze.

"Don't move," a voice from behind said.

The irony that Tristan had already stopped any motion faded into a chagrined grinding of teeth that so much kept going wrong. Was it bad luck? This planet? That yokel?

Fire bolted through Tristan's body—pain ripped through convulsing muscles. He dropped to the ground, unable to even scream. Then all went black.

= = =

His body thudded on a hard floor. Trembling. Nausea. Tristan opened his eyes. At the sight of Slap's face he closed them and shuddered. A nightmare.

9

A foot prodded his side.

"Is he awake?" asked a gravelly voice.

The detonators! Tristan's eyes flew open. How long had he been unconscious?

"Yeah," a second voice said.

"Get him up. The other one too. Search them for weapons and get something to tie them up with. You others, shoot them if they try anything."

Hands hauled Tristan to his feet, and he saw they were inside a dimly lit building. From the size, probably the ones where the munitions were stored. Great. More bad luck.

Slap stood, face pale, eyes unfocused. Tristan glanced down and saw the belt still around his waist. Not much time had passed, or no one would be here. What now?

Hands pawed him, removing his hidden stim-blade and the ammo belt.

Slap scowled as he was searched, and his steel knife taken away. He shook his head as if to clear it.

"Well, if it isn't our old friend, the homesteader. So, cowboy, we meet again."

Slap's head jerked up, and he spun to face a pale, slightly overweight man. "Lyssel! You murdering lizard! I'll kill you! I swear I'll kill you!"

Two men grabbed his arms but barely held him back. The ones holding weapons on him jabbed the air, yelling for him to be still as he lunged toward their boss.

Tristan took in the sneering man's sheened trousers and matching jacket—no standard pack-vest, the usual garb on this warm-climed planet. He watched Slap with interest, yet part of his brain tried frantically to figure out the time.

"Now, now, my oafish friend." Lyssel pulled a slender file from inside his jacket. He pointed it at Slap then began to clean under his nails. "You can't blame me that you lost your ranch and family. I offered you a chance to leave peaceably and you chose to stay."

"It was my home!" Slap yelled, tears streaming down his cheeks. "You burned it down. You made me watch them die, you murdering—"

One lackey punched Slap in the stomach with the butt of his weapon, doubling him over. Anger boiled up in Tristan. These men had taken everything from Slap. His own losses were nothing in comparison. If only he had a chance to break free—

A low growl grew into a roar and Slap straightened, fists smashing out to the sides. The men holding his arms hit the ground. He swung around and knocked one guard down—Tristan didn't wait to see more. He smashed the kneecap of the man to his right with his heel. His left arm snaked around his captor's, and he twisted to bring the elbow over his shoulder. He yanked downward and the man screamed.

Tristan dropped to a squat as a body flew overhead, then jumped into the air and shot a foot out to catch a guard aiming at Slap. The man tumbled, and Tristan scooped up the gun. He fired quickly, taking out the rest of the men.

His weapon and Slap's lay on the floor near an unconscious man. He sheathed his stim-blade and grabbed the steel knife, then took the ammo belt and slung it back toward stacks of boxes further inside.

Lyssel lay on the floor, trapped under a body, moaning in pain.

Slap stood, silent and shaking, face wet, gazing about him as if lost. Tristan had to get them away. If they didn't leave now, they'd be in orbit without a ship. He called the tall cowboy's name.

Slap turned, and Tristan pointed at the door. "Get out! Hurry!"

His friend grabbed his pack from the ground and joined him running for the exit.

"Don't stop," Tristan called.

They raced across the property, only able to distinguish outlines because of the moon. Tristan expected guards or the blast to knock them down, but nothing happened. Had Lyssel called all his men inside when he caught the trespassers, or did the dark cover their escape? A rover sat near a gate; Tristan veered toward it and jumped aboard. Slap dove inside as Tristan pressed the ignition.

The explosion rocked the rover as it rose, lighting up the sky. Tristan gripped the controls and fought to stabilize the craft. His lips thinned, and his knuckles turned white. The vehicle responded and he sighed with relief. A glance at the navigation console

11

almost made him chuckle. He looked over his shoulder to see Slap wiping his face on his sleeve. He held out the steel knife, hilt first. Slap took it with a nod.

"I found our way off the planet." Tristan pointed at the console. "This has an auto-direct to a private pad at the space port. I don't think we'll have much trouble acquiring Lyssel's yacht. What do you think?"

Slap gave a shaky sigh and a slight smile.

Reluctant Allies, *part two*

Tristan banked the rover, and Slap could see the spaceport's lights glowing against the night sky. They neared the entrance to the private pads on the south side. Slap blinked and wiped his face on his sleeve again. "Are you really going to steal Lyssel's yacht?"

"Of course."

"I don't know how I feel about stealing..."

Tristan glanced back for a moment. "It's not stealing to steal from a thief—especially a dead one."

That seemed to make sense. Slap remained quiet, fingering the knife Tristan had returned to him. As the vehicle approached the pad, he asked, "What are you going to do?"

Tristan landed the rover without even a bump. "Just play along."

"How can I, if I don't know what you're doing?"

The dark man closed his eyes for a second, then glared at Slap. "You're my bodyguard, all right? So just act the part and be a 'yes man.' You can do that, can't you?"

"Yes." Slap grinned and sheathed the knife.

Tristan jumped out of the rover, hailing the guards, who brought their weapons up. Slap clambered out and came up behind him, hoping he looked tough.

"Lyssel asked me to check on the ship." Tristan nodded toward the vessel.

"He didn't say anything to us," one guard said. "And we don't know you."

"Would I be using his rover if he didn't send me?" Tristan flashed a grin—a friendly, charismatic grin—and Slap found himself almost believing him. Brago's Bands, who was this guy, anyway?

"He's hired me to take care of some of his off-world business. He'll be along in a bit. He had a foul-up at the old Tellum factory, so told me to come ahead and check the ship."

The guard shook his head. "He can check all he wants, but nothing's changed. The parts haven't come in yet so the engineer hasn't been able to finish repairs. It'll be a week." The guard gave them a hard look. "Why would the boss send you when he already knows all this?"

Tristan scratched his head then smoothed down his hair, looking confused. "Why, I don't know. Does he have more than one ship?"

"Only the cargo ship."

Tristan snapped his fingers with a grin. "Ah, that's it. Makes more sense, too. Don't know why I—well, I guess it was because he said the rover had the coordinates, and I just..." He shrugged, his grin widening. "Guess I should have asked for clarification." With a wink he added in a stage whisper, "You won't tell on me, will you?"

The guards snickered. The one who had been talking lifted his rifle a bit with a nod. "The freighter is on the northeast end, at the cargo docks."

Tristan gave a jaunty salute and hopped back in the rover. Slap climbed in behind him, unable to believe his companion could so smoothly ease in and out of what should have been trouble.

A voice cracked over the guards' comm system and in the rover as well. "Rory, Gale—everyone! Lyssel is dead! We found him at the factory, and the rover is missing. Be on the lookout—"

The guards shouted, and Tristan muttered in a foreign language, jamming the throttle forward. Slap grabbed the seat as the rover rose, screaming. Pings hit the underside and rocked it as they flew off.

Slap whistled through his teeth. "That was close!"

"I can't believe they found Lyssel so quickly." He grumbled quietly—most likely cursing in his native language. "We need a place to hide and regroup."

Slap chewed his nail for a second. The Zendians wouldn't be happy at his bringing an outsider, but Tristan had saved his life and according to their ways, that made him a brother. "I know a place."

"Where?"

"The Zendi Mountains."

Tristan twisted to look full at him. "Aren't the Zendi one of the native races on this planet?"

"Yeah, they only live in that one mountain range."

"I've heard they can be unpleasant and don't like dealing with humans."

"Not usually. But they'll let us stay there." Slap met Tristan's gaze and saw the distrust, then added, "For a little while anyway."

"Which direction?"

"Only way is to walk. You can't bring any vehicles or equipment near the Zendians."

"Walk? How far is it? We don't have any supplies."

"Couple a days." Slap patted his pack. "Everything we need is in here or I can get as we go along."

"You're telling me anything we need to get safely to the aliens' mountains you have in that pack?"

"Yep."

"Forget it. It's crazy."

"Look, I know the land—"

"And I don't." Tristan veered the craft and flew it lower. "Hold on. We have to ditch the rover. I don't know if they can track it or override the controls."

Tristan set the vehicle down at the back of a warehouse in an industrial area at the edge of the city. Smart move. No one would be here this time of night—or rather early morning. Dawn couldn't be more than an hour or two off.

They hopped out, and Tristan whispered, "Follow me."

"Where're we going?"

"Away from this area. Just in case."

Slap followed him in the dark, almost bumping into him and once stepping on his heel as they wound around buildings and through alleys, sometimes backtracking. After Tristan hissed at him for stumbling into him for the umpteenth time, Slap grumbled back, "Maybe you got eyes that can see in the dark like a cat, but I don't!"

"Then put a hand on my back, and by Orion's belt, try to be more quiet!"

Slap sighed as they continued on, heading who knew where.

= = =

Tristan didn't want to worry his companion, but twice they had nearly fallen into confrontation. Lyssel's men seemed everywhere. Where could they hide? He couldn't see going into the mountains, especially on foot. Too easy to track and find while on the way. That—if he trusted his companion. He supposed he did, to the

15

limited extent he ever trusted anyone, but walking across unknown terrain to find some strange aliens? With no supplies?

However, Tristan was running out of options. They would be recognized by the Mordas anywhere they went. The answer struck him like a shock prod. He stopped short, and the cowboy knocked into him again, nearly sending him sprawling. He steadied himself with a hand against the side of a building, flaring his nostrils in irritation.

"What's the matter?" Slap asked.

"Quiet for a moment, while I think."

"Oh great," his tall burden muttered.

Tristan didn't deign to reply. He stared into the dark, trying to recall gossip and where he had heard it. What was the woman's name? Betts? Could she be trusted? Her story recalled another one, from long ago. That woman had been trustworthy. Tough call, but his choices were limited. He glanced over his shoulder. "Let's go. I think I know how to keep us safe and get us off planet."

"Good. Cuz I'm tired of wandering around and wondering if you've got us lost."

= = =

Slap grunted as consciousness seeped through his exhausted body, and he fought to stay in the blissful, dreamy cloud. A sharp smack on his backside made him roll over. "Hey!" He sat up, blinking and scowling at Tristan.

The woman, Betts, stood by the door; he clutched the silk sheets up to his waist. "Don'tcha know how to knock?"

Tristan tossed garments on the bed. "Get up. Here's your clothes. We're going to slip out of here after dark, disguised as a young scion and his servant. We'll take a sedan to the port, and once inside, we can commandeer one of the idle rich's yachts."

"You gotta be kidding!" Slap looked at the gold embroidery on the deep blue vest, and the jabot that would ruffle down the front. But it was the tights that made him shudder. The handsome woman walked up to stand next to Tristan and grinned. This had to be a joke!

Betts, with too much make-up and not enough clothing by Slap's standards, had cautiously taken them in. By the time they had eaten, news hit the street that Lyssel was dead, and she readily agreed to help them. The vicious gleam in her eyes at the mobster's name Slap could understand. He didn't know what had been done to her, but Lyssel had been greedy and heartless.

Slap scratched his curly hair with a scowl, one eye on those tights. The nap hadn't been enough, plus he was hungry again. Both tended to make him grumpy. "Can you do it, Betts?" Tristan asked.

She crossed her arms across her ample bust with a wry frown. "I'm no Henry Higgins."

"He isn't Eliza Doolittle, either."

The woman sniffed and brushed a wisp of blonde hair off her brow, then wrinkled her nose. "First step is a bath." She pointed to the tub in the corner of the bedroom.

Slap narrowed his eyes. "Now wait a minute—"

"If you can promise to wash thoroughly, I won't stay and scrub you. Although you might enjoy it."

Betts' voice was at the same time humorous and condescending. Slap couldn't decide if she was serious. But his face flushed hot. "I certainly ain't getting in a tub with you in the room, ma'am."

The corner of her mouth twitched, and she turned to Tristan. "I'll be back in awhile. Have fun."

When the door shut, Slap crossed his arms. "You ain't serious about this plan, are you? And how do you know we can trust her? I mean, I know she hated Lyssel, but that don't mean she's not going to turn us over to the Mordas."

"'The enemy of my enemy is my friend.' I think I can trust her—just as I think I can trust you."

"Think you can trust me? Thanks a lot, pal."

"How much trust should I give to a person I've known for one day? We have a common goal, but what, when that's over?"

Slap shrugged, conceding the point.

Tristan nodded at the tub. "Get in."

"Now, wait. I ain't said I'd go along with this crazy scheme."

"Do you have a better idea?"

"Well no, but I won't be party to stealing a ship. I don't care if it is some rich dandy who can afford the loss."

Tristan muttered in that foreign language again. "Then we won't steal a ship." He paused and shrugged. "Not exactly anyway. Now wash. And use the scented soap."

= = =

Slap stood, glowering, curly hair slicked down, as Betts adjusted the jabot.

Tristan straightened his own new clothes. Or lack thereof. Slaves of the high class wore only a loinwrap, sandals, and armbands, plus their House tattoo. Betts had stained his skin dark to pass as sun-bronzed and provided an ink that would last through water and sweat for the tattoo.

"Now," Betts said, brushing lint from the tall cowboy's embroidered vest. "Who are you?"

They had been reviewing this all afternoon. Slap sighed loudly and intoned, "I'm a visiting nephew of Amilie, late wife of old Lord Barthew's second son, Philip."

"You must remember to use a clear, strong voice when you speak."

Slap scowled, pulling at his neckline. "Yeah, yeah."

Betts snatched at the jabot. "Stop it—I had it straight. And don't say 'yeah.' You say, 'yes.' And if you can sneer as you talk, that's even better."

Betts stepped back, finger to her chin as she looked him over. "Tip your head up and look down your nose. Be condescending."

Slap did as ordered, his frown turning supercilious. Betts grinned. "Perfect! And you do look cute in tights."

Slap's face turned bright red.

Betts chortled. "Now, if you can remember to enunciate and use proper language instead of slang, you'll be fine. And if you do run into anyone unexpected, you have never visited Zenos before so you don't know all the customs here. That will buy you leeway. Cash should take care of the rest."

"That's no problem," Tristan said. "Speaking of which, are you certain I can't pay you?"

Betts' face hardened. "We discussed this already. You took out Lyssel. I know someone else will take his place, that's the way of

18

things. But my way is clear now." She stuck out her hand. "I'm glad to have done business with someone after my own heart."

"I have no heart."

"Precisely."

Tristan had no doubt she spoke the truth. He shook her hand, his eyes meeting hers.

She smiled. "I hope we meet again someday."

Tristan didn't. For now they were allies, but he wouldn't bet which side of the sheet this woman's loyalties lay from day to day.

= = =

One did not expect to see the high classes on this side of the city, but Betts' establishment was one of the few exceptions. Tristan wondered at the delicate balance between the rich and the Mordas that held Betts captive by Lyssel on one hand, yet relatively safe from his reprisals on the other.

In any event, the sedan driver saw nothing amiss that a young, rich scion would exit such a place late in the evening. Betts stepped up to the driver and pressed a gold piece into his hand. "Milord wishes to be driven to the private yacht gate."

Not the best solution, but it got Tristan and Slap to the space port itself, if not inside or near the shipyard. Betts leaned into the back, her endowments at full advantage. In a stage whisper sure to be overheard by the driver, she said, "Come back next time you're on-planet, milord, and I'll show you some exotic ways used by the Saurans."

The young man slouched, blushing, and Tristan, kneeling on the floor by his feet, clouted his ankle. Slap straightened, and cleared his throat. "I'll...I'll do that."

Betts grinned and winked, then nodded to the driver. She backed away, and the sedan rose slowly. The city fled under them and the spaceport lights glowed ahead, illuminating the sky. They neared the private gate, and Slap leaned back with an audible exhale. Tristan looked up, frowning, and gave a slight shake of his head. He never relaxed until he knew it was safe.

"Which yacht, milord?" the driver asked as they approached the gate. "I need clearance to fly to it, or else I'll have to land you at the gate."

19

"Land at the gate. My uncle expects me to be waiting for him."

Tristan winced. Arrogant, rich, young men did not offer explanations. But the driver merely nodded an affirmative.

The sedan landed within the lights flooding the entrance to the private pads.

Tristan jumped out, unfolding the step and bowing, eyes darting about, keeping alert. But the driver didn't move, and the guards at the gate stayed at their posts. All seemed normal.

Slap descended with a mincing step, head high, looking around as if the place reeked. Good. Tristan grabbed the bags and followed his 'master.' The sedan flew off.

Slap approached the gate with a prim strut, stopped, and put his hands on his hips. "Open up."

The guards exchanged glances.

"We haven't authorization, young Sir," said one.

"Insolent lizard! If you don't know who I am, you should at least know to use 'milord.' I demand to know your names! I will see that Lord Barthew knows of your disrespect!"

Tristan kept his face impassive but could not believe this ignorant cowboy was pulling it off! The guards stammered as Slap railed, shifting weight hip to hip as the fops often did. Finally he slowed his barrage and took out a handkerchief. He patted his face then fanned himself, huffing all the while. Tristan rarely had the urge to laugh out loud, but in this case, he had to restrain himself.

"We meant no offense, milord. Please! Enter!" The one guard keyed the switch and the gate swung open. "Lord Barthew's yacht is on the northeast side—"

"Now, wait, Joe!" The second guard threw out his arm. "We can't just let him go in without authorization. I don't care who he is."

"But Lord Barthew—"

"Call him. The union will back us up even against someone with his influence."

"I have authorization." Slap reached into the fancy vest and pulled out a pouch. He tossed it to the second guard.

The man stared at it for a moment then tossed it down. "A bribe!" He brought up his gun, but the tall local lived up to his name: he slapped the weapon out of the guard's hands with a growl. He then picked him up by throat and crotch and tossed him across the yard. The man hit hard and rolled, then lay still.

The first guard, Joe, stared with round eyes. With a blink, he lifted his sidearm, but Slap wrenched it out of his hands and threw it away.

Tristan didn't wait to see Joe's fate. He grabbed both weapons. A pitiful cry made him look up. Joe lay against the guardhouse, whimpering. From the angle, his leg looked broken.

That galoot was a one-man army!

Slap snatched up the pouch and tossed it at Joe. "For your trouble."

Tristan lobbed one of the guns at Slap then led the way as they ran into the dark. They had to avoid illuminated areas while they headed toward their destination. Sirens soon blared, and lights flooded the port, leaving few shadows to hide in.

"Now what?" Slap asked, ripping off the jabot as they hid on the dark side of a building. He wiped his face with the ruffled material then dropped it.

Tristan eyed it for a moment. "We have to get rid of these clothes." He peered in a window and saw lockers. Was his luck actually changing? About time. He couldn't wait to be quit of this planet!

"Glad to do it. But if we put on our regular clothes are we safe?"

"I wouldn't count on it. Wait one minute."

= = =

As Tristan melted into the dark, Slap stripped off the dandy clothes—those tights had to go! He scratched his legs and tender areas, wondering how the rich wore that stuff. His buddy returned a minute later and shoved clothes into his hands.

"What's this?"

"We're maintenance workers now. Hurry up."

"Brago's Bands! You never are short of ideas, are you?"

"Just get dressed."

Slap sighed and pulled on the overalls. They gathered at the waist, and had a vest-style top with open sides, a plus in this climate.

Tristan opened the bags and gave Slap his pack. Slap tucked the one guard's gun inside the waistband of the overalls with the fleeting thought that he was glad it had a safety. Especially considering where the muzzle was pointed.

His partner shed his slave get-up and quickly donned his new guise. He tossed his black vest over one shoulder and arm, hiding the tattoo and the gun. He carried his bag on his other arm. With a jerk of his head, he indicated they should start walking again.

Two maintenance workers shouldn't be noticed—Slap hoped anyway. They walked through the gate to the shipyards without anyone batting an eye. Tristan even waved to crewmen loading cargo.

"Which ship is it?" Slap asked, glancing at the dock-pad numbers. "Betts did get that info, right?"

"Yes. It's just ahead now."

Two men stood in front of the ship. It was small, a private cargo vessel rather than the typical huge freighter Slap had imagined. An older model, too—perhaps Canary class, probably one hundred years old, refitted at least once. It didn't look very space-worthy.

They walked toward the ship, Slap waiting for Tristan's nod. Just outside the circle of light from the dock pad, they pulled the guns and fired. Slap couldn't feel sorry—two more Mordas dead.

They ran up the ramp to the door and listened for a moment. Tristan nodded, then ducked inside. Was he taking a chance or could he hear that well to know no one lurked nearby? Not waiting, Slap entered and closed the hatch behind him. As a precaution, he closed the inner lock too. Tristan had found an access console nearby.

"I've locked out the cargo hatches," Tristan hissed over his shoulder. "No one can enter from outside now. Make your way aft on this deck, then around and fore to the bridge. Check all the rooms, the crews' quarters, galley, heads, everything. And don't get skittish and shoot before looking. It might be me."

Slap rolled his eyes. He turned and headed to the back of the ship, his heart pounding as he expected to find a Mordas henchman at every turn or inside each room. He sighed with relief when he finally got to the bridge.

Tristan lounged in one of the chairs, now wearing his black pants and vest. "Glad you finally arrived."

"I've been searching the ship, and you've been sitting here?"

"I checked the lower deck—cargo bay, engine room, then made my way up here. There's still a chance that someone is hiding aboard, but we're safe in here for the moment. I can change the registry after we lift off—Lyssel loaded a program that allows it. Makes sense in his line of work. Anyway, it frees us to go. Hook your pack and strap in."

Slap secured his pack, and the gun, then sat in the chair indicated, pulling the straps tight.

Tristan called for clearance, and when the tower questioned him, he reminded them whose ship it was, and that although Lyssel was dead, his business wasn't.

After a pause, the reply came. "Cleared for departure."

Slap swallowed, gripping the arm rests as the ship lifted off. What bothered him more—leaving the only planet he had known, despite the sorrows it contained, or the unknown in front of him?

Tristan looked over at him, a glint of amusement in his eyes. "You know, you looked quite natural mincing about in those tights."

Slap scowled. "They were binding."

Reluctant Allies, *part three*

"Occupants of the freighter *Manta*, this is spaceport security. You have pirated that ship. Return to the spaceport. This is your only warning."

Slap gripped the armrests even tighter, his eyes widening. "Brago's Bands! What now? Freighters don't have weaponry."

"Only defensive turrets. And they are"—Tristan's lips thinned as his hands flew over the panel—"engaged. Unless you have something against protecting yourself against your planet's space patrol."

Slap snorted. "You do know that most of the cops are on the Mordas' payroll?"

"I always assume such things. Makes life much simpler. My current worry is outrunning them. I wish we had a better ship."

"Well, why did you take this piece of junk?"

"Because someone's high moral stand against stealing left me few alternatives. Stealing from a dead man didn't offend your sensibilities too much." Tristan shot a cutting glare at Slap for a second before returning his gaze to the controls.

The ship rocked and shuddered, flinging Slap sideways. He grabbed the sides of the chair. "Hey, they're shooting at us!"

"Remarkably perceptive." Tristan peered at one of the readouts. "The turrets are operational. But there seem to be blind spots."

Two ships slid past their bow. Slap gasped. "They're cutting us off! We gotta get outta here!"

"I'm trying."

The ships now before them turned. A red light on the panel drew Slap's attention. "Incoming! I sure hope those turrets are working!" Slap leaned forward as he figured out the screen in front of him. "We have four behind, plus these two in front! Can't we go faster?"

"You want to get out and push?" Tristan snapped.

Slap ground his teeth. He knew he sounded like an idiot but he was helpless, no more than useless cargo. He knew how to fight on land—barehanded or with weapons. But being in space, on a ship with nothingness outside and no way to combat, he felt out of control, almost hysterical. If only he could do something.

A bright flash directly ahead made Slap wince. "What was that?"

Tristan chuckled softly. "So. The turrets aren't just defensive—they're offensive as well. Look at the display."

Slap glanced down. Two ships remained behind, and only one in front. He looked out the port again. Another explosion made him shut his eyes. "Brago's Bands! Lyssel knows how to refit a ship!"

"Indeed. I noticed when we came aboard that this thing has two capacitors for the jump engine, not one. And it's not the old-style heavy fusion reactor, but antimatter."

Slap laughed. "Not your typical cargo ship."

"No." Tristan sat up a bit straighter. "Hold on, we're at a Lagrange point. I'm going to engage the jump engine."

This was it! Slap was leaving his home. He had never wanted more than his family, his homestead. Others had looked up at the sky, watched the ships roar up into the atmosphere, and longed to leave, but not Slap. Yet here he was.

He wished he could see behind, see the planet. He closed his eyes for a moment in remembrance. Pale hair and blue eyes, a smile that could melt hearts—oh, sweet Shallah. Tiny arms waving above a happy baby face—little Evan, so innocent, given no chance. A long, grey visage emanating patience and wisdom—good-bye Ol' Pa. He swallowed hard and opened his eyes to see stars swirl then settle into place.

"What happened?"

"We jumped. I need to change the registry before we do anything else."

"So we're safe?"

"For now." Tristan didn't look up as he worked.

With a nod, Slap unstrapped. "I'm going to the galley. Want me to bring you something to eat?"

"No. But getting acquainted with this ship is a good idea. Take the gun and be alert in case we were wrong about being alone."

Slap grabbed the weapon and his pack and headed out the door.

The *Manta*, only needing a handful to man her, had merely one deck for the crew. Slap began checking the crew quarters and heads on the exterior wall, trying to tread softly on the metal floor plates so his boots didn't give a hollow *thunk* with each step. He left his pack in the port cabin next to the head and across from the galley. Nothing like convenience. The ship had six cabins for crew and two heads total. Four ladders led below, one fore and aft on both port and starboard sides.

When he had come full-circle to the bridge, he checked the interior rooms—the captain's cabin right across the hall, behind the bridge, a room that looked like a combination dining area and lounge, with doors that opened to the starboard and port sides of the hall. Lastly, the galley—his ultimate destination. His stomach rumbled in anticipation.

He opened the door and felt for the lights. They came on and he blinked. He walked across to doors he suspected were storage cabinets and opened them. Empty. He went over to the next doors—empty as well. Uh oh. He snatched another door open, then another. Shelf after empty shelf. A lower cabinet revealed bowls and utensils. He went to the corner closet, but a scraping sound made him pause, his stomach lurching. He pulled out the gun. *A rat. Has to be a rat. Those critters find their way everywhere.* But he hefted the weapon before yanking open the door.

A woman huddled inside, eyes wide, and curly hair falling around her face. "Don't hurt me."

"Who are you?"

"I'm an engineer." She sniffled and wiped her nose. "Who are you?"

"An engineer, huh? I was hoping you'd say you're the cook. Get out."

Slap backed up, his gun trained on her, as she crawled out and stood. He stepped sideways to the wall and keyed the comm. "Hey, Tristan, I found someone. An engineer."

"Space him."

The woman gasped, and her lower lip trembled. She looked ready to drop to her knees.

Slap sighed. "Uh, I don't know that I could do that. But anyway, it's a her."

"Even worse. Space her."

"I ain't gonna space no woman!"

"Then I will. Where are you?"

"The galley."

"Be right there."

"Now wait—Tristan? Tris? Awww." Slap keyed off the comm and glared at the woman for complicating things.

She burst into tears.

Great.

Slap wasn't going to let his guard down, tears or not, but he couldn't believe this woman was Mordas. She seemed too vulnerable.

Tristan soon entered, his own weapon drawn, and she backed against the wall, whimpering.

Slap held out his arm to ward off his dark companion. "I won't let you space her."

Tristan narrowed his eyes at her and gave Slap a disgusted look. "Her sex makes her no less dangerous. Probably more so. And if she is an engineer, locking her up is taking a chance. Who knows what mischief she could devise."

Could Tristan really mean to just kill her in cold blood? "But, you can't just space her!"

"Why not? She's Mordas. She'd space us if she could."

"I'm not!" The woman pushed her curly hair out of her face. "I'm not Mordas. Honest, I'm not! I'm just an engineer."

Tristan's lip curled. "Working at night?"

"They said they wanted the ship readied as soon as possible."

"I saw no tools or evidence of work being done in engineering, or anywhere else on the ship. And why didn't the Mordas use their own engineers? And what rate of pay does your union recommend for such unusual hours, hein?"

The woman stared at Tristan, mouth open.

He took a step closer, teeth gritted. "Who are you really?"

Slap held his breath. Tristan's voice had grown cold and hard, sending shivers up Slap's spine. Who *was* this guy?

With a snarl, the woman spun, one foot hooking at Tristan. He blocked. His fist shot out so quickly that all Slap could see was the result—the woman on the floor, unconscious. Slap whistled through his teeth.

"Pick her up."

"I won't space her."

"She's Mordas."

Slap clenched his teeth and hissed, "I don't care who she is. I won't space anybody!"

"You're going to get us killed with this attitude!"

"I mean it!"

Tristan's nostrils flared, and his eyes bored with black ice into Slap's. Finally he muttered to himself and said, "We can't leave her here. Pick her up."

Slap hesitated. He wasn't about to cart her away to space her. But Tristan was right; they couldn't just let her be. He started to put the gun in his waistband, then thought better of the idea—if she woke up, the weapon would be within grabbing range. He held the butt end toward Tristan. After the dark man took it, Slap leaned over and picked the woman up. She didn't weigh much, but from the kick she threw, she must know how to fight. Well, not against Tristan. Remembering how they met, he knew that his companion could take on several men at once and come out on top. She hadn't had a chance.

But what would Tristan do with her? He followed along until Tristan started down the ladder to the hold.

"You gotta be kidding!"

"Pass her down then."

Slap shook his head. He didn't trust Tristan. With a sigh, he shifted her weight and tossed her over his shoulder. He made his way down, feeling for each rung with his feet, and letting go with his one free hand to grab at the next crosspiece. Once at the bottom, he turned to his buddy. "What now?"

"We'll stow her as cargo."

"Why not just lock her in a cabin?"

"She might find a way out. But since this isn't an ordinary cargo ship, the hold has some special, hidden compartments that can be locked down."

"She'll smother if she's sealed in!"

"We can regulate air supply."

"And what about food and water?" Slap blinked, remembering. "Oh, forget about the food. We don't have any."

"We don't have much fuel either. We have to find a place to refuel and restock. And soon. We can dump her when we do."

= = =

"But who is she?" Slap dogged Tristan's heels all the way to the bridge. "I mean, if she were a guard, she'd have a gun, right?"

"I don't care if she's the captain, the captain's mistress, part of a cleaning crew, or the mascot. She's Mordas." Tristan keyed the lock and entered the bridge. He sat, his eyes scanning the read-outs.

"But we can't—"

"Look," Tristan twisted to look up at the tall irritant. "I have more important things to worry about. Like getting fuel."

Slap nodded. "And food."

Tristan turned back to the controls, not deigning to answer.

"Where can we get fuel and supplies?"

Leaning back, Tristan said over his shoulder, "If you see a flashing sign for a quick-stop way station on an asteroid, let me know."

The chair spun, snapping Tristan around to face the cowboy. Slap's face snarled close to his. "Stop treating me like an idiot. I'm outta my home pasture, and I know it, but I ain't stupid! I think I asked a fair question. Where can we get fuel?"

Tristan nearly retaliated but held himself in check. The cowboy had a point. But Tristan's temper tended to be proportionate to his stress level. And being saddled with this sidekick definitely had spiked the latter. He inclined his head in acquiescence.

Slap slowly straightened.

"Let me check our position and see what might be nearby." Tristan hesitated, adding, "Nearby being relative. Keeping this ship operational until we can refuel might mean limiting power."

"Wouldn't it be a good idea to do that now? Just in case?"

"Can't hurt." Tristan pointed at the other chair. Might as well teach the man something so he could earn his keep. "You can pull up the power read-outs and see where we can conserve. But don't cut power to anything without asking, it might have repercussions you don't realize."

Slap sat with a grateful look, glancing over the board. "How do I access 'em?"

Tristan bit back a smart reply. Instead he tried a small smile. "I bet you can figure it out."

29

Slap looked surprised, then snorted and pored over the board. Good deed for the decade done, Tristan turned his attention to the nav display. There had to be some place near—a colony, base, mining operation, something. He checked the distance of the choices the computer presented. Not good.

The blessed quiet broke when Slap shouted, "Ha! Got it!"

Tristan closed his eyes for a moment, before resuming his search for something close and workable.

"You know, it looks like we could cut most power to this deck. The rooms are all empty." A low rumble made Tristan look over. Slap glanced down toward his stomach and shrugged with a sheepish grin. "Even the galley isn't being used."

"Makes sense. I'm sure you'll want to keep power to that aft compartment where the stowaway is."

Slap shot him a dirty look, and nodded at Tristan's board. "Find anything yet?"

"Our choices are spare. And dicey. I'd suggest we shut down anything we can."

Tristan didn't mention spacing the woman again although that would save energy. Slap didn't understand the danger they were in, and had enough morals to get them killed. He had to find a place to leave the cowboy. And soon.

"So what is it we need? The hydrogen or anti-hy?"

"Hydrogen. The anti-hy is only available at deep space depots, for obvious reasons. They had filled up before landing."

"I don't get it. Why didn't they have the hydrogen tanked up?"

"Same reason the galley isn't stocked. They weren't planning to go anywhere, so they didn't have the ship ready."

"Great. Do you usually run into this problem when stealing a ship?"

Tristan glared. "I'm not in the habit of stealing ships." *Often.* "We were a bit pressed for time and limited in choices, if you remember." Tristan let his breath out in a sharp exhale. "If I keep this ship for any length of time, I'll have to outfit this tub with a hydrogen scoop."

"What's that?"

"Just what it sounds like. A large portion of solar wind that flows out from a star is pure hydrogen plasma. If we had a scoop, we'd not have to worry about running short of fuel. But Lyssel must only have used this ship for specific, short trips."

"So do we have any other alternatives? I mean, is hydrogen all you can use for the matter?"

"Anything that can be turned into a gas can be used, if the ratio of matter and anti-matter is adjusted. But other than the ship's atmosphere, we don't have much available. And I don't want to give up breathing just yet. Now if you don't mind, I'm trying to calculate which is our best destination."

"Um, wouldn't that be the one that's closest?"

This is why I prefer solitude. Tristan took a deep breath. "Not necessarily. The closest is a low-tech colony, agricultural. They have a reputation for not liking visitors. The next is a military installation."

"Agricultural, huh? Just farming, or do they have ranches too?"

Oh, what an easy solution if he could just dump the cowboy on those people! But no. He shook his head. "You can't just land and ask for a homestead. They have about a year's worth of red tape to get approved. They're Separatists."

Slap sniffed. "So were my folks. But it didn't stop others from trying to horn in on them. You think they'd help if I gave them some pretty patter?"

Tristan whirled around in the chair and stared at the cowboy. "You don't seem to be a very smooth talker."

"Yeah, not like you. But I know these type of folk." Slap scratched his chin and grinned. "I can talk their language."

"If they don't help us, we're stuck."

Slap chortled. "If they don't help us, they're stuck with us."

Tristan looked the cowboy over as if seeing him for the first time. Was there more to the man than met the eye? Blue eyes sparkled as if Slap knew he held a winning hand. What the hell, let the kid try.

"We have just enough charge in the one capacitor to make a short jump. From there, we'll be near enough to the colony to do a quick burn on the plasma drive and drift in. That saves just enough fuel that we should be able to safely land. So that puts our ETA at five hours."

Slap nodded, frowning. "What about the woman?"

"Let's worry about fuel before we worry about her. If I were you, I'd take care of any personal needs now. Once we're drifting, we'll need to be strapped in. I have to cut inertial dampers, or we'll lose too much velocity. And if you're a praying man, pray. Because we're vulnerable the whole time we're adrift."

= = =

Tristan closed his eyes. He hadn't slept yet since meeting his new companion. No wonder he felt so testy. He could doze for a few hours and might as well, since he couldn't do anything until they reached the colony. He let himself fade into blessed oblivion—

Tp tp tp t-t-t-tap. Tp tp tp tp t-t-t-tap. Tap.

Tristan's eyes shot open, and he glared at the cowboy's fingers drumming on the arm of the chair. "Do you have to do that?"

"Hm? Sorry. I'm bored." Slap subsided, sighing, then sat up straight with a gasp. "Say—what about the woman?"

"What about her?"

"We didn't warn her. What if she gets hurt?"

"That's her tough luck. If she stays still, and nothing hits us, she'll be fine."

"But—"

"It's moot. We can't go warn her now."

Slap leaned back. Tristan closed his eyes again.

"So where are we going after we get fuel?"

Tristan blinked. "Look, I'd like to rest a bit before we reach the planet. Do you mind?"

"Huh? Sure. No problem."

Slap hummed to himself, and Tristan gritted his teeth. Only four and a half hours more.

= = =

"What's the new name of this bucket?"

"Giselle."

"What's that?" Slap asked, wrinkling his nose.

"A name. Now go ahead and call."

"Um." The cowboy keyed the comm. "Cargo ship *Giselle* calling Voolmurra Colony. Request permission to land."

After a wait, the answer came: "We have no record of cargo due, *Giselle*."

"Yeah. I know. I'm sort of in a bind. I just need fuel and supplies. I can pay."

"We don't do much off-world trade, and we don't like outsiders."

"I hear ya. My folks were Separatists too."

"Were? You're not?"

"Were meaning they're dead. And I was turned off my homestead. Guy who sold me this ship cheated me on top of it. That's why I need supplies."

"You were cheated, yet you have money?"

"I hired on a captain, seeing as I don't know much about ships." Slap cut his eyes over to Tristan. "He has a little stake he'll give, seeing as his belly is as empty as mine, and he's as stuck in space as me if we don't get some fuel."

"And you're really a Separatist?"

"I had a great spread. Third generation. Fertile land, lots of cattle, and some pretty mustangs too. I lost it all." Slap's voice caught, and he continued on in a softer voice. "I lost my family."

Silence. Tristan held his breath. The cowboy had to be convincing; he was telling the truth. But would these people believe him?

"Switch on your viewer."

Slap did, and a man's weathered face peered through the monitor.

"Young one, aren't you? But your face is tan, not pale like a spacer." The man hesitated then asked, "You aren't looking for a new stake here?"

"Naw. No offense, but I wanna get farther out. Know what I mean? The Dusties are all over this sector."

Tristan frowned for a moment then realized that Dusties was a slang term for Industrialists. A term to note and remember.

"Yeah. Hold on." The Separatist looked down for a moment and sighed. "Permission granted. The beacon will guide your ship to its dock. But only you are allowed off the ship. Your captain will have to stay aboard."

"No problem. Thanks."

After transmission ended, Slap slumped back in the chair, letting his breath out with a loud *whoof.*

Tristan silently agreed. And he had to admit, the kid did a great job. Now if those Separatists just didn't change their minds.

He leaned forward and passed an e-pad to the cowboy. "Here. I anticipated they wouldn't let me aground. I made a list of what we need. And don't let them try to trick you into deuterium—we need cheap. I'm not worried about a more efficient energy yield."

Slap nodded, reading the e-pad.

Tristan tapped the cowboy's arm to make sure he had his attention before continuing. "Now, they may not take the quel from your planet or credchits. Ask, but be prepared if they say no. I have an account they can pull from, or if they demand cash, I have enough stellars to buy whatever we need. They'll probably hike the price, and I don't know how much dickering you can do—they know we have no choice."

Slap stood and crossed his arms. "I was bargaining horseflesh and selling cattle for my father when I wasn't but two spits tall. I'll get what we need."

= = =

Slap shook his head, trying not to sweat. "I'd have expected those prices for deuterium, not hydrogen. I can't spend that much on fuel. We need food, or we ain't going nowhere."

"That's my best deal, son." The man leaned back on his desk. "Take it or leave it."

Slap let his shoulders slump and scratched his cheek. "Then I guess I'll be seeing about hiring on somewhere. My captain won't be happy, but if it's a choice of sitting on a ship and starving, I'm sure he'll work to earn extra so we can buy what we need. How long do you think it would take for us to earn the difference between what I've got and what you're asking?"

The man straightened. "You serious?"

"Dead serious. I told you. I was cheated when I bought that bucket. I wouldn't have this much to spend if my captain hadn't had some stake put away. I'll be back." Slap turned and put his hand on the door. "Some time."

"Wait."

Slap hesitated, and slowly turned, keeping his expression sorrowful. Would the threat of outsiders stuck here outweigh this guy's greed?

The man rubbed his neck. "If I cut the price much lower, I'll take a loss."

"I understand. I just can't pay. Thanks anyway." Slap opened the door.

The man groaned. "All right. But it's got to be cash up front."

Slap squinted, hunching his shoulders. "All I've got in cash is quel. My captain has some stellars. Are they all right?"

"Yeah, I'll take both. Quel is as good as stellars, being so close to the Three Systems."

= = =

The dock hands left, and Tristan checked the cargo one more time. All the supplies were aboard. Everything was going well. Only one problem remained. Gun in hand, he went to the compartment where the woman was and unlocked the door.

She sat huddled in the corner, arms around her knees. Blinking, she covered her eyes against the light. Then she began cursing.

"Softly, softly." Tristan backed away from the opening. "You can leave."

"What? You lock me in the dark and leave me forever, then I get bounced around and bruised—"

"You're lucky that's all that happened. I said you can go. Or I can turn you over to the port authorities as a stowaway."

She lifted her chin while rubbing her arm. "Who do you think they'll believe?"

Tristan gave her a cold smile. "I know whose story they'll buy. So it's your choice."

The woman bit her lip, doubt on her face. She stood and sidled past him, eye on the gun, then ran across the cargo deck and down the hatch.

Tristan sighed in relief. Now, where was that cowboy? He secured the bay and headed up to the bridge. He opened the door and stopped. Slap sat, chewing and gulping.

"Hey, Tristan, lookee what I got!"

Tristan slid into his chair, and secured himself. "Don't tell me you bought something that wasn't on the list."

"Strawberries!" Slap grinned and held up the box. "Not many cuz they go bad fast."

"Why in the world did you buy fruit?"

"When was the last time you had real strawberries?"

"I can't remember. What did you spend?"

"Altogether? About one hundred less stellars than you expected."

Tristan stared. The cowboy might just come in handy. He nodded. "I've taken care of our other problem."

Slap scowled then his eyebrows lifted. "The woman? What did you do to her?"

Tristan shrugged. "I let her go."

"You what?" Slap's eyes bugged out. "Why?"

"I told her she could be turned over to the authorities as a stowaway—and who would they believe, us or her—or she could make a break for it. She took off." Tristan paused a moment as he scanned the read-outs. "Too bad we can't stay and find out how she likes being stranded on a Separatist planet."

"But, what if she tells them she's Mordas? That we stole the ship?"

Tristan smiled. "Doesn't matter. We're leaving. Strap in."

Knight Errant

Slap descended the ramp from the ship, pack on his shoulder, taking his first look at a space station. Beyond the security gate, humans and aliens jostled each other, all in a hurry to get someplace. Shops and restaurants lined the inside wall of this level of the civilian docking ring.

As Slap approached the gate, he held out his ID. Tristan had told him who to contact to get a new, forged one, but now that he was off Zenos, he didn't think the Mordas would still be looking for him.

With a bored nod, the guard let him through.

Slap turned to Tristan, who followed him.

"This is it. Good luck, cowboy."

An empty feeling sucked at Slap's insides. "What?"

"You'll be safe here. You have enough money to buy a homestead on any of several colony planets. Won't have to indenture yourself."

"But, but I thought..." Slap's voice trailed off at Tristan's expressionless gaze. He swallowed. "Never mind. G'bye."

Slap took off, cursing by stride, not caring where he went in the crowd. He didn't need Tristan. It's not like they were friends or anything. His long gait took him past stores, offices, hostels, restaurants with tempting odors that made his mouth water, and finally, anger abated, he stopped, lost.

Sort of lost anyway. The concourse circled the entire ring, unbroken. Eventually, he would find himself back at his starting point. He didn't want that. Tristan might be there—might see him and think he was hanging about.

So. What now? Slap took in the nearby businesses. Tourist traps. Not that he knew from experience, but Tristan had warned him about them. All glitz to blind gullible travelers' eyes and take their money. He needed a cheap place to flop for the night—when was night on a space station, anyway?

He began looking for hostels. The first one he found was fancy, and the prices made him back out of the door, the man behind the desk giving a knowing smirk. He nearly fell over two people, dressed in rich, frilly clothes. The man wore tights—Slap shuddered. They shot him looks of disdain.

Reason kicked in. Slap looked around and found what he needed. A map of the ring near an entry gate. Private yachts docked in this section, and luxury liners in the next. So...to find a cheap room and food, he needed...what? He ran down the list. Most likely, the section of the ring they came in on—cargo. Yeah, figures. Great. Back where he started. Well, maybe he wouldn't see Tristan and have to ignore him.

= = =

Tristan breathed in relief as the tall hick strode away, not allowing himself to look after the man. *Out of sight, away from me. Safe. Safe!* He walked with a deliberately casual air into the ring. Appearing to window shop, he made his way along the concourse, toward a little café.

He slipped into a chair of a corner table, back against the wall, and punched in an order for café au lait.

His contact sat at almost the same time the dispenser disgorged the drink. Tristan noted with absentminded irony that the man's weasel-like looks and mannerisms matched his character.

His skinny contact leaned close. "Took your time getting here, MacCay. You were due days ago."

He glared at the presumptuous little git. "I come and go as I please, Hadley." Tristan picked up the cup and sipped. With a grimace he set it down; surely someone could program the computer to know what lait was. Café, too, for that matter.

"J-just so." Hadley's Adam's apple bobbed a few times before he plunged ahead. "My employer is more than anxious to hire you for a transport job. You still have the Cutlas?"

"No."

The little man blinked. "What ship do you have now?"

"Old Canary class cargo ship."

Hadley's mouth dropped open and moved wordlessly for a few moments. "That...that is not acceptable. We need a yacht or at least an upscale cruiser to get...this merchandise to its new owner."

Tristan didn't change his expression, but he had the feeling this was a job he wanted to walk away from. He had never carried cargo for these people before and this didn't seem like a good time to start.

He took another sip, continuing his thoughts. Merchandise didn't care how it was transported unless sentient. What, no, who in the name of Dallor's moons did they want him to sneak off the station? And was the merchandise really willing cargo? Or was the merchandise running from someone who didn't want to lose possession? Unless perhaps—no. No further speculation on the merchandise. It would only cause a headache.

Pushing back his cup, Tristan stood. "I can't help you." He left the café, ignoring Hadley's stuttered protestations.

= = =

Tristan adjusted the black evening jacket and sat back in the cushioned chair. He sipped his wine and listened with great appreciation to Mozart's "Die Entfuhrung aus dem Serail."

He cut his gaze at a man approaching his table. Dressed better than most of this establishment's patrons—brightly colored silks cut in the loose style of Eridani. Strange planet, bound by caste, ruled by an Emperor. Too hot, too dry, too stifling—no free trade. Not in the sense Tristan enjoyed anyway. One visit had been enough.

The man bowed. To a non-Eridani? A servant. Tristan gave a slight incline of his head, and the intruder sat, his eyes darting about the room.

"Sir. My master wishes to speak to you on a most urgent matter."

Ah, high Eridani accent, yes. Not servant then. A thrall. A cultured, educated slave—one trusted and highly favored.

"And who is your master?"

"He...begs his privacy. I am to take you to him."

"No."

The thrall blanched, licking his lips. "But, Sir—"

"I am preoccupied." Tristan nodded toward the orchestral chamber and actors. "And am under no constraint to bend my neck to the whims of some spectral perspective employer."

Tristan turned his attention to the opera, dismissing the wide-eyed slave.

= = =

One positive aspect about a space station was that it never really became dark. No black alleys in a moonless sky, no shadowed doorways allowing predators to lie in wait. Only a dimming of the lights.

Tristan left the dinner-theatre relaxed, alert, and prepared. Polite invitation rejected, he would be summoned more forcibly.

Two massive men with swarthy features, wearing silk pantaloons, wide sashes, and vests, loomed beyond the marquee of the establishment next door. No weapons. Kudos to station security. They stepped out to block his path.

He sighed.

= = =

Muscular guards in silk vests and pantaloons and carrying scimitars flanked the entrance to the ship. Tristan eyed the yacht as he was led through the corridors. Gilded panels, woven matting on the decks—high nobility.

His hulking escort eliminated the force screen, and ushered him through a curtain of beads into a chamber meant to impress lesser beings. Traditional Eridani music dominated by mewling pipes and plucked strings haunted the air. Icons to the Seven Holy Sons of Afanasi stood on pedestals along walls, and at the far end, a niche with the image of Afanasi herself. A slight haze from incense hung in the air, candles flickered from tiered tables, large cushions littered the floor. At the far end, a throne sat on a dais. Tristan regarded it warily, his stomach sinking.

Not good.

Four guards came into the room. They took their places two on each side of the dais. Two more entered, a glowering dark-haired man perhaps in his twenties walking between them, the arrogant tilt to his head emphasizing his large, square jaw. He stood in front of the throne, his eyes coming to rest on Tristan. The Emperor, Vasso Istvan himself. Off planet.

Definitely not good; his chances for living through this encounter were less than winning the galactic lottery—without having bought a ticket. Istvan was known to reward a job well done with a knife in the back. Figuratively, and occasionally, literally. At least it was quick. Those who failed while in his service bought it much slower.

His escort prodded him in the shoulder. "Kneel."

Tristan ignored him, returning the imperial stare. He wasn't going to give more to this madman than necessary. He needed to try to keep an edge. Perhaps find a way to survive. "I am not a subject of His Majesty, or in his service. My required attitude of respect is a bow." He bent at the waist, lowering his gaze. When he rose, the Emperor had seated himself.

"It ill suits you to bend your neck, does it not?"

The corner of Tristan's lip quirked. "Your Majesty knows me."

"I begin to. But not well enough, I warrant." The monarch's eyes narrowed. "Why does only one guard accompany you when I sent two?"

"The other is awaiting medical attention, Sire." Tristan hesitated and added, "Whatever you have been told about me, it hasn't been very accurate for you to send a mere two goons to compel my attendance."

"Indeed? So why didn't you take out both?"

Tristan shrugged. "I needed one to bring me to you."

Istvan sat back, his expression less saturnine and more pensive. "And reports that you are able to be...subtle and discreet, are they exaggerated?"

"Your Majesty," Tristan resisted a small smile, but one eyebrow lifted slightly in amusement. "I can be invisible, if necessary."

The Emperor tapped his knuckles on the arm of the throne, his eyes still glued to Tristan. But Tristan just stood with sang-froid. He knew this game, and was its master.

Istvan broke the long silence by clearing his throat. "You might do." He gestured to a cushion at his feet. "Come. Sit with me, and let us talk."

"You are assuming I seek employment."

The ruler of Eridani drew up, his face darkening. "Do not think you can play with me, Derek Malcolm. You will serve me willingly or unwillingly."

Tristan's gut tightened. He hadn't used the Malcolm alias for several years. Who had Istvan gotten his information from? And he was known here as MacCay—that name would probably have to be abandoned as well. He ground his teeth—no, he mustn't appear perturbed. He consciously relaxed his posture and gave a hint of a smirk as he came forward and sat on the cushion. "You tell me what you need, Your Majesty, and I will see whether I think I can assist you."

Istvan's eyes gleamed as he leaned forward. "It is my sister. She has been kidnapped. I want her returned."

Tristan frowned. "What ransom have they demanded?"

The Emperor hesitated, his gaze flicking away. "None."

Uh oh. What's really going on? "Who has her? Do you have any idea?"

"Well, yes." Istvan frowned. "No."

Tristan waited, hiding his amusement at the sovereign's apparent obfuscation.

"You must understand our politics," Emperor Vasso rubbed his chin. "My cousin Abbra is behind a movement claiming the throne. Based on faulty reasoning about succession concerning both our grandfathers."

Tristan nodded, not offering his opinion of the 'faulty' reasoning. He was reminded of the Carlist faction ages ago in Spain. "The Orrilan movement. Yes." Puzzle pieces clicked into place. "Abbra has her." His eyes narrowed. "To marry. It would consolidate his Imperial claim. For himself, if anything happened to you, and even more so for a son. Plus name himself regent." Vasso had only sired daughters—no males to name heir. But a son of Vasso's sister could claim the throne when he came of age. If he came of age. Would Abbra's bride and son live long once he was named regent?

Istvan's eyebrows raised. "You have a quick mind."

"So you want me to rescue your sister from your cousin?"

The Emperor looked pained. "It's not that simple. I had a man in Abbra's camp. Pella. He was to send information to set up my cousin so we could arrest him for attempted kidnapping. Be done with him once and for all. But, he...double-crossed me, and Abbra as well. He has Nadi. It is a race now as to who finds her first."

"What is this man's interest in your sister?"

Istvan shrugged. "We can only speculate. My intelligence hasn't anything solid yet. Some think he likely wishes to make a deal with whichever of us will pay the most. But we have received no ransom, not even any message. We have traced them here, but the station authorities will not permit us to search." His fists clenched on the arms of his throne. "And they are doing nothing. The insolent peasants will not even let my men on the station armed."

Tristan resisted a smile. It wouldn't do to irritate His Royal Haughtiness. "So you know Pella and your sister are here?"

"The ship Pella stole is docked here. Since it has Imperial Eridani registry, we confiscated it. No one was aboard. Pella hasn't been seen. Neither has Nadi. We don't know if they are still here, or if they've booked passage and left."

Tristan inhaled slowly, thinking of Hadley. He looked up at the Emperor. "A man trapped might become desperate. I feel we must move fast. Sire, give me what information your intelligence has on this, and I'll see what I can do."

Istvan sat back with a smug smile.

"I cannot promise. And"—Tristan raised a hand—"threats cannot force me to do more than my best."

Emperor Vasso barked a small, nasty laugh. "It seems you know me."

Tristan wished he didn't.

= = =

Slap peered at the numbers on the doors along the dim corridor. Twenty-three. He had to find the room soon and lie down. Twenty-five. The cheap meal sat heavy on his stomach. Ah. Twenty-seven. He passed the key over the reader. The door slid open, and a dim light came on.

A bed with a chest at the end, and a small comdesk across from the bed. Slap peered into the lav. He snorted. Tiny but at least it had a sonic shower. Well, he'd only be here until he could decide where he was going. He'd checked with the Bureau of Colonial Affairs and getting a homestead on a colony planet was complicated. Lots of red tape even with the money to buy one outright. Might take a year or more.

And, after some thought, Slap decided he didn't want a homestead anyway. Lonely and alone on a strange planet with no family. No wife. His stomach knotted. He tossed his pack on the bed, forcing his mind away from agonizing memories.

After shucking his clothes and a cursory cleaning up, Slap stretched out on the narrow bed and rolled up in the thin blanket.

Muffled loud voices pierced the haze of near-sleep. Slap opened his eyes a slit. How can noise travel through metal walls? The voices continued, then a girl started crying. Slap pulled the pillow over his head.

The crying continued. It turned into a wail, and Slap sat up with a sigh. He didn't like to intrude, but he needed some sleep. He dressed and walked to the door. The key! With a snap of his fingers he turned and snatched it from the desk and stuck it in his pocket.

The noise came from twenty-five. With a sleepy sniff, he headed down the hall. The wail rose to a shriek, followed by a crash and cursing in some unknown language.

Before Slap could knock, the door slid open and a girl lunged at the opening. Two men dove at her, one missed but the other trapped her legs and she fell forward. She lifted tearful eyes to Slap's in a silent plea for help.

Slap wedged a foot in the door. He reached down and caught the attacker by the back of the neck and the clothes on his back. The man let go of the girl with a shocked look, and Slap hurled him across the room. He slammed into the wall head down, face first.

The second man had grabbed the girl, his other hand reaching into his clothes—likely for a weapon. Slap didn't give him a chance. He seized him by the throat and squeezed. A strangled cry and the man stopped struggling. Slap dropped him.

He looked down at the figure cowering at his feet. She wasn't really pretty—well, hard to tell with all the crying she'd been doing—but she was dressed fancy. Strange fancy. Colorful silk robes sort of, but wrapped around her. Sort of. How old was she? Younger than Slap, but not a kid. "You all right?"

"I–I think so, yes." Her dark eyes glanced about the room. She lifted a hand to touch her bruised face. Slap bit back a growl that those brutes would hurt a girl.

"I can't stay here," she whispered, wiping her face.

"Um." Slap thought of his narrow bed with a sad sigh. But what else could he do? "You can stay in my room for a bit. It's tiny, like this one. It's right down the hall." He extended his hand and after a moment, she timidly took it. He lifted her to her feet.

Once back in his room, he gestured to the bed. "You can rest there, miss. I'll uh, I'll bunk by the door. You can clean up in the lav if you wish."

Before long the girl was curled up on his bed, eyes closed. Slap propped against the wall near the door, watching her. Chivalry, he decided, wasn't very comfortable.

= = =

Hadley slipped into the seat across from Tristan, wearing a slight smirk, and clasped his hands on the table. "Change your mind?"

Tristan stared into the contact's eyes, making the man swallow and blink. "Who hired you to move this merchandise? I know it's not your regular employer. This whole enterprise is not his style."

"I–I don't know what you're—"

Tristan snatched the little man's pinkie and bent it back. Hadley moaned, his face pale.

Teeth clenched, Tristan leaned forward, speaking in a hiss. "I can do much more to you than this—before you could scream for help. Or I could decide to let you go now, and find you later. Cat and mouse. You know the kind of work I can do. I'd make it slow."

Hadley broke into a sweat. He whispered, "Please, no. Please. No!"

"Then tell me."

= = =

"Just down this corridor. Twenty-five. Please, let me go now!"

Tristan kept his vise grip on Hadley's upper arm. "You are staying within my sight until I know you aren't scamming me."

"What are you going to do? Just knock on the door?"

Tristan stopped several feet from the room, backed Hadley into the wall, and growled through his teeth, "You stay put. If you run, it won't be far enough to avoid me. I'll find you anyway. Understand?"

Hadley nodded like a spastic bobble doll, body tense, hands splayed against the wall. Tristan fished one of his favorite toys out of a pocket and set it by the reader. After a few moments, the door slid open.

Tristan stared at the body on the floor, throat crushed, and saw the other crumpled on the bed, head down, neck at an impossible angle.

Hadley crept closer, peered in, and gasped. "What happened?"

"Are either of these men your 'employer'?"

"Yeah, the one on the floor. But who could have done this?"

The last time Tristan saw bodies in this condition—no. It couldn't be.

"Get lost, Hadley. Find a hole and pull the dirt in on top of you."

"The ones who did this are that bad?"

Tristan had been thinking of Istvan. If he discovered Hadley had been in contact with Pella... "Just go. Now."

The small man pelted down the corridor and disappeared around a curve.

Tristan gazed again at the bodies. *I have to find Slap. And fast!*

= = =

The girl sat up with a gasp, staring around with glazed eyes until she saw Slap.

He stretched his aching back with a grimace, nodding at her. "Feeling better?"

She hugged her arms. "Who are you?"

"Me? I'm a knight in shining armor. Who were those guys?"

"Kidnappers."

Slap's eyes widened, and he whistled through his teeth. "You must be Somebody." He wrenched his neck to the left, then right, trying to get rid of the crick. "Well, I don't think those two will be bothering you anymore."

"No," she whispered.

He stared at her as she stared back at him. Finally she said, "Thank you."

Slap gave a slight smile. "What about getting home now? Can you do that? Let someone know where you are?"

"I...suppose. I don't even know where I am."

"Well, I can tell you where you are, but I can't say as I know where that is. We're on Perseus Station."

"How far is that from...Eridani?"

Slap shrugged. "I don't know, miss."

The girl's slender shoulders straightened, and her head lifted, looking for all the world like a woman about to take a man to task. Slap knew—his late wife could grind him into meat. *Shallah! I miss you!*

"I am not 'miss,' I am—" She stopped and frowned, and bit her lip.

Slap waited a moment before prodding for an answer. "Well, who are you?"

She shook her head, her lower lip trembling.

Brago's Bands, no tears! Please, no tears! Slap got to his feet, pushing away the ache of his wife's death and concentrating on the girl, on something to take her mind off crying. "You're hungry, I bet. I can go get something."

She half-rose from the bed. "No!" With a grace that made her seem older she sank back down, and curled her feet up next to her. "Don't leave me alone."

Slap rubbed his stubbly chin. What was he going to do with her?

= = =

Tristan hesitated outside number twenty-seven. If he knocked, the cowboy would likely use the comm to ask who was there. Voices heard, maybe overheard. But how fast would he react to his door opening without his leave? That knife of his might only be an old-style steel one, but it was deadly enough.

No time to wait. He had to chance it. He overrode the key-reader and stood ready as the door slid open. Slap, standing by the door, twisted in alarm then relaxed. The girl on the bed cried out, scrambling away. Despite bruises on her face, she matched the vid he'd been shown of her—Nadi.

"Quiet," Tristan ordered as the door closed.

Slap raised his hands in a placating gesture. "It's all right. He's a friend." He glared at Tristan. "Sort of."

"Get your things. We have to leave now."

Slap frowned. "What?" His lip curled into a sneer. "What do you mean 'we'?"

"No questions. Too dangerous. We have to get her back to her brother and get out of here."

Nadi rose from the bed. "You're taking me back to my brother?"

"Yes, Your Highness."

"Your Highness?" Slap exclaimed.

Tristan lifted his palm toward Slap. "No time. Let's go."

"Now, wait. You know I don't play that game—"

Tristan clenched his teeth. "We don't have time for this. We have to leave now!"

Nadi stepped forward. "Don't take me to my brother."

Tristan turned and stared at her. Slap fell silent and crossed his arms.

"And what shall we do with you if not return you to Emperor Vasso, Your Highness?"

A smile flashed, showing white teeth, and the illusion of vulnerability faded, not prey now, but predator. She lifted her head in an arrogant tilt much like her brother's.

"What do you know about my brother?"

"Enough to know I won't cross him." Tristan paused for dramatic effect. "Do you know, Your Highness, how he often rewards not only failures, but faithful service from his hirelings?"

An eyebrow lifted. "Ah. So it is not from any sense of loyalty to him, but only your pitiful life that would keep you honor bound to him?"

Tristan hesitated. Which way was she going with this? "My loyalties are only to myself. He has not earned them. Or bought them. No price was discussed, therefore I consider myself a free agent, not his hireling. He may not agree, however. So I intend to offer what service I can and still stay alive."

Nadi bit her lip, looking thoughtful. "So I could not beg or bribe you to not return me to my oh-so-horrible brother?"

"No."

"He's a monster." Her voice was matter-of-fact.

"That's not my concern."

Slap uncrossed his arms. "Now, wait. We can't—"

Tristan didn't take his eyes from the girl as he cut off the cowboy. "Yes, we can. Stay out of this. I know what I'm doing."

"Do you know what happened to her? She's been kidnapped. They were beating her when I—"

"I got the picture when I saw the room next door." Tristan took a breath and in his deadest voice said, "Stay—out—of—this."

Slap subsided, leaning against the wall with a hissing breath.

Nadi hadn't moved, but her gaze rested on Slap for a moment with a slight smile. "Archaic type, isn't he?"

"Indeed," Tristan said.

"Still believes in rescuing damsels in distress."

Tristan met her calculating eyes. She didn't want rescue; she was testing him. True pleas would have been accompanied by tears and playing prey.

A predator. Like her brother.

"I don't," Tristan said flatly. He nodded to Slap. "Get your pack. We're taking her to her brother and getting out of here before he can chase us down to 'reward' us."

Nadi smirked. "I like you. And your archaic friend. I think I'll ask Vasso to let you go."

Tristan believed that about as much as he believed the Eridani emperor was a philanthropist. He had to get Slap away from here.

Slap strode to the desk and grabbed his pack. He frowned down at the princess. "Mi—Your Highness? Why didn't you tell me who you were?"

Her smile softened. "I was afraid to trust you, even though you played 'knight in shining armor.' I'd been passed between several kidnappers. But he"—she nodded at Tristan—"knew me. And I know him."

Slap looked confused. "You do?"

"I know his type, I mean. I understand him." Her smile widened. "And I do thank you."

Tristan wondered which girl was the real one, the soft one that emerged for her rescuer, or the hardened one now facing him, eyes glinting.

"Take me to my brother."

= = =

Tristan burst onto the bridge and dove for his chair. Slap sat, ready, in the other seat.

"So she got on her brother's yacht all right?"

Tristan nodded and sought departure codes. "Yes." He strapped in while waiting for confirmation. "I saw her go into the ship from across the concourse. It's the best I could do."

"So...why are you taking me with you when you wanted to dump me off here?"

Tristan thought of the rumors of Vasso's sadism. Manacles, hot tongs, medical experiments, chemicals that melted skin, leaving raw muscles and nerves intact. He imagined the stench, the screams...

"Because." His voice came out a hoarse whisper.

Slap snorted, staring at him, but said nothing more.

A voice came across the comm. "Cleared for departure."

Tristan sighed in relief. After they jumped he relaxed into the chair.

Slap broke the silence. "She seemed so different with you. I don't understand her."

Tristan sniffed quietly and glanced over at the naïve cowboy. "I hope you never do."

Steel Trap

Tristan tapped off the comm and left the bridge, satisfied to have found buyers for both their official and unofficial cargoes. He'd had to leave Perseus Station in a hurry, but their next stop had been uneventful and, now that he had buyers lined up, successful. In Confederation space, smuggled goods brought great price due to the embargoes against all but government-sanctioned suppliers. This stop at Tania should be lucrative.

He frowned at a muffled pounding and walked toward its source—Slap's quarters. After receiving no answer to his chime, Tristan overrode the lock.

The door slid open to reveal his tall companion, tears streaming down his face, pounding the bulkhead over and over with one fist then the other. Sweat tightened his dark, curly hair into tiny ringlets. Red splattered and smeared on the metal wall.

Tristan watched, leaning against the doorframe, arms folded.

Slap's blows slowed, and finally he stopped, his shoulders slumped, his breathing heavy rasps. Without turning, he muttered, "What're you looking at?"

"You tell me."

Slap squeezed his eyes shut. Through clenched teeth he hissed, "I see them die every day. Every night. My beautiful Shallah." He inhaled raggedly. "My baby, my son, Evan. And Ol' Pa. Dead. All dead. Burned. Murdered."

Tristan lifted his head slightly, frowning. "You had said the Mordas killed your family. I thought you meant your parents, siblings."

A sob shook Slap and he gulped, stiffening his shoulders. An admirable effort at control. The cowboy shook his head. "Naw. My folks died when I was younger. It was only Ol' Pa, Shallah, the baby, and me on the ranch when the Mordas came." His lip curled. "They even killed Ol' Pa. The Zendians weren't happy over that. They said their god would send an avenging angel to stop the evil. That's why they sent me to the city. I was supposed to hook up with the angel." Slap's eyes cut to Tristan, the blue almost glowing from the water in them. "Instead I found you." He stopped and broke into a low chuckle. "I don't think you qualify as an angel, but you did stop the evil. Blew 'em all to dust. The dirt-sucking lizards." He continued to laugh, a low, malevolent sound.

"Go back." Tristan rubbed his forehead, trying to make sense of Slap's ramblings. "Why were the Zendians upset over Ol' Pa's death? Who was he to you?"

"He was a Zendian. I'd helped him when I was small. I found him hurt. It's not often the Zendians have anything to do with humans, but after that Ol' Pa became my friend. He said we were brothers, best translation from their language anyway. After my Ma died, he came and stayed with me. Trying to help me run the ranch—which was funny sometimes cuz he wouldn't have anything to do with any electronic machinery, no Zendian will— and just...being there so I wasn't alone."

Tristan stared at the cowboy. Finally he pushed up from the doorjamb. "Wrap up your hands and come down to the cargo bay."

= = =

Wiping his sweaty face on a towel, Tristan watched Slap chin himself on the pipe. Why was he doing this for Slap? Not because he cared, certainly. But listening to a man smash his fists into the bulkheads would get on his nerves. Better this way.

The cowboy had been working out steadily for over an hour. His arms trembled as he pulled himself up again. He held himself face level to the metal bar, teeth bared with effort, and dropped to the deck. Tristan tossed him a towel.

Slap took it without a word. After drying and pulling his shirt back on, he nodded upward. "Where'd you get that pipe, and those rings hanging there?"

Tristan shrugged. "If I keep this thing for long, I'll get mats and more equipment. Plenty of room. I can even get weights or a punching bag if you'd like."

"Yeah." Slap looked around. "I've been bored to tears the last few days. Not much to do aboard ol' Bertha."

"Her name is *Giselle*."

"And the next time we get in a scrape, you'll change it again. I'll just call her Bertha."

Tristan didn't deign to respond but changed the subject. "If you want something to do, I can show you various jobs around the ship."

"Maybe later. Right now I'm hungry."

Things were back to normal. For now.

= = =

"So you gonna dump me now that we're on a planet again?"

Tristan blinked in the sunlight as he walked down the ramp. "No. It would be in your best interest to stay with me for the time being."

"Oh, would it? How nice of you."

Tristan took a deep breath. Emperor Vasso knew by now Slap had been the one to rescue his sister. As a reward, that madman would likely kill the cowboy in capricious amusement. "I mean it. Stick close to me. And watch your back."

Slap snorted but followed as Tristan left the spaceport and headed into the city.

Selling their freight and arranging for a new legitimate cargo took very little time. Tristan hoped he could make other, more profitable dealings on the side, but that would have to wait for a time when Slap wasn't tagging along.

They walked through a market, Slap purchasing fresh vegetables and fruit. Tristan trailed as the cowboy exclaimed over various types of produce and grumbled at the high prices. *This is a Confederation planet, boy, get used to being robbed.*

A movement between stalls caught Tristan's attention. A pair of steel grey eyes glinted and disappeared from the top of potato crates. Oh, no. Not again!

Tristan watched Slap shopping as if he hadn't seen that execrable observer. He would have to meet with him later, if only to find out what Confed Sec wanted now.

"Hey, broccoli!" Slap picked up a large bundle of green florets. "D'you like this stuff, Tristan?"

"Do you know how to cook all these fresh vegetables you're buying, or are we to eat them raw?"

"I ain't no Shallah, but I can cook." Slap frowned and dropped the broccoli. His shoulders hunched. "Let's get back to Bertha."

53

Tristan eyed the cowboy as he followed him back to the ship. What had he done to deserve having his pleasant solitude disrupted—much less by someone with such wounds?

= = =

The steely-eyed Confed Sec operative would expect Tristan to make contact at first opportunity. So Tristan stayed aboard ship. He owed those people no loyalty or consideration. He wasn't a citizen of the Confederation, and didn't care what their secret security's schemes were.

He played checkers with Slap, and was surprised—the kid had a sharp mind.

Kid. Was he? At times he seemed so young, despite his size. But he had been married, owned a ranch. A man then. Young, but—a man.

"How old are you?" Tristan barely kept his face from registering shock at asking the question. What had made him inquire? He prided himself on his lack of interest in any person. People were annoyances to be tolerated or ignored, or marks to be exploited. Nothing more.

Slap didn't glance up as he studied the board. "Nineteen."

A kid. A man. A tall ox with a heart that had seen more grief than he should have had to endure. Fate, or perhaps some Zendian god of irony, had saddled Tristan with this burden. But he owed Slap; the cowboy had stepped in, risked his life for Tristan. Tristan knew betrayal, and expected nothing less from others, but could not make himself betray such a sacrifice. He couldn't leave Slap until he knew the ki—man would be safe.

Slap jumped Tristan's king and looked up with a grin.

Rubbing his chin in a mixture of quiet astonishment and chagrin, Tristan met his opponent's gaze with narrowed eyes. "Ever hear of a game called chess?"

Slap shook his head.

Tristan smiled.

= = =

The ops man browsed booth to booth, glancing over silks, jewelry, baked goods, but his gaze darted about the crowd. Tristan's lips twitched up, and he sidled between stalls until he came around behind his target, who was pretending to examine local ceramic artwork.

"I'm not interested in another job," Tristan murmured, picking up a decorative pot from the table.

The man didn't jump. "We just want information."

"I'm not inclined to give any."

"We understand you were recently on Zenos at just the time their local underworld was thrown into turmoil by the death of their kingpin, Lyssel. You wouldn't happen to know anything about that, would you?"

"No." Tristan turned the pot over in his hands, tracing the intricate designs. The Three Systems weren't neighbors of the Confederation. Why the interest? It couldn't be due to trade routes, or plans of the Confederation's so-called 'expansion' known anywhere else as conquest; the Xanthus Commonwealth lay in between the two. Had Lyssel been dealing across Confed borders, perhaps? Or was Tristan the connection?

"Even though it appears your ship was blown up at his orders?"

"Was it?"

"And who is this bumpkin with you?"

This required more privacy. Tristan put the pot down with a nod to the vendor and strode off. He wound through streets until he found a small alley. There he waited, leaning against the wall.

Steel Eyes soon came around the corner and jerked to a halt. "We need your help."

"Sorry. I'm not available. And not for sale."

"You were the last time."

"We merely had a common goal. Getting paid to do what I would have done anyway was ironically pleasant. Is that prostitution or expedience?"

Steel Eyes' lips thinned for a moment. "You were on Perseus Station about a week ago. Did you have a meeting with Emperor Vasso Istvan?"

Panic gripped Tristan's heart, squeezing it in a vice. What the—? Perseus Station wasn't in the Confederation either; it was within Xanthus. What were these serpentine idiots up to?

In an even tone, he said, "I didn't know the Emperor ever left Eridani. That would seem to be a nightmare for his security."

Jaw muscles twitched as Steel Eyes glared at him. "Let's go back to the hayseed traveling with you. Who is he?"

"He is none of your business. Neither am I."

"My superiors need your cooperation. We are ready to deal."

"Not interested." Tristan pushed up from the wall.

"Don't you even want to know our offer?"

In lieu of an answer, Tristan walked away.

"We're willing to do an identity search," the man hissed.

Tristan turned. "I know who I am. Who I was born is of no consequence to me." He spun and left before any more conversation could be thrust upon him.

His mind raced as he returned to the ship. Blast Confed Sec! Had he merely stumbled across two concerns of theirs with both the Mordas and Vasso, or were they studying him? They knew something if they had found out about his searches for his heritage in his younger days.

And why the curiosity in Slap? If Confed Sec knew about Tristan's enforced visit to the Eridani emperor, how much did Vasso Istvan know about both him and Slap? His neck tingled in expectation of danger. He wished he hadn't promised to take the cowboy on a local tour before they left Tania.

= = =

"Y'know..." The cowboy's eyes were wide as he took in the low, rambling buildings with brightly colored canopies and tree-lined streets beyond the spaceport marketplace. "I haven't seen one alien since we left the space port."

Tristan gave a small, brittle smile as he glanced up at Slap. "This is a Confederation planet. You won't. They don't like aliens here, and don't allow them on-world except at the ports."

Slap had seemed to understand his basic warning before, but now, in the sunshine, amid shoppers, families walking together, he gawked, seemingly unaware.

"But laying aside that detail, most port cities are the same."

"This place doesn't look nothing like Zenos' port. At least, not Zanti City, where we met."

"I'm not talking about climates or architecture, or the races of beings one might encounter. Port cities attract certain types of unsavory characters and illegal dealings."

"Like smuggling, you mean?"

Tristan nodded as they side-stepped two women hurrying toward a shopkeeper's door. "For one. The trappings might vary, but the foundations are always the same. I keep telling you to be on guard."

Slap nodded, but didn't seem to take it to heart. They approached a bakery, and he sniffed with obvious appreciation, his body half turning as they passed the doorway.

Tristan stifled a sigh. "You really need—" Tingling paralysis halted his words and steps. Buzzing filled his head. A stunner! The ground rose up to meet his face before all went black.

$$= = =$$

Muscles trembled and ached. His head thudded. Nausea passed through him in waves, making him swallow convulsively. Brago's bands, what happened? Slap opened his eyes and blinked twice before realizing the room wasn't sideways, he was. The side of his face pressed against a cold floor. His hands were tied behind him, the bindings cutting into his wrists.

Tristan lay across from him, eyes shut, a slightly glowing net wrapped around his torso. Where were they? From the metallic, slightly oily smell, he'd guess a ship. And from the narrowness he could see, they'd probably been dumped in a hallway.

Boots appeared near his face.

"That's the one he wants all right. Keep that energy-mesh on him—he's a slippery one."

"We got him easily enough," a second voice said with sneering disagreement.

"Don't underestimate him. I won't rest easy till he's off our hands and we've got the reward."

"What about this other one?" A boot prodded Slap's forehead. "There's no reward on him. Shall I kill him?"

"When we could make a side profit? Look at his size! Sell him to a press gang. There has to be freebooters in port. Now help me get this one locked up. Then you can get rid of the big one."

Several men lifted Tristan. Footsteps faded away.

Slap struggled against his bonds and a hand grabbed him by his hair.

"He's awake." Laughter. A foot nudged against his ankles. "You're going on a trip, boy. A real luxury cruise."

Fury rose in Slap. He swung his legs and contacted flesh. A yell and thump. He lifted his head to see his victim scrambling against the bulkhead, holding a hand to his bloody nose.

Hands grabbed Slap's shoulders from above his head. He sat up and twisted. A body flew over him and flipped, landing on his back. Slap shoulder-dropped onto the man's chest.

The other man leaned against the bulkhead, one hand still on his nose. Blood dripped through his fingers. He dropped his hand to his holster.

Slap scrambled to his feet and dove at his captor. They crashed to the deck—the man softening his own landing, but Slap still struggled to get his breath. His cushion wasn't so lucky; he was out cold.

"Good for you, lizard," he muttered. He rolled off the body and managed to get to his feet again. His first victim lay unmoving, gasping shallowly. He bet he broke the man's ribs and sternum, and despite everything, he winced in sympathy. He'd been kicked by a horse once and suffered broken ribs. It'd been agony. He'd been unable to move or breathe without it feeling like knives were driven into his chest.

He strained his arms, but couldn't loosen the bonds. He eyed the corridor. Not far down to his left a hatch promised a way out. They'd likely been brought aboard and dumped unceremoniously until the captain, or whoever, had checked them over. So—that was the way out. But he needed cover, and a knife. His knife! He could feel the sheath on his back, but he'd bet it was empty. No way to tell with his hands tied—Brago's Bands, how was he going to get untied?

He looked down at the gasping man with what he hoped was a convincing snarl. "You gotta choice. You untie me, or I stomp you."

The man's mouth worked like a fish out of water, and he lifted a hand. Hoping he wasn't going to be stabbed in the back, Slap knelt next to the man. Fingers fumbled at his bonds, and as he felt the cords slacken, he strained and pulled his arms free.

Blood welled from gashes the cords had made in his wrists. He rubbed the circulation into his hands as he stood. "Thanks," he said to the downed man. "Maybe when we're through with you, we won't sell *you* to the freebooters."

Empty bluster, but perhaps because of Tristan's reputation he was at least half-believed; the man on the deck turned pale. Slap remembered his sheath and felt for his blade. As he thought, gone. "Who's got my knife?" he asked himself aloud.

"Braddon," whispered the man on the deck.

Slap grinned and bent over, taking the man's stunner. "Amazing how a little pain can make you rethink your position, huh?" He stepped to the unconscious one and relieved him of his stunner as well, tucking it in his waistband. "These'll do instead of my knife for now." He looked down the corridor and back down at his ersatz helper. "How many men are on your ship?"

"Twenty one."

"You two down, that's nineteen to one." If the man were telling the truth. Slap would soon find out. "I wonder what Tristan would say to these odds?" Without a further glance down, he muttered to the man, "Wish me luck."

This ship was larger than ol' Bertha, and who knew what doors led where. Hefting the stunner and starting down the hall, Slap wondered where Tristan was locked up. Two men came out of a door ahead of him, and Slap shot them. One fell immediately, the other staggered against a bulkhead, his hand fumbling at the gauss gun holster on his back. Slap fired again and snorted at the heavy thud. "Sack o' potatoes. Seventeen."

The first man wore a stunner. Slap tucked it in his belt. Slap swallowed taking the gauss gun—a nasty weapon. He gazed about. Where might they have Tristan? He opened the door the two had exited. Tristan! Blind luck!

His dark companion leaned upright against the bulkhead, awake, dark eyes glaring. The energy-mesh hissed, almost a sizzling sound. It must be set to max.

"What are you doing here?" Tristan asked.

"Looking for you, what else? How do I get this thing off you?"

"The controls are on a belt."

"Gotcha. I'll check the two guys who just left here." Slap peeked around the doorway and dragged one then the other into the room. He found a small box with several switches on it and yanked it off the belt. He thumbed a switch and the hissing stopped.

Tristan tossed the thing off with a look of disdain and rose. "What are you doing here?" he repeated. He took the gauss gun from Slap.

Slap scowled. "If it slipped your mind, we were both stunned and brought here."

Tristan narrowed his eyes. "I meant, why did you come looking for me. No time now. Let's go." He started through the door and jumped back—a blinding flare hit the left side of the doorframe. The entire edge of the jamb twisted in glowing ruins— the door within the scorched bulkhead destroyed. Tristan muttered a sharp word in his native tongue.

"PBG?" Slap hissed, fear rising through his gut.

Tristan eyed the damage and shoved backwards into Slap. "Or rifle. Get back."

"You're trapped in there," a voice called. "It doesn't matter to us if you give up or not. We get our reward dead or alive."

Slap's gaze darted around the room—no other doors. He grabbed Tristan's arm. "What do we do now?"

Tristan jerked free, lips thinned into a line. His gaze went to Slap's waist and he snatched one of the stunners from him. "Play them," he whispered. "Stall. Tell them the PB got me and you'll give yourself up, but only if they let you go free."

Slap licked his lips, a feeling of certainty, of trust in Tristan welling up in him. "You got your reward then," he shouted. "The particle beam got him. But I have stunners and a gauss gun, and I'll use them if I have to. Let me go, I've got no part in this."

"You'd just walk out when we killed your friend?"

Slap eyed Tristan prying the stunner's case open as he answered, "He wasn't no friend, just someone I hitched a ride with. 'Smatter of fact, with him dead, I can take his ship. I figure you've done me a favor."

Silence for a moment. Tristan was still diddling with the stunner, his slender fingers working quickly, face intent.

Then, from the hall, "And if we don't want to let you go?"

"Well, I figure being dead now is only hurryin' what I'd get in a press gang. And I reckon with this gauss gun I'd take a few of you with me, anyway. So what's say? You get your reward, I just inherited a ship. Call it square."

Tristan looked up, his voice low, urgent. "When I say 'now,' you rush with me, cover our backs—stun anything moving."

"Thing is," the voice called, "how do we trust each other?"

Tristan gestured as if tossing the stunner out the door and winked.

Slap grinned. "For starters, how about if I throw my stunners out to you?"

"Sounds fine."

From an angle, Tristan lobbed the stunner to the right, the direction the particle beam had come from. Shouts of alarm—a burst of light.

"Now!" Tristan hissed.

Slap almost tripped charging out the door, one hand on Tristan's back, spraying stunner fire behind them. Bodies fell, and he turned to see where they were going just as Tristan skidded and pushed against him. "Back! Back!"

Slap needed no urging—he could hear footsteps running their way from beyond the curve in the corridor. He trampled over bodies and felt a pull on his arm.

"Up!"

He saw the stairs and leaped up the steps, his breath ragged with panic. Behind, below, he heard a scream. He jumped up to the deck, belatedly checking for people. Tristan surged up to join him, eyes darting about. He waved a command to follow with the gauss gun and sprinted to their right. Slap stayed on his heels.

Tristan pulled up by a door. "Get ready to stun."

Before Slap could nod, the door slid open, and he peppered the room—the bridge from the look of it—with stun bursts. Two men slumped in chairs.

"Overkill, but effective," Tristan said, as he locked the door, glancing around.

"What do we do now?"

Tristan went to a small cabinet embedded in the bulkhead and pulled out several tools. With one hand, Tristan hauled a body out of a chair and let it flop to the deck. He fell into the seat and began working on the console's cover.

Slap leaned back against the bulkhead on the other side of the room. The better to keep an eye on Tristan, the unconscious men, and the door. "What are you doing?"

"Taking advantage of opportunity and buggering their ship."

"Do we have time for this?"

"You have any place to go?"

"Yeah. Away from here." Slap put his hand up to push back his hat and realized it was gone. Great. He ruffled his curly hair instead. "Preferably alive."

"This won't take long. You have a few moments to catch your breath before we make a run for it."

Slap jerked a thumb at the door. "Just don't forget there's eighteen guys standing between us and a way out."

"Most are piled up on the deck. Just wait."

Wait. Right. Like Slap had a choice. He twirled the stunner then stiffened. "Hey, one of them has my knife!"

"If you want to go out there and ask kindly for its return," Tristan said, head bent to his work, "be my guest."

"But—"

"They took my whole bloody vest." His voice sounded bitter. Slap could understand why. Tristan's vest had lots of little secrets and unusual devices hidden in it. "We can replace whatever we've lost, but not our lives."

Slap leaned against the bulkhead. Tristan was right. But still, it burned. That had been a good knife.

"So what are you doing, anyway?"

"Let's just say I'm increasing the odds that they won't get this ship off planet any time soon." His lips spread in a grim smile. "Just in case we don't escape, they can't either."

Tristan set the cover in place and swiveled to access the communications console. He studied something for a bit, then seemed to be nosing in files.

Finally he stood. He returned the tools to the kit in the wall and turned. "Get ready!" Lifting the gauss gun, he walked toward the door.

Slap pushed up from the bulkhead.

A deafening flash—shock knocked him back against a console, his neck and spine recoiling like a whip. He blinked, unable to see, his body tingling with electricity, his back screaming with pain, his ears ringing. What? *What?* An explosion? He tried to straighten and fell to the floor. Smoke and burnt-metal tang invaded his nostrils, choking him. Crawl. Move. His hand bumped into something and he grabbed, felt. An arm. He squeezed his eyes shut and opened them. Things seemed furry and like negative images, but he saw Tristan, face pale, eyes closed, bloody. *No!*

Hands jerked him to his feet. With a roar, Slap swung fists, connecting with flesh. Three men, two down. The third he grabbed by the throat and crushed until he felt soft tissue and cartilage give before throwing him against the far bulkhead.

The ship fell silent except for Slap's gasping breaths. He looked down at Tristan and knelt by him. Blood poured from a wound in his chest. Fingers felt for a pulse at his throat. Weak, but there. *Brago's Bands, Tristan, don't die on me!* He pressed his hands against the wound, trying to staunch the flow of blood.

Footsteps thudded in the corridor. Slap fumbled on the floor with one hand for a weapon, any weapon. He snatched up a stunner, but before he could aim it, the first of two men skidded to a halt and called, "Don't shoot! We're here to help."

Slap didn't lower the stunner. He looked over the two intruders. They weren't dressed like the mercenaries. No space vests, and their dark blue clothes had straight lines, the jacket a high collar. They had a military air about them. "Prove it."

The man nodded toward Tristan. "He's hurt. We'll take him to a hospital."

Slap looked down at the bloody, still figure and licked his lips; his worry for Tristan battling with his fear to trust. He looked up and nodded. "Help him. Don't let him die."

= = =

Sharp pain. He gasped and the pain spiked into searing hotness. He experimented with shallow breaths...relief. A hazy, dark cloud seemed to envelop his mind. Various stringent odors permeated cool, dry air. A monitor softly beeped body responses, heart rate, breathing...he was in a hospital or medical facility. His throat felt raw.

He opened his eyes. White ceiling tiles. Motion drew his attention to the right. The tall form had been lounging in a chair but now sat up. Curly hair disheveled, eyes sunken.

Slap stood with a worried look and approached whispering, "How ya feeling?"

Tristan tried to speak but his dry mouth and throat fought him. He swallowed, licked his lips, and swallowed again. "What happened?" His voice came out a hoarse croak.

"A piece of metal tore into your chest. You almost died. But these Confederate guys"—Slap waved a hand across the room—"showed up and brought you here."

Tristan turned his head to the left. Steel Eyes and another man, stockier and older. Great.

"We saved your life," Steel Eyes said. "You owe us."

"I didn't ask for your help."

"He did." Steel Eyes nodded at Slap.

"He doesn't speak for me, and he can't make deals for me."

"He asked us to save your life. We figured it would be worth something to you."

"You figured wrong."

"Now look—"

"Enough," a new voice said from beyond the foot of the bed. "He's still far from recovered."

"We need answers," Steel Eyes' partner said.

"My patient needs rest. Now get out of here."

The two men hesitated then left. A stern man of slight build walked up and peered at Tristan. "A little worse for wear after your adventure, but you should be up and around in a day or two." He gazed up at Slap. "Now that you know he'll be fine, why not go get some rest yourself? At the rate you're going, you'll end up a patient too."

Slap frowned, shaking his head.

"Don't argue or I will throw you out. Now, go!"

Grumbling, Slap complied, with one last troubled look before heading out the door.

Tristan let himself fall back down into forgetful sleep.

= = =

Slap took a deep breath, enjoying the fresh breeze of the open-air café. Now that Tristan was released, they'd be heading back into space too soon, he was sure. Ol' Bertha seemed to get smaller and smaller each day he was confined to her. Well, at least it made him appreciate being on a planet.

He swirled the last bit of meat in the spicy green sauce and shoved it in his mouth. Good stuff. He hadn't thought so when the plate was first set in front of him. The café boasted foods from many planets, each dish with a strange name, and expensive to boot. Tristan's choice from the menu had been a mystery to Slap. He didn't know what hobbits were; Tristan said the name was a reference to some classic literature from ancient Earth. Whatever the source, the dish had lots of mushrooms.

Tristan sipped his tea, his gaze, as usual, darting around, always alert.

The meal had been quiet, but now, with Tristan seeming a little more relaxed, perhaps Slap could ask a few questions. He finished chewing and swallowed. "So who hired those mercenaries?"

"I'm not sure, and I loathe leaving without knowing, but those men are all in the Confed's custody. They have refused to talk, which has our erstwhile benefactors pulling their hair out." Tristan's teeth flashed in a grin. He took another drink of his tea. "It can't be Istvan, he'd want me alive, and be after you too. These fellows weren't interested in you. And Dray wants me dead. I don't think the Mordas have gotten their feet under them yet to come after us, and again, they'd want us both."

Slap tapped the table lightly with his knuckles. "Istvan? Why would the Emperor be after you or me? You returned his sister to him."

"A quirk of his."

Slap gritted his teeth. "Could you chew it fine, please?"

With a shrug, Tristan put down his teacup. "More often than not, his rewards are painful. And fatal."

Slap grimaced as he pulled out Tristan's meaning. "That's crazy!"

"So is he. The best thing that could happen to Eridani would be for the royal palace to be blown up with him and all family inside."

Slap thought of the girl, the princess, blown to bits, and pushed aside the image. "Who is this Dray you mentioned?"

"Someone to avoid."

He banged his fist on the table. "Why can't you give me straight answers?"

Tristan looked off, as if seeing something far away. "He's someone I used to...know. He taught me a few skills and felt that obligated me to him. He wasn't appreciative when I left and has been looking for me."

"You know..." Slap whirled his glass in the water ring. "You have the most...understated way of saying things. Of saying nothing." He sighed. "So how many people want you dead—or alive?"

"Unknown." Tristan's dark eyes bored into his. "Unfortunately, some of them are now aware of you. I thought keeping you with me for a while would guarantee your safety from the Mordas. It was a mistake."

Slap dropped his gaze to the table. *Here it comes. He's dumping me.*

"Now answer me a question."

"Yeah?" Slap mumbled, wishing he could pretend he didn't mind being chucked like an old pair of boots.

"Why did you come back for me?"

Slap squinted over at Tristan. "Huh?"

"You broke free. Why didn't you just leave while you could?"

"Without you? Are you crazy?"

"I wonder sometimes. But why? And why did you ask the Confeds to save my life?" Tristan's eyes probed his for answers.

Did he honestly not get it? Slap turned his hands palm up. "You're my friend."

Tristan's expression froze for a moment. He took another sip of his tea, looking very thoughtful. After a silence he said, "I've paid the medical bills—we owe the Confeds nothing. I'd like to get off this planet before they get more insistent that I help them."

Slap grinned. "So where're we going next?"

"Out of Confederation space," said Tristan, his voice flat. "I was thinking of going to the Cygnus Hegemony or perhaps to the Aquila Freehold. You might get a landstake on one of the Aquila worlds." He lifted his cup in a throwaway gesture. "That's what they call a homestead."

With a wrinkle of his nose, Slap said, "I knew that. But...naw. I don't want a homestead."

Tristan sat back, his brows rising.

Slap suppressed a smile. It wasn't often he could get a reaction out of his friend. He liked the feeling. "A strange place, all alone?" He shook his head. "No. I'll stick with you."

Tristan's expression grew slightly dyspeptic, but he nodded. "Wise. For now."

"Sure is." Slap paused for a second. "You need a bodyguard."

Boring Ol' Bertha

Tristan left the bridge, glad one more jump would get them out of Confed space. He'd had enough of them. This was tricky territory though, near the border. Dangerous. Freebooters often lurked, waiting for hapless, helpless ships. Not that *Giselle* was as helpless as she appeared, but the old cargo ship wasn't up to Tristan's standards and that made him feel defensive.

And Tristan did not like a defensive position; he preferred being on the offensive.

He also did not like boredom, and that was one thing he had plenty of right now. Slap suffered seriously from the malady, and not quietly. The cowboy found pleasure in irritating Tristan—had from the beginning. It spoke volumes that Tristan was bored enough to look forward to it.

Well, for now, he'd alleviate the tedium by working out, then perhaps surprise Slap by cooking for once.

= = =

Slap continued pounding the bag while he sneaked peeks at Tristan working on what he called aerial rings, his black hair damp, hanging on his forehead. This was the only time he wasn't perfectly groomed. His friend's well-defined muscles strained as he assumed various positions and held them. He might be a bit on the short side and lean, but the man was no weakling. Watching Tristan stretch and warm up before a work out made Slap wince, especially those splits. Ouch.

This had been the longest without a stop at a station or planet. To keep busy, Slap sweated his guts out exercising in the cargo bay, cooked, played games with Tristan, and read manuals about the ship. He cleaned, checked various systems, and could now handle communications quite well, if he said so himself. But still, he felt closed in, and if he didn't get out of ol' Bertha soon, he'd go loco.

Slap toweled off and left to get a shower—he couldn't wait to get to a planet and have a real shower not a sonic one. He'd have to fix some grub in an hour or two. Tristan never cooked for himself and rarely said anything about Slap's cooking except to grumble about the clean up they'd have if their gravity failed, but he never passed up a fresh meal for packaged food. And shared meals often led to time spent playing a game of chess or cards. Not that Tristan talked much, but at least Slap wasn't alone.

Just for fun, he had considered not talking to Tristan to see how long his friend would go without speaking, but he already knew from the short time they'd been together that Tristan preferred solitude and would bask in the silence. Slap would easily lose that game. Besides, it was more enjoyable irritating the quiet man and watching his subtle changes of expression. The thinned lips and even-more-stony-than-usual face and, when really aggravated, flared nostrils.

Slap finished the shower and lay back on the bed with a sigh.

He awoke from an unintentional, boredom-induced nap. With a groan, he rose and pulled on his jeans and a shirt. Delicious odors drew his nose—and the rest of him—toward the galley. He stopped, shocked, in the doorway. Tristan cooking? He sauntered around the island to the counter where his friend was working and peered at the plate of...something. They looked like flapjacks but almost thin as paper. A bowl sat next to them. Slap started to unlatch the lid but Tristan slapped at his hand with a spoon. Slap hid a grin.

Tristan moved a pot off the induction hob to a cool spot and stirred. Red broth with lumps of some sort of vegetables he guessed—er, hoped. Soup?

Slap sniffed appreciatively. "Gotta be a first time for everything, I always say. What about open containers and what-would-happen-if we-lose-our-artificial-G?"

"You aren't the only one who can cook. I just haven't bothered in a long time." Tristan's gaze cut to Slap with a small, ironic smile. "Gravity, you know." He dipped the spoon and tasted the broth. "And you aren't the only one who gets bored on these long jaunts. With my possessions all ashes on Zenos, I don't have my library. I have to recoup my losses to not only replace that, but get back into business."

Slap hitched a hip up to sit on the edge of the counter. "And what is your business?"

Tristan quirked an eyebrow while he stirred something in a bowl. He poured it into the pot, and the red broth turned pink. "Surviving."

Slap rubbed his chin, considering. Now was as good a time as any to open the subject. "So how does smuggling fit into survival?"

Both Tristan's eyebrows rose slightly. Ha! A hit. Tristan hadn't known he knew about that.

"It's lucrative." His eyes flicked to Slap as he pulled the plate of pathetic pancakes toward himself and took the lid off the bowl. It was filled with some creamy-looking glop. "Another moral judgment?" He filled one of the flapjacks with the creamy stuff and rolled it up.

Slap hesitated. "I guess that would depend on what you're smuggling."

"Isn't the fact it's illegal enough to pass judgment?" Tristan's sarcastic tone made Slap want to grin, but he had serious questions, so now wasn't a good time to bait his friend.

"Illegal and immoral ain't always the same thing. I want no part of"—Slap's lip curled—"bio-weapons, or things like that."

"I have, at times, run weapons, but I won't touch biologicals." Tristan turned to meet Slap's gaze, his teeth flashing in a smile. "I have, though, stolen and destroyed both."

"Is that what Lyssel was doing? Selling bio-weapons? Is that what you stole?"

"The first time, yes. And I destroyed them in space, where it was safe." His black eyes bored into Slap's. "Don't try to attribute any virtue to that, or me. I was merely trying to irritate Lyssel's buyers."

Slap bit the inside of his cheek to keep from saying anything. No baiting. No baiting...

"The second run," Tristan continued, "was for all the standard armament, just to put a dent in his business for awhile." He shrugged. "But they got me back, destroying my ship."

"I'd say you got the last word, with Lyssel blown to bits."

"Even so, it won't be long before the Mordas are back in full strength. And finding us is probably one of their highest priorities."

"Yeah..." Slap frowned and rubbed his neck, thinking of their most recent adventure. "So who do you think hired those mercenaries to kidnap you?"

Tristan put the rolled-up flapjacks on a plate, clicked the cover into place, and took them to a table in the adjoining rec lounge. "I've been thinking about that quite a bit. And I've about decided it must have been the Confeds."

Slap's mouth dropped open. "The Confeds? Why inna world would they do that? They were the ones who rescued us, remember?"

"Indeed. But it doesn't fit. They don't rescue people. Not that bunch. Their local constabulary might, if not overworked and not paid off. But those men were Confederation Security. Their...secret police, you might say. They specialize in espionage." Slap followed his friend back into the galley and watched as Tristan filled two bowls with the reddish soup and fit the lids on. "They had tried to recruit me for a job and I said no. I think they thought I might change my mind out of gratitude." He returned to the rec lounge and put the bowls into lock-spots on the table.

Slap sat down with a snort and removed the lid from his bowl. "Well, why not? You were grateful when we met."

"That wasn't gratitude. That was a life debt. You risked your life to help me. I couldn't leave you to be killed."

"You have some strange ideas, you know that?"

Tristan shrugged, opened a napkin, and placed it in his lap.

Slap blew on the soup and took a taste. "Hey, this isn't bad. What's it called?"

"Borscht."

"Well, that tells me a lot."

"Beet soup." Tristan lifted his shoulders a bit. "It also has cabbage, carrots, and tomatoes in it."

Slap nodded and chewed a large mouthful. Very different from any soup he'd had, but tasty. "So," he asked, after swallowing. "Is that the only reason you think the Confeds did it?"

"No. I know of quite a few people after me, and none want me 'dead or alive.' One or two might want me alive, like the Eridani emperor, but most want me dead and would pay handsomely for proof of the deed done. And think about this, we were stunned in the middle of a busy street, in the daytime. Not subtle. You probably aren't aware of the way the Confeds rule, but anyone planning a kidnapping would likely want to be very discreet. The Confeds don't like any disorder they haven't created or don't

71

control. And that was as subtle as a nuclear going off. Besides, they hid a tracker on the ship."

"How'd you know?"

Tristan looked at him as if he were stupid. "I did a sweep."

"No, I know, I mean how did you know to think of that?"

"I'm paranoid, haven't you figured that out? Procuring a sweeper wasn't easy, either." His eyes glinted. "Not exactly a stock item. I replaced one essential item that had been in my vest while I was about it, too. But most of my toys are best found outside the Confederation." He gestured at Slap's chest. "We'll need to get you a new knife."

"Yeah. Hey, since the Confeds arrested the mercs, why didn't they give us back our stuff?"

"'Confiscated for evidence.'"

Slap grimaced. "Evidence of what? The mercs were the bad guys."

"The Confeds weren't about to give me back my little specialty gadgets, or your knife. Dangerous, old-fashioned weapon. A stunner they might have returned." He paused, his eyes narrowing. *"Might."*

"Very different from the way things are run back home," Slap muttered.

"The Three Systems don't have a government, not as such, you know. They started with guilds, merchants, and you Separatists. But the mobs took over, corrupting everything. The Mordas consolidated the underground factions, and the wealthy, for all their class-based arrogance, are in bed with them. Your people, until recently, had been left alone. They were considered backcountry hicks, not worth bothering."

Slap nodded. The Separatists ran their own affairs—until Lyssel got land greedy. Slap wondered how many other ranches had fallen to the Mordas now. Or had Lyssel's death stalled their expansion?

Tristan swirled his spoon in the soup and captured several little chunks of vegetable. "But back to our current problem, from the limited facts I have, Confed Sec is the only thing that makes sense. I don't insist I'm right, just my best working theory."

"Is that why you've been busting tail to get out of their space?"

Tristan took a spoon of soup, chewed, and wiped his mouth. "Yes. I didn't even pick up cargo. No stops except for fuel. I want to get out of Confederation territory—and far from Eridani too."

Slap could understand that. He applied himself to the soup, and helped himself to a second bowlful. Tristan, as usual when Slap wasn't prying conversation out of him, remained quiet as he ate.

"So what are those?" Slap asked, pointing at the rolled-up flapjacks.

Tristan stared at the plate but he seemed far away, like he was remembering, and a slight smile flickered on his face. "Depends on who you ask. Blinis, crepes..."

Tristan's voice took on a strange accent on that last word. The same as it did when he muttered to himself in whatever-language-it-was when he was really angry or upset. Slap doubted he could come close to saying that word like Tristan did. "What was the word? Bli-blinis?"

"Yes." Tristan's eyes crinkled at him. "Blinis would be fine." He pushed the plate at Slap. "Try one."

Slap did. The sweet, creamy filling oozed out as he bit, and he moaned in appreciation. "This is good stuff," he said, his mouth full.

Tristan's smile twitched wider for a moment. "We can play chess, if you want, when we're through."

Slap felt a slight rush as he nodded. Why he liked the stupid game, he couldn't say except he'd gotten good enough to make his friend frown and sigh in irritation, and for Tristan, that was about the same as anyone else throwing a royal fit. His best had only been a stalemate, and he'd've thought his buddy would've gotten angry, but he'd had a proud gleam in his eye.

He didn't think he'd ever figure Tristan out.

Dinner over, the two cleaned up in the galley.

As Slap wiped off the counters, Tristan said, "If you'll finish up in here, I'll get the chess board."

"Got it." Slap tossed the cloth into the sonic scrubber chute and looked around. All clean. He eyed the pot of borscht and unlatched the lid to take a sniff. Hmm, good stuff all right. He'd not put it away yet; it would make a good snack later. He set the lid back on and went back to the rec lounge.

Slap sat, and they settled in to play. They studied the board, and Slap found his mind wandering again to his companion. Who was this man anyway? He could be so many things. He could fight like a tornado, charm lizards out of their hides, outthink bad guys, pilot ships, buy and sell cargo like a merchant...

Slap made his move. "Tristan?"

After a delay he got a quiet, "Hmm?"

"You've..." How could he put it? "I've seen you do lots of things...and I was just wondering..."

Tristan took his rook. Slap stared. He hadn't seen that.

"You were saying?"

Slap blinked. "I was wondering what you are."

Tristan didn't look up and didn't change expression. Should Slap explain what he meant? But how, without sounding even more like an idiot?

In the ensuing silence, Slap wondered if Tristan would even answer.

His friend cleared his throat and said, "I'm a survivor."

Slap sighed and concentrated on strategy. He moved his knight. "Check."

Tristan lifted his eyebrows slightly, then his eyes crinkled in a smile.

Slap grinned in return and decided to try again. "So if you like surviving so much, why do you get involved in things that make that so chancy, like taking on the Mordas?"

Tristan didn't answer. He took Slap's knight. Good, good, maybe he was actually falling for the gambit. Slap made his move and waited.

"Because I can. Because I'm good at it," Tristan said.

Slap frowned and struggled to regain the thread of conversation. "But why dangerous things?"

"The challenge."

Tristan moved a pawn, and Slap stopped his mouth from falling open. Dang, he hadn't—

A loud, blatting sound jarred his thoughts. Slap jumped up, his leg banging the table. Like all the furniture aboard, it was clamped and didn't move.

"What inna world is that?" he asked, his heart pounding.

Tristan glanced over the game with an irritated look and stood with a sigh. "We're being attacked."

"What!" Slap ran out and forward to the bridge. He could read most of the telemetry now, but had no idea what to do. Gah, that helpless feeling was like a burr under his saddle!

Tristan sauntered in, glanced at the displays, and sat down. "Huh. Freebooters."

"Freebooters? Why aren't you worried?"

"Who says I'm not? But let's worry about things in order. Remember Lyssel's refit of this ship? Those turrets are doing their job. That's a Scorpion Quick Strike Frigate. Our cannons have taken out three of their fighters. If we get the fourth—"

The lights went out. With a gut-churning jolt, Slap's weight disappeared, and he began floating.

"Hmm." Tristan's voice was irritatingly calm. "Guess the fourth got us first. EMP torpedo."

Slap held down his hysteria with the same determination he was trying to hold down his meal. Zero-G didn't agree with his stomach. He gave a slight audible gulp.

"Don't you dare," Tristan ordered. "I'm not going to deal with *that* floating around."

Slap gulped again. He could just make out his friend in the dim glow of the emergency lights embedded in the bulkheads.

Clang! Slap started, looking around at the bulkheads as the sound reverberated through the ship. *Clang!*

= = =

"Right on time," Tristan mused, his mind racing. Defensive strategies weren't his strong suit. But how to make this offensive? With Slap's life to worry about, not just his own, he couldn't take the daring chances he'd like.

"Huh?"

"Standard procedure," Tristan said, "as we just heard and felt, is for the frigate to grapple us. Then they initiate their boarding strategy. Ships like this are helpless for about an hour, so they likely won't hurry. Psychological edge, make their victims squirm, waiting for the unknown."

"So what do we do?" Slap's hands scrabbled the air to find something to hold on to.

Tristan grabbed him and hauled him toward the chair. "Strap in for the moment."

"Strap in? Those are freebooters out there! We gotta do something!"

"Not yet."

"Whaddaya mean, 'not yet'? We can't just sit here and—"

"Yes, we can. I have to think before we act, and we have some time yet. So strap in."

Awkwardly and with a few gulps, Slap tried to maneuver his body into the seat. "But we're dead in the water, er, space. What can we do? How do we get our power back on? Isn't our computer fried from the EMP?"

Tristan stared over at him in the dim light. "The computer's optical. That's standard." He frowned. "How old were the ones you used on Zenos anyway?"

Slap shrugged, fumbling with the straps. "We didn't use much electronic equipment. Breaks down. I had a small com for some personal stuff, but it quit working not long after Ma died." His eyes scanned the bulkheads as if freebooters were going to blast through. "How long till they board us?"

"That will take some time. They have to match and seal airlocks before they break through and board. They might go through the hull—this ship is so old, they may not want to salvage it. However..." He paused, trying to think like a pirate. "They do know *Giselle* has some updated systems, like the turrets—which shouldn't have been able to take out their fighters so quickly. So if they're smart, they'd want to keep her intact as much as possible."

"But what about us? We are going to fight, aren't we?"

"Better than the alternative. But we don't know yet which airlock they'll use. Chances are they'll use a stun grenade when they enter, saves lives on both sides that way."

"So they can sell their victims to pressgangs?"

"If their victims are lucky." Tristan clenched his jaw; he shouldn't have said that. No need to have Slap worry even more. "But we'll deal them a few surprises."

"How so?"

Yes, Master of Ingenuity, how? Defensive. What—hide in the dark, avoid the stun grenade, fight the armored freebooters as they swarm over the ship? Faugh! If he could only take the fight to the enemy. Strike first. Hard enough to finish it...

"Dammit, Tristan, don't leave me in the dark! Tell me what you're planning!"

Tristan let his breath out loudly. "If only we could attack, instead of having to—" He stopped; the ship's status panel was glowing pale yellow. What? How could the grid be showing signs of a power-up?

"What's wrong?" Slap asked.

"Hold on." The glow increased. Tristan's mind reviewed the ship's specs. Only one thing made sense. "Lyssel, you sneaky..." He barked a short laugh. "Nothing is listed in specs, but I would bet *Giselle*'s anti-matter reactor is shielded against power loss and is recharging the power grid. I don't know how long it will take though." Tristan sat back in the chair, his mind whirling with possibilities, plans. A seed of hope grew.

"Does that...how much edge can that give us?"

Tristan frowned. "It should give us the element of surprise. From what I'm seeing, my best guess is that our power will be back on within five minutes."

"And then?"

"Once the computer comes online, it will start allocating power to critical systems, beginning with life support. If I can access it quickly enough, I can program the turrets as highest priority. When they realize we're not 'dead in the water,' they'll launch more fighters. Our biggest problem is going to be more EMP torpedoes."

"Yeah. If the turrets didn't stop the last torpedo, they probably won't stop the next one."

Tristan pursed his lips, shaking his head. "No, I think we have a better chance this time around. Their fighters are docked, and the frigate's defenses are laser turrets. They depend on their fighters for offense. Since we took out three, that leaves nine, unless they were already under complement."

"Us against nine fighters?" Slap's voice cracked. "How can ol' Bertha's turrets take on the frigate's lasers and all their fighters?"

Couldn't the cowboy at least use the ship's proper name? "The lasers are comparative pea-shooters to *Giselle*'s"—he emphasized the name—"turrets. And don't forget the upgraded armor she has."

"But the fighters—"

"We have military turrets, with a military tracking system. I doubt if their fighters are used to that sort of...aggressive assault. Anyway, once *Giselle* begins attacking, it will take a full two minutes to launch the fighters, one at a time. The cannons will be targeting the ships as they launch, as well as pounding the frigate. We do have a chance." Tristan leaned back in the chair. "I know it's difficult, but all we can do is wait."

Tristan tried make himself appear comfortable, to ease the cowboy's fears. But his mind raced—scheming, worrying, thinking of contingency plans for a dozen variations on Things That Might Go Wrong. Offensive. He needed to make an offensive strike...

In the silence, Slap chewed his nails.

A slight *whoosh* indicated air circulating as the lights slowly brightened. Down began to feel like down. Tristan dove forward to access the computer. Come on—hurry—override—reset... He straightened. "Turrets have priority." He glanced at Slap, allowing himself a slight smile. "Things should begin to be complicated for our friends."

The cowboy nodded and rubbed his stomach in relief, his face fading from green to pale. His eyes flicked between the telemetry displays and the external monitors. A shudder shook *Giselle*. And another.

"The cannons are targeting our conjoined assailants," Tristan said, a quiet glee rushing through him. "They must be scrambling to ungrapple and get clear so their fighters can launch."

The ship trembled again.

Tristan continued his running commentary, knowing Slap couldn't read the displays very well yet. "Ship away." He leaned over the console.

"Bet it's taking a pounding from the cannons," Slap muttered.

"Definitely. First fighter launched. Turrets targeting..." Tristan stared intently at the frigate's image, turning the map grid to show an alternate angle, waiting for just the right distance. "Come on... A little farther away... I'll show you offensive fighting, you—"

"What are you doing?"

"I'm going to use the turrets to take out their launch bay."

Slap chuckled. "Can you train a monitor on it? I'd like to see the mess a cannon would make."

"You require such simple pleasures." Tristan fingers moved with easy practice over the controls. "Monitor three...and... Now."

A fighter spewed out of the frigate. Behind it, the launch bay erupted in a bright explosion.

Slap whooped, and Tristan almost joined him.

"Ha! Hey, that Scorpion doesn't look in too good a condition. For an old cargo ship, this thing packs a wallop—whoa! Is that frigate going to make it?"

Tristan shrugged. "She's taken some heavy damage. They're backing off fast. Only that one fighter left. Now if only the cannons can take it out before it launches another EMP torpedo."

A tiny flash lit on a telemetry display. Slap pointed at it. "I think that means it's over."

Tristan saw the dot approaching from where the fighter had been.

"Not quite."

Darkness and weightlessness hit.

Slap groaned. "Aw, shoot."

= = =

"Well, I hope we don't have that sort of fun too often," Slap said, unstrapping as the lights came up.

"What, I would have thought you'd prefer something to break up the boredom," Tristan said with a slight smile.

Slap snorted. "Well, right now, I think I want a snack."

Tristan joined Slap heading to the galley, his mind pondering *Giselle*. She had some possibilities. He suppressed a chuckle at the thought of an old, Canary-class cargo ship defeating a Scorpion QSF. Not bad. *I might keep you for a while, old girl.*

The cowboy stopped dead as the door slid open, and his mouth dropped open. Tristan glanced beyond him into the galley. Pinkish-red globs and splashes stuck to bulkheads, appliances—Tristan doubted any surface had escaped.

He glared up at his companion. "I hope you know who's cleaning this up."

Slap rubbed a finger under his nose in resignation.

In the Lap of the Gods, *part one*

Two chimes and no answer. Tristan weighed Slap's privacy against his last memory of Slap not answering. If the cowboy'd had another nightmare of his family being killed in front of his eyes, what might he do? Surely he wouldn't do something stupidly fatal?

Tristan stared at the door, licking his lips.

Surely not.

He overrode the lock.

A twisted shape lay before him, tangled in a blanket. One bare arm and shoulder hung off the bunk, and one leg. A mass of dark, tight curls nested on the pillow, and from under it came muffled snores.

Tristan sighed quietly in relief. He took a deep breath and loudly called, "Slap!"

The snoring shifted tone, into a soft buzz.

He called again.

"Snrt?" The head lifted, eyes still shut. "Wht?" The body began to move, and Slap flopped onto the deck with a loud *whuff!* He groaned and scratched his head, one eye blearily opening. "What is't?"

"Morning."

"Mornings," Slap said through a yawn, "come too early in the day."

Tristan suppressed a smile. "This from a rancher who had to rise at dawn every day?"

"Didn't mean I liked it." Slap peered at the chrono and scowled. "It ain't morning either."

"It is planetside. We need to get moving."

"Sadist," mumbled the cowboy.

$$= = =$$

Slap glanced up at the tall, grey buildings looming menacingly over them. He shivered. Dulesh, what little he'd been on it anyway, had frosty, metallic-tang air, and little greenery. *A Dusty planet, and a cold one at that.* He hunched inside the just-bought jacket, hands stuffed in his pockets. His nose felt icy and began to run. He sniffed.

Tristan opened a door, and Slap stepped inside behind him. He was never let out without a leash. A loyal dog following its master. "What am I even doing here?" Slap asked in a plaintive whisper. He looked around the huge metal-walled warehouse. One of many in this part of the port city. It wasn't much warmer inside.

Tristan didn't answer. With a sigh, Slap trailed his friend as he headed for a small office to one side.

An older man with a slight stoop to his shoulders looked up from his desk. Curiosity lit his round face. "May I help you?"

"I hope so," Tristan said. "Name's Philips."

The man held out his hand. "Howard Kane."

Tristan shook his hand. "I need some equipment for my ship. A Bussard collector, for starters."

Ah, Slap thought, *then he's going to keep ol' Bertha for awhile. He said he'd install a hydrogen scoop if he were going to keep her.* Did that mean he was truly going to keep Slap around too? He realized he still tensed up when they landed on a planet or stopped at a station, wondering if he was going to be left behind.

"Hm," Kane said, "we can help you out with that. What sort of ship?"

"Canary class freighter with a custom refit."

Kane's eyebrows rose. "An old Canary? Well, I'd need the specs on her."

Tristan handed him a data crystal. "Take a look."

The man pulled up the specs on his desk screen and his eyes widened. He whistled through his teeth as he read, muttering to himself. "Two Type II assault turrets with twin plasma cannons...twin capacitor jump drive...Mark I matter/anti reaction assembly and 906 terajoule power grid?" He gazed at Tristan and, with a very dry look, said, "This isn't a Canary. She might *look* like a Canary...but I don't know that I'd even call this a refit. This ship has the armor, power, and weaponry to rip apart a Light Patrol with a few salvoes or shred a wing of fighters within seconds."

If only you knew. Slap kept his face straight, but the image of the turrets demolishing the launch bay of the freebooters' Quick Strike Frigate burned joyously in his mind.

Kane shook his head. "Why didn't you have the Bussard installed when you refitted her?"

"I didn't. I recently inherited her."

Slap didn't even blink at the smooth lie. Well, was it a lie? Could you call it stealing when the owner was a gangster and dead to boot?

"I see." Kane's face seemed thoughtful. Too thoughtful, Slap mused, and shook himself mentally. He was getting paranoid, hanging around Tristan.

"Well, I have Bussards in stock. My crews are a bit overworked, however. We can't start until..." He looked at his screen, and scrolled a new read-out to the surface. He blinked. "Is three days all right?"

Tristan shook his head. "I've already made arrangements for cargo. But that's not all I wanted, so if you can't do the Bussard on a tighter timetable, I doubt you could handle a particle beam installation."

Kane's expression grew intense. "You want to add to the armament?"

You betcha, Slap wanted to add, but stayed silent. Tristan shrugged.

Kane scratched his head and smoothed his thinning dark hair. "We could do it—all of it, but the time..." He squinted at Tristan. "I could have crews on overtime, but it would add to your bill."

"How much?"

"Twenty percent over total cost."

Slap inhaled sharply, but Tristan barely hesitated. "That's acceptable. Can you have the ship ready in four days?"

Kane hissed through his teeth. "Let me talk to Carter. He's supervisor of all weaponry installation. He'll want to see the ship first." He rose with a smile and left the office.

"He seemed awfully curious about things," Slap whispered.

"Later." Tristan fingered the edge of the desk absently.

Slap ambled to the wall and looked over the hanging blueprints, trying not to yawn. The day might be half over planetside, but by ship's time he should just be waking up.

Kane soon returned. "He says he can be at your ship by fifteen hundred."

"Good. We're dock pad NE fifty-three."

The two men nodded at each other, and Slap followed Tristan out, pulling up the collar of the jacket.

"Well," Slap asked as they walked along the street, "think you can trust him?"

"I picked him for his reputation. Any fallout from his 'curiosity' would happen after the job's done, and we won't be staying around."

"That's good. Where next? To the ship? Any chance you'll let me look around a bit on my own?" He knew the answer, but had to ask.

"We're still too close to the Confeds. It's too risky."

Slap sighed in defeat.

An apologetic look crossed Tristan's face. He added, "I thought we'd stop and eat before returning to *Giselle.*"

Slap perked up. "Sounds good!"

= = =

"Oh yeah, I can have you hooked up in no time, Captain," Carter said, wiping his hands on a rag as he sauntered across the cargo bay to Tristan. A gangly, silvering blond with a prominent Adam's apple, his weathered face wore a constant grin.

Slap leaned against the wall, arms crossed, playing—what? Bodyguard? Not that Tristan needed one, but with their sizes, it made a reasonable assumption, especially since he usually had Slap follow him around and never introduced him.

"Which system do you suggest?" Tristan asked.

"That's a piece of pie. The TLACorp Mark III."

Tristan's eyebrows rose. "That's a bit on the heavy side."

Carter nodded. "I'd agree, but this baby"—his hand slapped against a bulkhead affectionately—"can handle it with the antimatter reactor." His grin widened. "She's sweet! If I wanted to ship out, I'd ask if you were looking for crew."

"You weren't born here," Slap said. It wasn't a question.

Carter shook his head, still smiling. "Nope. I've traveled all over, tried lots of things. Learned lots of skills. Rolling stone, that's what I am." He tipped his head. "You a Separatist? Three Systems?"

Slap nodded. How did he know?

Carter snapped his fingers with a laugh. "I can call 'em."

Tristan cleared his throat. "Back to the Mark III. You really think this ship should have that rather than the Mark II?"

"Oh, yes, Sir! See, it has its own built-in spectrograph scanner and battle computer and does the frequency control automatically without the ship's MBC and spectrograph being involved. The smaller ones more often require a tie-in, and you don't want that."

Slap had been with Tristan long enough to know the subtle changes on his face. He was playing this guy to see if he was on the level. His voice maintained a neutral, almost questioning, tone. "I don't?"

Carter shook his head, his eyes narrowing knowingly. "No, Sir. It'd mean letting outsiders—meaning me—diddle in your computers. With all you have here, you don't want that."

"And what do I have here?" Tristan asked, his voice lower and sharper than usual.

Slap winced.

Carter's smile took on an edge and he seemed less buffoon-ish. "I don't know exactly, but I wish I did." His voice was quieter, less manic. "This gal's rough exterior hides an inner beauty. And I bet your cargo runs aren't run-of-the-mill. Boring can be good, but sometimes a guy likes to see things stirred up." He frowned down at the deck for a moment, but when he raised his head, the grin was back. "Anyway, I'll get to work on this. And bust the boys along on the collector too. Boss said you had a tight timetable." He nodded, his Adam's apple bobbing, and almost skipped to the cargo hatch.

Slap scratched his cheek, waiting until the engineer had left. "Whaddaya make of him?"

Tristan shook his head. "I'm not sure."

= = =

Slap shrugged on his jacket and checked for Tristan; his friend was immersed checking something or other on the bridge. One more day and they'd be gone. This might be his last chance. He grinned and strode down the cargo hatch. Squinting and holding a hand up against the sun, Slap peered up at the crew on the hull. Carter waved a spanner in greeting and bent back over his equipment.

"Hey, Carter," Slap called. "Can you let Tristan know I went out for supplies? I shouldn't be gone long."

"Sure thing."

Slap walked off, chuckling to himself. Finally, he was alone. Not feeling like a kid needing supervision. He'd shown he could take care of himself in a fight. Now he'd show Tristan he could do something as simple as shop for groceries.

$$= = =$$

Tristan checked all the cabins and the galley. No Slap. He descended to the hold. The collector crew worked diligently, finalizing the installation, but no Slap. He descended the ramp and glanced up at Carter and his men. The engineer, grinning as always, called down, "Captain? Your buddy said to tell you he was going for supplies."

Tristan's insides froze, and his brain buzzed into overtime. "When did he leave?"

Carter squinted in thought and scratched his head. "Oh, about half hour or so ago. I guess. Maybe longer."

Tristan nodded and strode toward the gate, cursing silently.

Like most port cities, this one had an open air market just past the gate. Spacers would pay premium prices for fresh foods. Many also had local commodities available with, of course, the customary dockside prices.

Tristan wove through the market, peering inside and behind the stalls as well as over them. One of the vendors scowled at him while blowing on his hands to keep them warm. Tristan kept going, pushing past people. If only the galoot had replaced his hat as well his knife. But the curly, almost kinky, mass of dark hair rising almost a head above all others wasn't easy to miss either. Yet he didn't see it anywhere. No Slap. His gut churned as he continued searching. Damnation, why did the boy have to disobey? He knew dangerous people were after them. How could he take such a chance?

After a time, he slowed, thinking. Adrenaline was a great ally at times, but not when one needed to step back and use the brain.

To find Slap, he needed to know who had him. Was it someone after Slap, or trying to get to Tristan through him? The answer could give him direction.

Could the Mordas have come after Slap already? Or were the Eridani the culprits?

Or was it someone after Tristan? The Eridani and the Mordas were also hunting him, not to mention the Confeds dogging his heels, but it might be any of several of Tristan's old enemies, even—heaven forbid—Dray.

To ask for help galled him, but he needed backup, to watch the ships, for movement in the city... But he took a chance. The very men he would hire might be working for those who took Slap. He didn't have much hope, but he'd pull together whatever resources he could.

He pressed through to the city.

= = =

"A bigger reward if he's returned to you alive?" asked one of the men by the wall, his eyes alight.

Tristan let his gaze burn into the man, who hunched his shoulders and looked away. He glanced around the large, well-lit room, making sure he had the attention of every one of the men present, as well as their employer, seated comfortably behind a large desk. Truss controlled quite a few legitimate concerns. And a few illegitimate ones besides.

"No. No attempts. He could be harmed. Retrieval is my concern. Just the location."

"And if we find nothing?" asked Truss.

"No results, no reward."

Truss tapped the smooth top of his desk. "Who is he to you to post such a...generous amount for him?"

"Curiosity is a consideration?"

"Knowing who I'm dealing with is always a consideration."

"I would think," Tristan said, letting his eyes bore into the man, "that considering your...profession, you would understand the importance anonymity would play in some of your more delicate business transactions."

87

Truss leaned forward, lip curled. "In your case, I think knowing is an important consideration."

Gah! He hated having to play this game. Some of his enemies would make any local underworld organization quake with fear, and close doors to him. Or worse, make them think of bounty hunter fees. Meeting Truss's eyes, he said evenly, "Money usually speaks for itself."

Truss settled back in his chair with a contemplative look. "But...you won't say who has your friend. I don't want to bring negative attention to myself or my associates."

"I'm not asking for direct involvement. Only information. And you're not the only ones who will be given this opportunity."

Truss's nostrils flared as he inhaled deeply. "I still think I need answers."

Tristan considered his money situation. Upping the ante would likely work, but he was stretching his finances already. He sighed. This was like tap dancing on a tight rope. "I don't know who has him. If I knew, I might have an idea where to look. And this is wasting time. A ship might have already taken off with him aboard, or he might be dumped in a river or trash pile by now."

"For what reason? Who is after him? And you?"

Tristan shook his head and walked to the door. It slid open and he turned. "The offer stands, if any of your associates wishes to show personal initiative."

He left quickly. Walking through the streets, something felt wrong. He doubled back, checking to see if he were being followed. Nothing. The back of his neck prickled, the Not Right feeling increasing. A drizzle started as dusk fell and the dank, oily odor of this 'Dusty' city increased. Slap and his people had a point. Regardless of plans to create an aesthetic display, industrialization unchecked inevitably provided a polluted view and environment.

Tristan had seen planets that moderated industrialization, and kept themselves from sliding into an abysmal defilement of their world, but the moment the corporations got a toehold, the cause was lost.

He shook off his train of thought—no doubt Slap's influence—and concentrated on his surroundings. As he neared the port, the streets grew narrower and dingier. Detritus littered the street. Now he had to be extra alert. Silence grew, except for the sound of light rain spattering.

A shadow moved ahead, and Tristan readied himself.

The silhouette of a man stepped into the street, hands away from his sides. He stepped forward and light fell across his face. Steel Eyes.

Part of Tristan felt relieved. Chances were Slap was safe. Merely being held to blackmail Tristan into helping the Confeds in whatever scheme they kept hounding him about. But something was wrong. Steel Eyes had been beaten. He sported a black eye, his nose looked broken, his jaw swollen, lips split, and blood stained his shirt.

"We need your help."

"So you keep saying." Tristan walked a few steps closer. "But kidnapping Slap to try to force me—"

"We don't have him anymore."

Tristan stopped, staring Steel Eyes, fear rising from his stomach, threatening to choke him. "Explain."

Steel Eyes licked his lips and winced. "We took him, like you said, to get you to help us. But now, the enemy has him. Our enemy. And yours. The Eridani."

The fear rose, blinding Tristan with red rage. His hand shot out and seized Steel Eyes by the throat. "You bastards! You—" He choked, words inadequate to describe them or his feelings. Steel Eyes used a pressure point to release Tristan's choke hold.

Tristan struck twice swiftly, to the solar plexus then the throat.

Steel Eyes dropped to his knees and croaked, "We'll help you get him back, if you'll help us."

His mind whirling with plots, schemes, counterplots, Tristan spat, "I'll make you pay tenfold for every injury inflicted on that kid. You'll wish the Eridani had grabbed you rather than leave you to me."

In the Lap of the Gods, *part two*

Steel Eyes, who finally gave his name as Swain, took Tristan to the warehouse where they had been holding Slap. The inside looked like a war zone with walls half-melted and charred from particle beam bursts. The smell of burnt flesh and acrid, scorched metal filled the air.

Doctors were there, attending to several men. Several bodies lay covered with sheets.

"I knew you wouldn't believe me," Swain said. "So investigate all you wish. See that I'm telling you the truth. This isn't a set up. The Eridani did this. And they have your friend."

Tristan went to the first body and pulled back the sheet. He knelt and felt for a pulse at the neck. Cold. Dead all right. But how did he know this wasn't a cadaver brought here to make it look good? He walked to the next body and pulled back the sheet. Swain's partner. And he was dead. He didn't put it past the Confeds to kill their own people to further a goal; they had done it before. But Tristan somehow doubted they rated him high enough to go to this extreme. The third body was Eridani High Guard—their best soldiers. He had tattoos and loyalty scars—some many years old. This was not chicanery.

His hand dropped from the lifeless form, and he stood and looked across the carnage to Swain. "Let's talk."

= = =

Tristan remained silent as the Confeds discussed their invasion plans. He rubbed his face as the one agent rattled on about meeting their fleet at Orion Station. No. He was not going to be their pawn, and owe them for helping him free Slap. He shook his head. "I'm not going back through Confederation space."

"But—"

"We're already in the Xanthus Commonwealth, and I won't detour. I'm going straight to Eridani Prime. You know that's where they're likely taking Slap." *Were they?* He'd ponder that later—now he needed to deal with these idiots.

"But we need to coordinate our attack!"

"No." Tristan pointed at the man. "You might need to. And if your scheme isn't any better than this fiasco was, then I'll not worry about seeing you alive again. I'm going straight through Xanthus to Eridani,"—*perhaps*—"and I'm leaving tonight."

"One of our ships will take you, then," Swain said.

Tristan shook his head, arms crossed. His lips thinned. "I'm taking my ship."

"Our ships are faster," one of Swain's men said to Tristan. "You need to—"

"I need to gut the bunch of you for creating this situation." Tristan's voice cut across theirs, and they all fell silent. "You make whatever plans you want for conquest of Eridani or assassinating their Emperor or whatever else you are scheming. I don't care. I'm going after my friend. And if you get in my way, I swear by my black soul you'll each beg for death before I'm through with you."

He spun to leave, but Swain stepped into his path. "If you just go off on your own, how will we rendezvous later?"

"We're not. Get that through your head. I have one objective, and it doesn't coincide with yours."

"We can't just let you leave. And besides, what if the Eridani are outside right now, waiting for you?"

"If they were, they'd be in here, and you'd be dead. Look around you! They didn't care who got in their way to get Slap. If they want me, and I'm with you..." Tristan glared around the room at the expressions on the agents' faces; their arrogance began to be replaced by fear, and they exchanged nervous looks. Right. The knuckle-draggers finally got it.

Before anyone else could say a word, Tristan yanked the door open and left the warehouse.

His pace quick and senses alert, Tristan wove through the streets back to the ship. The Eridani could grab him right now. If they did, he wouldn't fight—futile given the scene in that building.

A shadow appeared ahead, and Tristan slowed. The shadow grew into several, then into silhouettes as five massive men stepped into the thoroughfare, blocking his way. Even in the dark, their outlines betrayed they were Eridani High Guard. Unlike Perseus Station, they had managed to sidestep security—they bore full arms. The emperor had learned his lesson; he didn't send a mere two men against Tristan this time.

He stopped. The urge to fight clenched his fists. One stepped closer and, in a voice heavy with the Eridani accent, said, "We were ordered to give this to you." He held out a white envelope.

Tristan could make out, barely, the royal seal of Istvan's house on the back. He took it. The guards all stepped back and disappeared into the shadows.

They could have grabbed him, but they didn't. For what reason? Just psychological torture? Wondering what was happening to Slap? If so, it was working. His teeth ground, knowing what that madman was capable of. He walked on, still acutely aware of his surroundings. At last he came to a place with enough light and tore open the envelope. The writing inside was a feminine script. The paper read:

This time you shall be the Knight.

What was the purpose of this missive—if one sentence could be called that? To make sure he knew who had taken Slap? But why did the emperor have his sister Nadi write? Only Tristan, Slap, and Nadi would know she had scornfully called Slap a knight in shining armor when he rescued her, so this appeared genuine. Perhaps that was the reason. But not, he didn't doubt, the only one.

= = =

"Hey, Captain!" Carter stood in the doorway of the cargo hatch, the light from inside casting him in silhouette. "My men are done. The equipment is installed, but needs some hooking up and testing. We should be able to finish up and have you ready before noon tomorrow."

Tristan ascended the ramp into the lit cargo bay, the crumpled paper and envelope still balled in his fist. "No time. I'll find a way to have it finished later. I have to take off now."

Carter said nothing, his Adam's apple bobbing as he eyed Tristan.

"Now, Carter. Get off. I'm leaving." He tossed a credchit at the man. "This is the second half of payment for your boss."

"Wait a minute, Captain. You look like you might be in need of an extra hand or two."

Tristan stood by the hatch control and glared at the engineer. "Get off."

"Where's your Separatist friend?" Carter's eyes gleamed in enlightened suspicion.

"None of your business."

Carter licked his lips, and planted his fists on his hips. "Now, listen, Captain. I can read a situation. And this is sizing up to be one. I can finish up on the equipment on the fly. And with your friend...missing, you might want someone to watch your back."

Tristan's eyes narrowed. "Why would I trust my back to you?"

"Well, considering you could shove me out an airlock, I'd say I'm taking as much chance as you. But I've been waiting for a way off this rock. My contract was up with my boss two years ago and he won't release it. And I know I can be handy to have around."

"You're indentured to Kane?"

"Not any more. It was up two years ago. But I'm still tagged, and the law here doesn't care. I get room and board, but no pay. Just take me with you, and I'll do whatever you want."

"If that's true, why is Kane allowing you to be here alone, now?"

"The crews know the work's not done, so you'll not be leaving, or I'd not be allowed to stay to update you on progress. There is a guard from the company by the gate though, waiting for me. Take me with you, Captain!"

Tristan shook his head, and Carter stepped closer. "My boss was contacted by the Confeds—they put word out about you. He told me to take my time on the installation, to keep you here. But I didn't." His blue eyes gleamed. "I thought I might finally get my chance. Please."

In a heart's beat of time, Tristan searched his instincts. Suspicion had kept him alive many times. One moment of misplaced trust not only risked his own life but guaranteed Slap's demise. He hesitated, not believing his decision. "It's going to get dangerous. Probably more so than anything I've ever been involved in."

Carter's eyes lit up, and he grinned. "Let's go."

"I'm not playing, Carter. I'm going to rescue my friend from the Eridani emperor himself. I really don't expect to succeed. This is a one-way trip. And I'm not stopping anywhere between here and there, so you can't jump ship on me. You come with me, you're in all the way."

The engineer's smile faded a slight bit. His Adam's apple bobbed as he swallowed. He took a deep breath and nodded. "I'm in."

"You're insane."

Carter's lips spread in a lopsided smile. "You're the one going into hell itself for a friend. It might be suicide, but then, I get the feeling you might have a card or two up your sleeve that might even things up. Let's go, Captain. We're wasting time."

What am I doing? Tristan wondered as he closed the hatch. He headed for the ladder, calling over his shoulder. "Get to the bridge and strap in."

"Yes, Sir!"

= = =

Tristan got clearance and lifted off. He brought up the comm display as he said, "Carter, you keep your mouth shut unless I give you the word."

"What are you doing?"

"Keeping options open. For both of us."

Kane's suffused, round face appeared on the display. "Captain Philips, what is going on? My man just called me that you took off. You still owe me, and besides, that madman Carter is on your ship."

"I have the credchit for you. I'm coming back. If I weren't, would I bother to contact you? I've had an emergency come up and couldn't wait. I imagine the Confeds will confirm that much."

"The Confeds? What—"

"Carter's tag comes off when we return. Then you get your credchit."

"And if you don't return?"

"Better pray I do. I have no next of kin to pay my debts for me."

Tristan cut the connection and settled into the chair.

Carter stared at him. "Why did you do that? You really are coming back?"

"I doubt it. I honestly don't think I'll live through this. But I always cover the bases if I can. Kane has a reputation for good work, and it could be I might need his services again. It also lets him know his hold over you is gone."

Carter gave him a calculating look and nodded. "And puts me more in your debt. I get it."

"Covering my bases."

A sad, lopsided smile flickered on Carter's face but he said nothing.

= = =

Jumps completed, Tristan set course and rose. "You can work on the installations if you wish. I think by now you know your way around the ship if you want to eat or rest."

Carter looked up at him, blue eyes wide. "I'll uh, clean up a bit and rest." He followed him off the bridge.

Tristan paused, feeling inexplicably lost. The ship felt...strange. Empty.

Carter passed him and headed down the hall on the port side. He watched the gangly blond walking away. This was all wrong; it should be Slap sauntering along that corridor. A surge of anger welled up in Tristan and he took a few steps toward Carter. "The cabin across from the galley and next to the head is Slap's. You can take one on starboard side."

Carter whirled, his eyebrows rising. "Sure, Captain." He gave a nod and pointed to the other side of the ship. "I'll just, uh, starboard, yeah."

Tristan unclamped his jaw with effort and stormed into his cabin to change into his sweats. He needed a workout.

= = =

Tristan chalked his hands. He hadn't had a place to work out in years anywhere near the size of this cargo bay; it was glorious. He stood before the beatboard, sizing up the static trap. The only flaw was the lack of height. Trapeze bars should be many meters off the ground. At least this close to the ground he only needed a crashmat.

He bounded off the beatboard, grabbed the trap, glided into a kip, and up to handstand. He pirouetted and held it, staring at his hands gripping the bar below him. Slap chinning himself on this trap burst on his sight, and he vented a growl. He began a giant, but his concentration wouldn't hold, and his grasp slipped as he swung around the bar. He landed on the crashmat with a loud *whoomp* and lay still for a second before scrambling up.

He snatched a towel from the stack and threw it, but that wasn't enough. He glared at the hanging bag and leaped in the air and kicked it as hard as he could. It jerked and thrashed spasmodically. His lips drawn back in a snarl, he slammed the bag with his fists and feet over and over. Finally, winded, sweat rolling down his face and stinging his eyes, Tristan quit and fell to the floor.

"Uh, Sir?"

He took a deep breath and glanced up to see Carter standing by the ladder watching him, eyes round. "I uh, I was just going to work on the final hook up of the Bussard. I figured you'd want that done first."

Tristan gave a nod, still trying to catch his breath.

"I need you to unlock the panel. I noticed you had them all coded."

Tristan got to his feet and picked up a towel. Wiping his face, he walked to the fore of the cargo bay. He looked over the new equipment and snorted. This guy knew what he was doing. "Did you intentionally not finish so you'd have a card to play in getting me to take you off planet?"

Carter's frown slowly changed to a grin. "You can tell, huh?"

"Like you, I'm knowledgeable in a variety of areas. I've had to be both pilot and engineer of my own ship for a long time." He waved at the collector. "Get this done."

Tristan walked away, Carter's "Yes, Sir," trailing in his wake.

= = =

The image wavered, and Tristan rubbed his eyes. He flicked off the display and leaned back. No useful information on the emperor's palace. From his one visit to Eridani Prime, he had heard the rumors of the horrors inside the huge fortress. He must have other places he used for his victims, but almost certainly those he wished to personally oversee must be at the palace. And with the trouble he'd gone through to grab Slap, he would surely want him close at hand.

He could expect no help from any of the Eridani subjects; they were conditioned from birth to accept their emperor as a god, and their lot in life was to do his will and fulfill his whims. He had to use a backdoor to get into the place. But how, if he couldn't access plans of the structure?

Backdoor. He needed a backdoor for information. His fingers flew over the panel and soon the information he needed appeared. The architect for the palace design. Alvarza. Ah, impressive credentials. And—ha, dead. He snorted. Why was he not surprised to find Alvarza's death came soon after finishing the palace?

Tristan began to read through the information. The architect had been famous for his love of old Earth castles. Probably what drew Istvan's grandfather's attention to him. His designs integrated technology with ancient aesthetics. Tristan did another search. No specific blueprints for the Eridani palace, but many of his other projects were available. At least examining them would give him the mind of the man. Couldn't hurt. Might come in handy. Tristan settled in to study.

= = =

Carter sat at a console in the rec lounge. From the adjoining galley, Tristan ignored him as he viewed the available food while twisting to crack his back. He saw leftovers from Slap's last culinary effort and ground his teeth. Well, waste not. He warmed it up and, only after a slight hesitation, walked into the lounge and sat to himself.

Slap had grinned offering this particular dish. They both enjoyed spicy, hot foods, and this was one of Slap's best achievements. Tristan had heard whoops and calls of "Brago's Bands!" and "Boy howdy—that's good!" while the cowboy had been cooking and taste testing the food.

Somehow the spicy rice and meat dish—Slap wouldn't say what kind of meat, just "tastes like chicken"—didn't seem so appealing now. And seeing Carter's surreptitious glances instead of Slap's mischievous grin didn't help. He pushed back the plate.

Why did this bother him so much? It wasn't as if he actually *liked* the galoot. That ingrained life debt was to blame. His people were their own subculture, floating from star to star. Over the centuries, they learned to distrust outsiders. But from young childhood they were taught that anyone who bore the weight of your safety was a brother, and you owed a life debt to that person. And within their culture, that meant everyone. He could see a hand grasping his wrist as he flew through the air, and hear a voice saying in Russian, "When his hand grabs yours, and saves you from the fall, then he is your brother, and you owe him the same."

Rarely did someone from outside rate a second look, much less ever incur a life debt. But life debts obviously didn't mean what they should, even to those inside. Or Tristan would not have been betrayed.

Even Dray had used the life debt to try to lock his young protégé to his side. But he had twisted the custom, and its meaning. And eventually Tristan saw through the twistings, saw the lies. The betrayals.

He would not do that to Slap. He owed him.

Carter eyed him, and Tristan sighed. He needed to discover if he could use the engineer, depend on him. He beckoned to him.

Carter came over, his lined face drawn, no goofy lightheartedness now.

As he sat, Tristan said, "I didn't have time to argue with you, but do you really realize what you've gotten yourself into?"

"I've been thinking of nothing else." Carter's smile flitted for a second, but disappeared when he swallowed. "It's kind of scary."

"It's our necks on the line. And you're in this up *to* your neck. You can't easily desert once we're on Eridani. They don't like non-subjects without a passport or working papers. They take a fatally grim view of it, as a matter of fact."

"I know." Carter stood. His lopsided grin slid onto his face again. "Got a poison tooth you can put in my mouth so I can avoid the alternative if I get caught?"

Tristan snorted in lieu of an answer. Carter did perhaps understand how serious this was. He just hoped he could count on him. If he weren't a Confed spy, or worse. Faugh! He shouldn't have brought him along. Another variable to plan contingencies

98

for. But back to the basics. "Getting into Eridani space shouldn't be a problem with this ship."

"Not with the military jump-drive," Carter said. "This thing doesn't need to look for Minkowski space like a civilian drive. We can create a wormhole and jump to any specific point we wish."

"I'm aware of that."

"Sorry. Anyway, this baby should be able *to* get us to the planet no problem. But getting *down* to the planet, that's another story. Their planetary defenses are nasty."

"I can change registry for this ship, but somehow that doesn't seem safe enough, in this situation."

Carter's eyebrows rose. "I agree."

"Any suggestions?"

Carter rubbed his chin, his eyes narrowing. "How good a pilot are you?"

Tristan pursed his lips. "Good."

"Well, what we try depends on your piloting skills. So how good is good?"

"Try me."

A smile edged onto Carter's face. "Well, if you're good enough to take us in precisely at a magnetic pole and keep us there throughout descent, I can do it."

This idiot was out of his mind! "You're talking about a vertical entry. Ever hear of entry burn-up?"

"I can tune the electromagnetic distortion shield to sweep the atmosphere away, so it flows around us." Carter made burrowing motions with his hands and shrugged. "The hull *will* get a little warm..."

"Wait. Wait..." Tristan leaned back, frowning at the engineer. "Electromagnetic forces need something charged to affect. The atmosphere below the ionosphere has a low concentration of charged particles, so the EMD will be limited in what it can do to shield us."

"That's why I suggested the magnetic pole."

"How much assuming are you doing as to the amount of charged particles present?"

"It's....iffy. I mean, it does depend on the amount of particles plus your piloting skills, not to mention my engineering skills."

"You think you're good enough to pull it off?"

Carter's smile broadened. "Try me."

Tristan glared. Carter's diffidence had evaporated. He had honest confidence in his skills. Or he was crazy.

The engineer cleared his throat. "If you're a *really* good pilot, we could avoid that by jumping straight in, under the ionosphere, in the stratosphere if possible, at the magnetic pole."

"And then?"

"Then I have the EMD cloak us from sensors by wrapping the magnetic lines of force around the ship. And, we'd have to jump in slow or it would be like hitting a brick wall."

"Jump in straight on the pole, wrap the field lines around the ship with no breaks, and at a low enough speed that we don't turn into strawberry jam? Just balancing those fieldlines to stay 'silent'..." Tristan shook his head. "That's almost impossibly exacting. And flying this barge in atmosphere at full throttle for thousands of miles with both fighters and orbitals targeting us? No."

"That's why I said you'd have to be a *really* good pilot. Oh, wait...." Carter frowned, his fingers drumming on the table, he began muttering to himself. "...forgot this had a double-jump....hm, subatomic particle cascade....EMP....perfect." He looked up, his eyes alight. "Let's try this. We jump in near the city using both capacitors. One to open and hold the wormhole, the other to create a field of negative energy around the ship. This will allow us to jump at a high speed so we have some momentum to get somewhere faster and not turn into strawberry jam."

Tristan stared in disbelief at the engineer. The man was certifiably insane.

Carter continued, "An added benefit would be we would create a massive EMP shockwave and particle storm from the stresses of space-time being ripped open in a gravity well. That should knock out the city's defenses temporarily and keep us from being tracked for a few minutes while we find a place to land and hide the ship."

After recovering his voice, Tristan asked, "What will this do to the ship, assuming I have the skill to pilot her through this scenario?"

"Er, the jump core will be glowing white-hot. We won't be able to jump again for about an hour. But I don't think you'd want to jump that soon once we're there. My only question is, can we hide the ship fast enough once we arrive?"

Tristan rubbed his eyes. *Insane. Completely insane.* "If this is really possible, has it ever been done before?"

"Um, yeah."

"And the results?"

"Well, less than favorable. The Confeds tried it and lost the frigate. I'm not sure how many others have tried it..."

"Considering it's not standard procedure, I doubt the maneuver is very practical."

"Or safe. But this is an emergency. How would you have tried to get to the planet if you'd been alone?"

"Backdoor. Public transport in a disguise most likely. I'm...rather experienced at that. But the Emperor appears to know enough about me that he'd be expecting me to try to sneak in."

"Well then, this is perfect! Totally unexpected."

"Totally unsurvivable."

"Not totally."

"You're insane, you know that."

"I wouldn't be a good engineer otherwise."

He gazed at the table. He had one shot to get in. He could take his time, try to get down to the planet invisibly, but what would be happening to Slap in the weeks it might take? And the Confeds were planning their assault. That might destroy his ability to sneak in if it coincided with their assault—and afterwards, make it impossible. And those idiots might blow up the palace, and Slap. Crazy or not, this was his only way in. Tristan knew he was a good pilot. A very good one. But was he that good? He'd done some tight, perilous flying, but didn't know if he could handle this. And he had no base to catch him if failed.

Was that hell he felt breathing heat on his heels?

He took a deep breath and looked up to meet Carter's gaze. "All right. We'll try it. And most likely die in the attempt. But assuming we don't, we have to hide this ship, and fast. The mountains should give us some cover. The land is pock-marked, filled with canyons and mesas."

Carter grinned, but it faded and he paused, staring at his hands splayed on the table. "You know, they wouldn't let me go knowing I came on a ship that had sidestepped all their defenses. And I'm no pilot—I'd never be able to fly this baby out of there, even without them trying to shoot me down." He looked up earnestly. "I really am in."

Tristan wanted to ask why, but Carter might take it as an invitation to go into his history and—by Orion's belt, no—his feelings. So he merely nodded and left to finish his studies of Alvarza's designs. He wondered if he might sleep, but doubted it. He couldn't get Slap out of his thoughts, and his mind lent itself to gory imaginings.

$$= = =$$

Slap awoke. Sensations whirled, fighting orientation. He blinked but everything remained dark. His throat hurt, his mouth so dry he could barely swallow.

He sat, naked, on a cold, hard surface, leaning against a wall, his arms splayed out in restraints. He yanked but cool metal cut into his wrists. Trying to stretch his legs brought sharp pain to his ankles—manacled to the floor. He shivered.

Vibrations and the metallic-oily smell told him he was aboard a ship.

What happened? Where was Tristan? What *happened*? Was this a freeholder ship? Had he been captured and sold to a pressgang? *Where was Tristan?* He called for his friend, but his throat barely managed a croak. He tried again and listened. No answer.

Doubts and fears congealed in his stomach. He stared with suppressed terror into the dark.

In the Lap of the Gods, *part three*

Tristan paced the hall between the bridge and the galley. Fifteen minutes until the capacitor charged for another jump. He'd discussed their entry to the planet with Carter, memorized the floor plans of the emperor's palace, and studied the topography of the area they were going to land in until he knew it blind. Nothing left to do.

Except wait.

He'd chafed on their fuel stops, and they'd have to make one more before arriving at Eridani.

Carter came up the ladder and watched him for a moment. "Captain, you really need to sleep. You can't pilot this gal through that last jump into the atmosphere like you are."

Tristan bit back a snarl. He knew the engineer was right, but sleep did not come easily.

"Three more jumps, Sir, and we stop for anti again. That refuel will take hours. It would be a perfect time for you to rest."

"I have to oversee that. It's a touchy business."

"Sir, that's one thing I can do and know I do it right. I know it's hard for you to delegate, but you need to be in top form, to get us to the surface alive. I admit I don't think you care if I make it, or even if you make it, but your buddy's only chance of rescue is you, so think of him."

Tristan blew out a sharp exhale, almost a laugh, and ran his hands through his hair. "You're right. After we dock to refuel, I'll try to take a nap."

= = =

Slap's legs shook as he set one foot in front of the other. If he fell, they might drag him again. Lack of food, and water, had weakened him, and with this planet's hell-hot heat, he felt ready to pass out.

Blood ran down his arms, chest, and back, from the tight-fitting stone stock encompassing his wrists and neck. The inside of the enclosures had been deliberately chiseled to grind and gnaw into flesh. To take the pressure off his raw neck, he had to lift the heavy stock-bar with his arms, scouring the skin off his wrists.

The heat of the bare ground had blistered his feet as he was led through the city to the palace. His pain, and dread of what was to come, overshadowed any embarrassment at being paraded naked through the streets. The natives pointed at him and chattered in their tongue, or hissed. Some spit on him. A few threw stones. "Barbarian!" several shouted.

The outer guard walls of the palace loomed. Should he want to get to the end of this trip? The little Tristan had told him made him fear the end as much as the journey.

The palace looked like an old castle; outer walls with towers, a fortified gatehouse, a courtyard, even crenellations on the tops of the walls, but the doors opened by modern magic. The air conditioning struck him, and he shivered as he was shoved and prodded through hallways. At least the place had lifts. He could not have managed stairs.

Finally guards shoved him into a dim, dank chamber, filled with overpowering organic smells. He retched, but not having eaten since...whenever he'd been captured, and being given little water, he had nothing to disgorge. Still, his stomach heaved violently as they hauled him to a wall, and chained his feet to the floor.

The door slammed. Slap fell against the rough stone, not caring that the rock sliced his back as he slid to the floor. He could not lie down; the stock would not let him. But at least he could lean back a bit and rest, after a fashion.

Slowly, he became aware of his surroundings. The shadows that hid most of the chamber in darkness became sharper. Small sections of wall divided the room into cell areas. He heard raspy breathing but because of the partitions could see no others. A gurgling wail rose, then fell into weeping, followed by silence.

Tristan. Where was he? Considering this place, Slap rather hoped he was dead. One man against all of Eridani? Not even Tristan could win this one. And the last thing he wanted was for his friend to end up in here trying to rescue him.

= = =

Tristan was a good pilot; he had learned under intensive tutelage and gotten his master rating—albeit under a name he

104

hadn't used in years. But was he good enough? They'd soon find out. First test, get them through the wormhole fast enough that it didn't collapse on them, and slow enough that they didn't disintegrate upon slamming into the atmosphere once through.

From the time they jumped in, which would inadvertently create an electromagnetic pulse, they'd have about five minutes to hide the ship before the power grid would come back online, allowing in-planet defenses to target them. The resulting ion storm should help block them from orbitals. He hoped.

With only five minutes, they were going to jump in near the capital, where Tristan bet, hoped, prayed Slap was being kept. Cavern systems pocked the desert planet, and many of the inhabitants lived in them. However, one not too distant from the city was considered taboo. From all the information Tristan could find, the superstitious natives avoided it, claiming it was home to their dead ancestors and gods.

Perfect.

Getting from their jumping-in point to the cavern—that was going to be sticky. They would need almost a vertical descent. He took a breath and rubbed his palms on his thighs. Now or never. "Ready for the final jump. Engaging first capacitor."

"Wormhole forming," Carter replied in a shaky voice.

"Engines idling down," Tristan murmured.

"Now entering wormhole."

Disorientation flowed over Tristan; tingling coursed through him, his skin turning inside out. He cleared his throat. "Engaging second capacitor."

Carter's distorted voice floated to him. "The negative energy field is steady, keeping the wormhole from collapsing on us, but it's overheating the core faster than I expected."

Tristan growled invectives and gripped the controls to pitch the ship as they emerged. They were low in the ionosphere—not good. Their speed was above Mach six. Almost too slow for the wormhole but way too much speed for this old freighter at this altitude. *So much for my piloting skills.*

Several warning klaxons blatted, bombarding Tristan's ears.

"Slow the ship!" Carter shouted. "The field is dissipating quicker than I—"

"Shut those damned alarms off." Tristan's lips peeled back and his knuckles whitened as he banked the shuddering ship left. *Giselle* creaked and groaned around him as they began a controlled—semi-controlled—spiral.

"What are you doing?" Carter called, his voice breaking.

"Trying to burn off speed and not overshoot our landing zone."

Tristan slammed forward against the restraints; the last of the field was gone. *Giselle's* groaning rose to a scream, and the controls barely responded. *Like flying a brick!* The vessel felt like she was ripping apart.

"We're still too hot!"

"Speed brakes."

"We might burn them off."

"Use them!" Amid the cacophony of what seemed like the ship nearly self-destructing, Tristan could feel and hear—barely—the rhythmic thunking of the wings automatically extending. "With this pitch, will we lose the wings?"

"Don't know. Get her below Mach three and we shouldn't melt the hull."

By all means, let's not melt the hull. "Do you have a death wish?" Tristan growled through gritted teeth.

Carter laughed, manic and shrill.

Not reassuring.

Carter's voice pierced the air in staccato tremor, in synch with the freighter's quaking. "I'm showing we caused an EMP just like I thought we would—didn't affect us because we were inside the field at the time, and the ionosphere cascade is beautiful. And— sand! There's a sandstorm below. But the wings could shear off in this turbulence! I can override atmospheric wing control—retract them."

"Don't you dare! I need them."

Carter quieted a moment, then chuckled nervously. "At least all this atmospheric disruption should cover us from the orbitals and any ships trying to track us."

"I have to fly this barge through 'all this atmospheric disruption' to find that cavern, you know. Assuming she doesn't tear apart first." And that was still likely. This wasn't flying, more like hurtling through the air and not hitting the ground. Yet. Terra was getting firma fast. Too fast. "Temperature?"

"Below melting point."

Just in time. Tristan pulled out of the spiral; Carter wheezed an audible sigh.

"Sir, you're sure that cavern is a safe place to hide the ship?"

"No. But it's a better bet than anywhere else near the city. These people—" Tristan stopped to concentrate on plowing the ship through heavy turbulence. As they dropped through the troposphere, he watched his heading, ground track, altitude, and airspeed closely. If this old freighter did survive, she'd need major work. *Concentrate on the immediate.* He zeroed in on the coordinates for the cavern. How could he slow and hope to navigate her into the tight cleft in the rocks without any visual reference cues and with the wind shear?

This was impossible. Why had he even considered it? To break pattern. Istvan had to know his usual style, and this front door battering wasn't his way.

He decelerated *Giselle*, trying to hold her steady as he closed in on his target. She lumbered, not as responsive as usual.

"What's that ahead?" Carter asked, squinting at the read-outs.

"Our destination. Hold on."

"Are you sure you can fly this ship into that small opening?"

Tristan barked a laugh despite himself. "After all this, now you're worried?"

Carter didn't answer.

The sand still whirled around the ship, obscuring everything. His eyes riveted on the instrumentation. The cavern's aperture seemed too small.

Tightening his grip, Tristan slowed even more.

= = =

Slap roused slightly from the dazed state he supposed could be called dozing when he heard a scraping sound from the door. A boy, skinny, dressed only with wrappings around his loins, padded to him, bearing what looked for all the world like a water bottle with a straw in it.

107

Keeping his distance as much as possible, the boy stretched his arms so the straw could reach Slap's lips. Thirst overcame any suspicions, and Slap took several deep gulps. The water was cool flowing through his mouth and down his throat. His stomach knotted in rocks as the water hit, and his body jerked in an uncontrollable spasm. The boy pulled the bottle away and stood, staring at him with a mixture of curiosity and revulsion.

"Th-thanks," Slap murmured.

The boy's lip curled, but he held the bottle out once more. Without hesitation, Slap drank.

After a few more gulps, the boy stepped back. Slap muttered his thanks again, but the boy only hissed, "Barbarian," and ran out.

Some time later, the dim lights—wherever they were hidden, recessed somewhere in the ceiling—blinked out. The complete darkness stilled all noise in the chamber until one thin voice began its piteous wail again.

The door slammed open, and guards entered, guns in one hand, hand lamps in the other. Without a word, they unshackled Slap's legs and hauled him to his feet. A confused walk in the dark, and being hauled painfully up stairs, took Slap at last to a wide archway. He was dragged inside to some sort of large chamber. Incense hung heavy in the air. Hands roughly encased his calves into some sort of upright, manacled braces in the floor. He would be unable to sit.

A bright light, held by an unseen person, flashed in his face, making him squint.

"So this is our bait, is it?" a sneering voice asked. The light, closer now, blinded him as the voice whispered. "You work well, Bait. Your friend has arrived on the planet, if the disruption to our power is any indication. But he shall find he is overmatched this time. We are ready."

Tristan? Here? *No!* Slap wanted to cry, but no tears formed.

"We shall keep him here," the voice said in an authoritative tone. "He might amuse Us."

A faint hum began and the air moved—circulation. Lights started to glow. Whatever Tristan had done to their power, it was back on already. Slap was reminded of the time that frigate attacked, its fighters sending an EM pulse to disable ol' Bertha. The power had been restored in a similar way.

The lights brightened, and Slap could see a slender man with dark features, large, square jaw, and silk robes standing before him. His grin was so predatory and gloating that Slap shivered. *Tristan,* he shouted in his mind, wishing telepathy worked. *Stay away. Stay away!*

= = =

"Partially retract the wings, or we won't make it."

Carter complied silently, and Tristan clenched his teeth as the ship maneuvered on thrusters through the narrow confines of the tunnel. The passage widened into a large cavern, just as the maps posited. And it appeared uninhabited. Perfect.

He deployed the struts, and let the freighter down as softly as he could. Barely a bump. The least he could do for the old girl who got them through alive.

Carter heaved a sigh of relief and almost clawed out of the restraints. Tristan followed him to the lower deck, flicked on the external lights, and let down the starboard cargo hatch. Carter ran out, fell to the ground, and began to sob quietly.

Tristan wasn't going to ask if he had that reaction in general to flying or only to Tristan's piloting. He descended the ramp, glad to see that at least some of the lights still worked, and turned to see what he had done to his ship. The radiator heat sinks glowed orange, and waves of heat rose from the engines. The hull had patches and streaks of charring, and the speed brakes were burned nubs. The plinking and thunking of cooling metal proclaimed the freighter's quiet disapproval of what she had endured. He rubbed his forehead.

"It worked!"

Tristan spun to see Carter capering and cackling. "It worked! It worked! It worked! It worked! Yes!"

A shriek of stressed metal made Tristan pivot in time to see the aft starboard landing strut slowly collapsing. *Giselle* groaned as she tilted and settled into a sullen, temperamental pose. *Sorry. Sorry, old girl.*

Carter walked up next to Tristan, blinking. "Mostly."

"I take it you'll be fixing things while I'm trying to find Slap."

"Well, I won't be fixing that strut. That's for sure." Carter scratched his head. "No way to lift the ship."

"Think of Archimedes."

"Too bad he isn't here," Carter said with an edgy laugh.

Tristan sighed and shook his head at the damage. "Since I can't leave until the storm lets up, we might as well see what repairs we can do."

= = =

Slap's body trembled with pain and fatigue. The leg braces kept him upright, yet he was to the point of crumbling beneath the weight of the stone stock still around his arms and neck. He would soon topple over, and when that happened, his legs would break.

The emperor sat upon his throne, eating dainties off a tray held by a servant, not even glancing at the "bait" he wanted to keep here for amusement. Strange music that sounded rather like cats killing flutes played softly, and despite the ventilation, so much incense burned that the air was slightly hazy.

"Ahh, Vasso," a feminine voice called. Slap didn't even look up at whoever had come in. The marbled floor had his full attention—as in not fallen onto it and snapping his legs in half.

"Oh, this is not acceptable," the woman went on. "He's mine, and you said you wouldn't harm him."

"I said I would not kill or inflict permanent damage to your toy. But until I have his friend, he is mine."

"That's not fair."

Slap blinked, glancing up at the dark, slender woman. It was the princess. Nadi. The one he'd rescued. He dropped his chin to rest on the stock; his muscles ached too much to even hold his head up. The two continued arguing.

"Release him to me!"

"You watch your place, sister."

"You promised! And I want him!"

"Do you want him in pieces?" the emperor growled.

"It seems that's what you have in mind already. At least don't break him. I want him for a bodyguard. Imagine such a tall barbarian for a bodyguard!"

"You think you can tame him?"

"Like a wild stallion."

Like hell, thought Slap.

Emperor Istvan laughed, long and low. "This I would like to see."

A silence fell. A pair of guards came over and began to fiddle with the stock. After they removed it, he leaned forward, resting his hands on his knees, taking gasping breaths. A guard pushed his shoulders back. He flailed his arms, trying to keep from falling, but in vain. He expected a sick crack of pain in his lower legs but landed on a stool. He shuddered in relief and stared with detachment at his bloody wrists.

Nadi swished over in her long robes. She took his chin in her hand and lifted his head. Her smile reminded Slap of a feral cat. "Tend him," she called over her shoulder and pranced away, like a child happily anticipating promised candy.

A man, a servant, he supposed by his plain clothes, came over and began to wash Slap's wounds. Not gently, but not overly rough. Slap tried not to wince. After his injuries were cared for and he was given broth, guards manacled his wrists to a wide wooden beam connected by a cable to a pulley system. When that was done, his legs were removed from the leg braces, and the stool taken away. He could be lifted off the ground to dangle helplessly, forced to stand, or allowed to lie down. For the moment he sat, trying to ignore the metal already cutting into his flayed flesh, and the cold of the marble floor against his bare skin.

Despite his pain and exhaustion, Slap looked around. Huge cushions littered the floor near the dais, and gold gleamed from the pillars along the walls and the cornices. Statues sat on pedestals at the edges of the room with smoke rising from the incense burner set before each one. Stands of graduated shelves held candles. Wooden panels like brightly painted picture boards lined the walls. Faux torches lit the room.

Guards, dressed in silk vests and pantaloons tied around the waist with wide sashes, stood on either side of the dais and the archway as well. They wore scimitars, but also carried a shock baton, and a needlegun. Particle beam rifles were slung over their shoulders.

A groove running through the frame of the archway and the threshold told of a hidden door that could slide out to seal the room. The wall between the archway and the dais sported a computer console. Braces and manacles spouted from the floor near Slap, and another beam hung from the ceiling next to his.

What did it say about the ruler of this planet that he had devices for restraint, even torture, in an audience chamber? What had Tristan once said? The best thing that could happen to Eridani would be for the royal palace to be blown up with the emperor and his whole family inside. Slap now understood.

Nadi re-entered the chamber, her dark eyes gloating. As Slap was forced to lie on his back, he felt somehow the princess was more threat to him than her brother could ever be.

He was right.

I only love Shallah. I only love my wife. Slap repeated the thought over and over, humiliation and loathing filling him not only at what was done to him, but in the emperor's audience chamber, in front of all present. He tried staring at the eyehook attaching the pulley to the ceiling as a focus, but the princess leaned over him with a predatory smile, blocking his view. He squeezed his eyes shut, but tears still ran down his cheeks and into his hair.

Finally, Nadi rose. And Slap continued to sob, his soul shattered.

= = =

Tristan glanced up at the pale engineer and the forlorn-looking ship, nodded, and charged for the exit of the cavern. Two days—two foul days—they had been delayed, waiting for the sandstorms to subside. Their arrival had caused the initial storm, but he didn't know if the progression of them was something natural or an aftereffect. He almost foamed at the mouth at the wait, and Carter had slunk around, avoiding Tristan for almost the whole last day.

A soft blush across the dark sky announced dawn. The trek to the nearest road wasn't all that distant, and the capital not far beyond that. He should arrive in the city by midday.

= = =

The thrill of challenge surged in Tristan's heart as he slid easily past the guards with the others bringing wares into the palace courtyard. The inspection was thorough, but Tristan was just what he seemed, a poor laborer in rough-woven clothes delivering baskets of ripe fruit for his merchant master, smuggling nothing, concealing nothing. He straightened after depositing his offering in the kitchen, and began to follow the other menials out. In the press, he bumped against a guard and bowed low with murmured apologies. The guard would soon find he was without both the shock baton and the master key that should be hanging from his side.

The guards were less attentive of leaving laborers than of arriving ones. With an easy grace he slipped from shadow to shadow until he found a side door in an alcove. The master key did its job and he was inside, in an empty antechamber. Perfect.

He took off his upper clothing and ripped the shirt into strips. He donned the loose tunic again, and was now a lowly drudge, carrying cleaning cloths. The card hung inside his pants and the baton under the rags. He found a bucket and spigot to fill it with water. Now he was in business. He descended the nearby stairs to the dungeons without passing a soul. The guards didn't bat an eye as he bowed, showing his cleaning supplies, and he passed on.

= = =

A scuffle as two guards dragged in a victim didn't interest Slap except that it would take attention off him for the first time in the forever he had been here. Nadi left him on the cold stone. At the edge of his vision he could see her settle onto a cushion with a cat-that-ate-the-canary look on her face. He stared at the cracks radiating from the eyehook in the ceiling, numbly wishing he hadn't tried to help her. He should have let those thugs beat her, perhaps kill her. He wished he were dead. If only he'd died with his family.

The man shouted vehemently, and although Slap didn't understand the native Eridani language, he knew the poor slob was cussing out the emperor. *Probably get his tongue cut out for his trouble.* Slap wondered what the guy had done.

Istvan laughed. He walked over to Slap and bent over, leering down. "Our guest cannot understand you, Kebba. Speak so he can know your plight." Stepping back to the wall, the emperor lifted a lever, and the manacle beam began to rise.

The pain in his bloody wrists kept Slap from letting himself be hauled upright. He scrambled to get his feet under him. The beam stopped at shoulder height.

He and Kebba stared at each other. The man's face had been disfigured some time ago, his nose and ears gone, but the wounds had healed. Like Slap, he'd been stripped of any clothes; old whip scars marred his body. His hands were cuffed together in front of him.

"Go on. Tell this barbarian."

"I care nothing for barbarians," Kebba said in a thick accent. "Only for killing you. You are no god. You are murderer. You took my wife. Made me watch while you tortured and killed her. Then did this to me. And you think I will be a good *slave*, go away, and be frightened into silence about what I know? I have told others what you are. And I will kill you!" His voice rose and he screamed. "I will kill you!"

Slap's insides curdled. In his mind he heard the screams of his wife and cries of his baby trapped in the burning house while he lay helpless on the ground, battered, back broken, unable to stop the murderers. His agony rose, threatening to choke him.

Istvan grinned into Slap's face and waved his fingers in the air. A guard gut-punched Kebba, doubling him over. The emperor waited until his victim straightened, his eyes gleaming with insane glee. In an almost bored voice, he ordered, "Debone him."

Kebba screamed as the two guards began dragging him toward the archway.

Incomprehension gave way to sickening realization. The choking in Slap's gullet boiled into rage. He dove at Istvan, and actually managed to grab the shoulder of his robe, but the material slipped through his fingers. The fleeting expression of fear as the emperor jumped back with a cry tossed fuel on Slap's burning heart.

Feeling like a chained dog, Slap threw himself forward in futile fury, cursing Istvan with every foul word he knew. He couldn't reach the madman, but he couldn't stop trying either—his soul wouldn't let him.

Istvan stayed just beyond Slap's reach, laughing quietly. Taunting him. With a growl, Slap lunged again and—something broke loose. Istvan's eyes widened; he gasped, leaping backwards. They both looked up. The eyehook hung askew. A snarl escaped Slap, and he dove again at his prey. A cascade of rubble fell as the pulley broke free. Slap landed on top of the emperor and cursed that his hands weren't free to choke the life out of the monster. He smashed his forehead into Istvan's face. Royal blood spurted from his nose—red, like everyone else's.

"Don't shoot!" Nadi screamed. "I want him alive!"

Guards pulled him to his feet. Unholy joy coursed through Slap. He used the long wooden beam as a weapon, swinging it wildly, knocking the guards about like rag dolls.

"Don't shoot!" Nadi yelled again and called something in her language.

The emperor struggled to his feet, holding his nose and shouting in Eridani. The guards stood, frozen, uncertainty on their faces. Nadi ran for the archway.

Slap would die in a few seconds when the guards made up their minds who to listen to, but he was going to take out as many as he could. He dove at the ones who ran toward him from the dais. He hit them like a battering ram, bowling them down.

Every moment, Slap expected to feel fiery pain explode his back or head, but he kept on, determined to fight to the end.

A PB rifle fired, and again. Wild laughter echoed in the room along with agonized screams. Slap twisted around to see Kebba shooting guards, his face glowing with fierce delight. Brago's Bands! How did he get hold of a weapon? No time to ask. He turned to find another target for his beam and saw the source of the screams—Istvan convulsing on the floor, minus his legs. Huh. Good. His mother would have chided him, telling him to have pity, and find forgiveness. So would Shallah. But Slap couldn't. He didn't want to try. Let the murdering lizard get some payback.

He spun to survey the room. The guards were all down; the archway sealed. Nadi huddled near the door, eyes wide.

Istvan continued to shriek as Slap's and Kebba's eyes met. The man grinned. "I said I would kill him," he said over the dying wails of the emperor.

Slap managed a shaky sigh. "So you did."

"You—you were like a, a god." He nodded at the ceiling. "You broke free."

Slap swayed. Blood dripped freely down his arms. Hoping he didn't pass out, he walked toward the dais. The cushions looked so soft. He sat with a moan.

"No man—" Istvan half-hissed, half-sobbed, "is...is a god—but me." He grabbed his wrist, his fingers fumbling at a small instrument there. He spoke into it, in his native language, and laughed. The lights dimmed.

Nadi screamed and ran to her brother. She grabbed his arm, and spoke into the device. Twice. She pounded on his chest, yelling something. The emperor sneered, and his face went blank.

Nadi shot up, eyes wild. "We will die! The palace. He has spoken destruction. To prove he is a god."

"Then we die!" Kebba raised the rifle and fired. Disbelief shone on Nadi's face, and she fell in a heap. Slap stared at her crumpled, burned body for a moment, wanting to feel...relief, fulfilled revenge—something. But he only felt empty. Her death didn't restore the honor to his soul.

An earthquake-type rumble shook the room. Slap met Kebba's eyes and saw his own desperation reflected.

= = =

Tristan dragged the unconscious guard into the room and locked the door. He sat at the computer station and, using the guard's code card, began trying to find Slap. He stared at the display in disbelief.

Nothing.

Not possible.

A code word? Knight perhaps. He entered it.

Again nothing.

A red light blinked at the bottom of the display, and Tristan's stomach tightened. Had he tripped some alarm in the system? His hands flew over the console. No, something was wrong with the entire computer system of the palace. What in the name of Dallor's moons was going on?

A trembling rumble began, and he jumped up. An explosion somewhere nearby shook the room and a wall bulged. Tristan leaped to the door. It took two swipes to get the door unlocked. He ran into the hallway. About twenty feet to his right—the way out—stones blocked the way. Another boom sounded above and rubble fell, pelting his body. Tristan tried to protect his head with arms as he swung around, thinking and trying not to panic. A third explosion knocked him off his feet. Rock fell around him, battering him, pinning him.

In the Lap of the Gods, *part four*

An explosion elsewhere in the palace shook the whole room, knocking Slap onto his back. He struggled to rise, not an easy feat with the beam still manacled to his wrists. "Kebba! Get the keys and get this thing off me, please?"

The native groped on the body of the dead guard by his feet and rushed to kneel at Slap's side. He ran the key card over the slot. "If we will die anyway, why do you care?"

The beam clattered to the floor, and Slap held his hands up in front of him, gazing at the bloody mess that used to be his wrists. From the dawning awareness of pain assaulting his body, the adrenaline was waning. He began to shiver. "Dunno. Just...the feeling of being free, I guess."

Another thunderous rumble shook the chamber. Slap stood. Only a few minutes ago, he had wished to die, now he wanted to live. But how? The door was sealed. Wait—he grabbed the key card from Kebba and ran to the door. "You give up too easily," he called over his shoulder as he swiped the card.

Nothing.

He tried again, growled in frustration, and finally banged on the door with his fists. There must be something, some way—he swung around and almost tripped on a guard's body. The particle beam rifles! He snatched up the weapon from the dead guard and ran back from the archway. Raising the rifle, he fired until the door melted into hunks of white-hot metal. "C'mon!"

He jumped through the smoldering hole and waited for Kebba. "How do we get out?"

"Follow me!"

Slap did, trying to keep his footing as the building boomed and shuddered. They turned a corner and saw several servants huddled, crying. He hauled them to their feet. The servants cringed away from him. "We're getting out. You understand? Follow. Kebba, tell them!"

The native called to them and gestured. They chattered an answer. He shook his head at Slap. "They say stone fell and blocked the way."

"Let's see if we can unblock it! Show me where."

They ran down another passage. Slap stared at the damage. Not just stone blocking the way, the whole area was gone. Brago's Bands, there had to be a way! Part of the floor had given way here, leaving a gaping hole. "What level are we on? How high?"

"Two above ground." Slap knelt and looked down the hole. The passage below was piled with stone as well. "I'm going to take a look below. We might be able to get out this way." He slung the rifle over his shoulder and carefully lowered himself. The ersatz stair held, and he squatted to peer into the hall. The way looked clear, but they had to move fast. The booming was increasing. This place was ready to finish falling around them. He scrambled back up and beckoned them. "C'mon."

He stood at the bottom and helped the natives down. The first one flinched from his touch, but he steadied her as she slipped. Her dark eyes wide, she allowed him to hold her hand the rest of the way down. The male servant said something to Kebba who translated, "There are two stairs near here. The south one is closer."

"Let's try it."

The servant led the way and, day of miracles, the stairway was clear. He heard the roaring of many people shouting and shrieking as they descended to the main level. He didn't know fear could be a tangible thing—a smell, a feeling in the air—but it was. Servants and guards clamored at the now-sealed exit. Slap met Kebba's eye and nodded at the rifle and the door. Kebba yelled, pushing through, trying to get the mob to back away.

He wasn't very effective. Slap took a deep breath and gave a wild cowboy whoop—the kind he used when rounding up cattle. Some turned to look at him and shoved at others with fearful expressions. Warning against the wild barbarian, he supposed. He must look the part, naked and unshaven. He climbed onto a fallen block of stone and whooped again. More turned, and now Kebba's voice could be heard. They all backed away, and Slap fired. Nothing happened. He stared for a second, and it hit him—a force screen guarded the door.

"Can't any of the guards override that thing?" he called to Kebba, widening his stance to stay on his feet. A giant boom rocked the building, and the wall to Slap's right began to crumble. He hollered for folks to move, but too late; part of the wall crushed

119

several people—including the girl he'd helped earlier. In what seemed slow motion he saw her agonized eyes as she disappeared under the rubble. Only a hand remained visible as the dust settled.

No! With a growl of rage, he aimed the rifle at the computer console on the wall between two buttresses near the door and locked it on. With a shock, he realized he'd done just the right thing—the shield only covered the door. But only the surface shattered; the rifle didn't have the power to break through the thick wall.

A guard ran forward, yelling, and fired his rifle. The other guards joined him, sweeping the wall until it disintegrated. The mob crushed toward the hole, some getting burned as they pushed their way outside.

Slap stopped for a second and knelt to touch the delicate hand of the dead girl with the dark eyes. "Sorry," he muttered. He jumped up and bolted for the hole.

He stumbled once in the courtyard and hands grabbed at his arms, bracing him. The crowd ran, some screaming, toward the outer gates. The guards were long gone.

Once beyond the walls of the palace, Slap and the others turned. Clouds of smoke, debris, and dust obliterated the sun. Most of the palace had already collapsed. The center of the structure, where they had been, was the last to go, as if the destruction had worked its way inward.

Several people pulled on Slap, murmuring to him, urging him to move farther away. He let himself be led through a small square archway without a door. He ducked under the low frame and down stairs. At first he thought it was a cellar, but no, those around him continued on, leading him through one tunnel and on to another. Finally they came out into a large, well-lit cave. He was taken to one of the small, curtained openings lining one side and found himself in a small room. It contained several small wooden stools, and shelves along a wall. One person beckoned to Slap and pointed to a stool.

He sat—gingerly; though his anatomy no longer bled, being forced to cooperate with Nadi had left deep bruising. His body trembled. And—now that escaping death wasn't overriding everything else—he blushed as he realized anew he wasn't wearing anything. A woman held out a cup of water. He gulped it down.

Kebba stepped forward. "They want to know what you need."

Slap glanced around at the men. They wore loose pants and tunics. He looked down at himself and doubted they had clothes in his size. "A blanket."

One blanket was set over his lap, and another draped over his back. Ask for one, get two. Slap wasn't going to complain. Another woman knelt before him and began to clean and bandage his arms. Her touch was gentle, but still he clenched his teeth to keep from wincing. The wounds went deep.

Clothes were shoved at Kebba, and while dressing, he began talking a mile a minute. As he did, the folks crowding by the door grew silent. This Kebba had a charisma about him, despite his mutilated appearance. The woman in front of Slap paused occasionally as she worked to give her charge an awed glance. Kebba finished speaking and, in the silence, everyone looked at Slap. He gazed at the floor between his feet to avoid the stares.

After his wrists were bound, Slap was given a bowl of some sort of soup and a piece of dark, heavy bread. He balanced the bowl on his knees and ate slowly, dipping the bread in the broth. He'd not had much to eat while a prisoner and didn't want his stomach to rebel. He met Kebba's eyes. "What did you say to them?" Slap asked, swallowing a bite.

"I told them how you broke free and attacked that false god of an emperor. How you saved us. You have come from the gods."

Slap nearly choked. "Brago's Bands! I wasn't sent by no gods. I'm a cowboy. And I'm only here because your emperor kidnapped me to use as bait for my friend. You were the one who killed Istvan and Nadi."

"Only because of you. The guards were watching you, not me, so I had a chance to grab a rifle."

"I'm a barbarian, remember? The one your people spit on when I was brought here."

"You look like a barbarian, and do not speak the gods' tongue, but you are not a barbarian. No barbarian could have done what you did."

"Ugh." Slap rolled his eyes. "I ain't gonna argue. Got no energy left."

Kebba nodded. "Yes, you must be tired. When you finish eating, we shall find you a bed."

121

"That'd be real nice."

= = =

It wasn't a proper bed, only mats piled high against the wall opposite the door, and not long enough for his tall frame, but despite all that, Slap curled up and found it indecently soft. He was asleep almost before the woman who had been hovering over him covered him up.

He awoke alone. His muscles ached, his wrists throbbed, and he was acutely aware of other parts of his body, too. He fought down the humiliation and rage at his memory of the indignities forced on him. Nadi was dead, buried under heaps of rock, but it wasn't enough. He took a deep breath, trying to shake off the trembling fury, and sat up. The Zendians had tried to teach him about giving away those sorts of feelings when his family had died. But he hadn't wanted to listen to the aliens' philosophy. Still didn't. He swallowed and looked around.

A stool by the bed held folded clothes. The loose-fitting pants were snug, and both the pants and tunic a bit short, but at least he didn't have to wrap a blanket around himself now. He wondered how long he had slept.

Light came from beyond the curtained archway. He ducked through into a...a courtyard was all he could call it, despite being underground. He would have expected torches or something more archaic, but niche lights set into the walls illuminated the place quite well. But that was about the only modern device he saw. In the center, a winch perched over a hole circled by rocks in the stone floor marked a well. Beehive ovens squatted in a wide half circle around this centerpiece.

Two women attended the cooking, wearing robes that wrapped around their bodies and over their shoulders and heads. One was the woman who'd mothered him; she was taking bread out of one of the beehive ovens on the far side with a long-handled paddle. The other knelt by coals, cooking something in a shallow pan. Several children ran about, laughing and chasing each other around the scattered stone benches and tables. They saw Slap and stopped, gaping. The only thing missing was livestock.

A man stood near the archway. He bowed to Slap.

"Uh, howdy." Slap squinted around the courtyard. "Uh, is Kebba around?"

The man repeated Kebba's name and, while continuing to talk, pointed away. Slap nodded. He got enough to know Kebba wasn't there.

The baking woman approached Slap and, with much bowing, touched his bandaged wrists, speaking in a soft voice, her eyes questioning.

"They'll be fine, most likely, ma'am. Thank you." He ducked his head at her, wishing he had a hat to tip.

She lifted her head slightly, perhaps acknowledging his thanks, and gestured for him to follow her across the courtyard. She opened a curtain to reveal a tiny chamber. He bent to enter. The facilities were a bit basic, but he wasn't picky. He could take care of a need he hadn't known how to express, especially in front of ladies. A basin of water sat on a ledge. Ah, good, he could wash as well. He smiled and nodded. She let the curtain fall and left.

Slap emerged, still dripping water off his bearded chin. He needed somehow to ask for a razor next time. And a toothbrush.

The same woman gestured to a table. An earthenware plate with slices of fried, red something waited for him. He sat, glancing at the woman, wondering how to ask for a fork. She bowed, backing up, her eyes averted. He sighed. Right. Fingers it was. Slap gingerly picked up a slice; hot, but not too hot. It tasted like sweet potato. Not bad.

Sounds of talking echoed in the cavern, and before long Kebba entered with three other men. They all were bald and dressed in silks similar to the stuff he'd seen Istvan wear, long robes over pants, with sashes at the waist.

The whole bunch of them bowed before approaching. Kebba stepped forward. "We...we don't know your name."

"Slap."

"S-Slap?" Kebba asked, his brow furrowing.

"Yep."

"We would like you to come with us, Slap."

Slap slowly straightened, wary, gazing at Kebba's earnest expression. They had been nice to him, but they were the same people who had spit on him. Look at Nadi. She had seemed nice the first time he met her. "Why?"

"We are having a...meeting. My people wish to meet you. To thank you for helping them."

"Um. No need. I mean, you've all been swell. But I need to find—"

"Please!"

Slap glanced at the remaining food on the plate and rose with a sigh. The woman rushed forward and spoke strongly to the men, pointing to Slap. They dropped their heads, murmuring what had to be apologies. It didn't take knowing a language to see when a woman had cowed a passel of men. She came around the end of the table and, reaching way up, pushed down on Slap's shoulders. He obeyed. She pointed to the food and told him to eat with mother-cluck scoldings—another thing that sounded the same even if you didn't know the language.

"Yes, Mother," he said with a small smile.

= = =

Slap found himself led through tunnels and into a large cavern, much larger than the one he'd been in. But the one end was an open cliff into a canyon, the sun shining, making him blink. Steps were carved into the face of the canyon, some leading up, and others down. The opposite wall of the canyon had openings and caverns as well. Like a neighborhood or village built into the ground, away from the blasting sand. He also saw steps through an open arch, going back into the rock. Perhaps into other chambers, or to other courtyard areas.

This place looked even more like a courtyard, animals and all; chickens scratched and bobbed, and a goat chewed something, staring malevolently at its surroundings. A dog padded after a boy. In the center, a round fountain provided running water. A few low troughs at the back of the chamber had fodder in them, and others water. So perhaps the animals didn't share the water from the fountain. That was good to know.

Most of the activity in the courtyard ceased, and they all turned to look at Slap. His face grew warm. The men hustled him across to more tunnels, and up stairs. Finally they emerged on the surface into the midst of an enormous compound. Buildings surrounded them, which was just as well, because the wind gusted, occasionally spinning up sand. Slap wouldn't want to be someplace without a windbreak if the weather got wild.

Under a tent near the center of the courtyard, a group of men waited, bald like the others and wearing the fancy silk clothes like Kebba and his buddies. Slap's mouth watered as he eyed baskets of fruit sitting on the tables.

"These are the priests." Kebba gestured broadly. "They all wanted to see you."

"You're dressed like them. You a priest too?"

"Yes. That murdering dog is now dead, so I am restored as a priest."

Slap blinked. "Now wait. You—but why would he treat one of his own priests that way?"

"Because I knew the truth. We all do, of course. But I was careless and was observed mocking him by one of his spies."

Slap shrugged. Made sense. Well, as much sense as anything on this planet. Things were much simpler back home.

Kebba turned to the other priests and talked in their tongue. The only thing Slap understood was his own name—repeated more than once.

Self-conscious, Slap dug the ground with his foot and stared at the buildings. They all had a rounded design, but whether that was intentional, or from the sand scouring them for a long time, he had no clue. He hip-sat on the edge of a table under the tent and made crosshatch patterns with his toe.

The priests continued to talk, sometimes quietly, sometimes more animatedly. Slap yawned and stood. He grabbed an apple from one of the baskets. Where on this planet would they grow apples? All he'd seen was desert so far. He sank his teeth into the fruit; it was sweet and crisp. He closed his eyes in enjoyment.

Munching away, he began to wander around.

The men still talked, curious glances thrown in his direction. He strolled about and, after passing several buildings, heard a noise that caused his heart to beat faster—a horse snorting.

He followed the sound and found a huge corral—well, he might as well call it a corral; it was fenced, although by some metal mesh not split rails. Inside, the most glorious stallion Slap had ever seen pranced around the circumference, his mane and tail plumed, muscular neck arched, muscles rippling. He was a coppery sorrel with a creamy mane and tail, deep through the withers and with powerful hindquarters. Slap rested an elbow on the top of the fence and whistled. The horse jumped, skittered back, and resumed prancing.

Huh. He'd need persuading. Slap hurried back to the center of the compound, snagged two more apples, and headed back, finishing the fruit he'd been chewing on.

Slap entered and closed the gate. He tossed the apple core over his shoulder and took a few steps toward the horse. He and the beast stared at each other. For the first time in a long time Slap felt at home. "Hello, boy," he said in a soothing tone. "We gonna be friends?"

The horse snorted again and shook his head, as if for all the world he knew what Slap was saying to him. Slap grinned. "You look like you need a friend as much as I do. But friends need names. So what's yours, huh? Príncipe. That's your name. We gonna be friends, Príncipe?"

Slap took one step closer, and Príncipe flattened his ears and stamped his feet. Slap took a bite of the apple as he regarded him evenly. He continued to chew as he waited for Príncipe to get used to where he stood. He took another step, waited for Príncipe to calm down, and took another step. When finally he was within touching distance, he held out the apple on his palm.

Príncipe blew, arched his neck, and danced away. Slap didn't move. Twice he trotted closer and snuffled at the apple, but tossed his head and skittered back. Finally, the third time, he took the offering. As Príncipe crunched the fruit, Slap murmured, "We're gonna be good friends, boy. You're a beauty. Got good blood in you. Yeah, you're a fine one. Bet you fairly fly over the ground."

Príncipe nudged him for more apple, and Slap reached up and patted his neck. Príncipe nudged again, put his nose in Slap's armpit, and blew. Slap chuckled. "Yep. We're friends now, ain't we?"

Slap continued with his breaking patter, as he rubbed and patted the horse's neck, and scratched his ears and between his eyes. Príncipe leaned toward him, nickering, and Slap rested his head on the stallion's neck for a moment, inhaling the wonderful smell of horse.

He fed him the second apple, still scratching and softly talking to the animal. Before long, he walked back a step. Príncipe followed, his ears still flicking back and forth. Slap began walking, and the stallion stayed with him. He stopped, rubbing and patting the horse's neck again, and started walking once more.

He repeated this scenario, wishing he had a saddle or at least a blanket. He didn't know how used to riding Príncipe was, or how skittish he'd be if Slap just leaped onto his back. Pa always said Slap had a way with horses. "Hope you're right, Pa," he muttered.

More walking and soft patter worked their charm and made Príncipe comfortable; his stance, eyes, ears—all his body language—gave Slap his cue. "We're gonna try a new trick, boy. I'm gonna tickle myself onto your back, and then you know what we're going to do? We're gonna fly together. You like that idea?"

Slap put both hands on Príncipe's back and pressed. The horse stood. He hopped a little the next time, pressing harder. Príncipe's ears flipped a bit, and he looked around as if asking Slap what he was doing. He repeated the hops several more times. Príncipe seemed unimpressed. If there had been grass in the compound, he'd probably be grazing.

Slap's aching muscles all told him mounting wasn't going to be easy. But now was the time. He leaped and settled on Príncipe's back. The stallion jumped and sidestepped, ears flicking back. But he didn't buck or rear. Slap sat still, petting his neck, talking to him—concentrating on the animal, not how straddling the horse brought a fresh reminder of the torture he endured. The pain would fade. If only his memories could fade too. And the burning fury. He took a deep breath, staring at the stallion's upright ears. *The horse—concentrate on him!*

He sat for a moment in pure enjoyment. Nothing in the world felt like this—the muscles, the energy, the aliveness of the horse beneath him. Grabbing the mane and using his legs, Slap clicked his tongue. Príncipe took a step, arching his neck. Slap tried again, nudging harder with his knees. Príncipe walked, tossing his head. Slap wanted to howl and whoop, but merely grinned.

Before long he had Príncipe trotting and leaned forward to whisper to him, "Time to fly, boy!" He gripped the mane tighter, dug with his heels, and yelled, "Ha!"

With a leap, Príncipe took off at a full gallop—the hot wind whipping in Slap's face. Exhilaration filled him, a shrieking joy that flooded his body at sensing the stallion's power released; Slap laughed aloud. They circled the corral several times before Slap tried turning him. Sweet! He turned him left and right, loping in a weaving pattern. Príncipe responded like they'd been working together for years. Oh, he missed this!

As they galloped around the perimeter again, Slap saw Kebba and the priests standing outside the fence, watching, mouths open. With a soft "Whoa," he brought Príncipe to a walk and approached the men, grinning. He patted Príncipe's neck. "He's a beauty. I didn't know you had any horses on this planet."

The priests all bowed very low.

Kebba slowly straightened. His voice was soft. "We would like to take you to our temple."

Visions of human sacrifice came to Slap's mind, and he muttered an earthy word. "I...don't see why you'd want me to go to your temple."

"We wish to honor you."

"H-honor me?" Slap gulped. *On an altar?*

"Please, it will not take long. Then we shall take you to rest. I know you must be weary."

That's better—doesn't sound like a one-way trip. But still... "Look, I didn't do anything. You did as much or more."

"You are most humble. But please," Kebba went down on one knee, "let us thank you and honor you."

Slap sighed. He swung a leg over Príncipe's neck and dismounted. Kebba was going to be a burr under his saddle until he got his way. He scratched between Príncipe's eyes and muttered, "G'bye, boy."

Príncipe whinnied as Slap exited the corral. He smiled back at the stallion before following the priests.

= = =

Slap ascended the stairs from the tunnel, walked through the archway, and gaped.

The structure in front of him had to be the biggest building he'd ever seen, totally comprised of white marble and gold. The front portion, a tiered structure with columns all around it, stood at least ten stories high and looked to cover over half a mile square. Rising behind it, a huge, four-sided stepped edifice blacked out the sky, and on every section of block on every 'step' stood a statue of someone or some animal. This thing made the palace seem like a shack.

The people lining the sides of the stairs must number in the hundreds or maybe thousands.

Slap turned to Kebba. "Is this your temple?"

"Yes."

"Brago's Bands!" He gaped for another second and asked, "How come it doesn't look weathered? From sandstorms and such?"

"Force screen. The peasants are told the gods protect it." Kebba chuckled. "Technology is wonderful, is it not?"

The priests surrounded him almost like guards—making his worry meter go up—as they approached the steps. He looked up, and up, at the colonnade far above, wondering if he could manage that distance. But a golden, hovering platform with carved, gilded rails floated over, a priest at the controls, and the men urged him into it. They rose slowly, almost skimming the steps. The people bowed as they passed.

They rode through the colonnade and disembarked to take a lift. Exiting, Slap found himself in a room with wardrobes, and screens partially hiding sunken tubs.

"What's all this?"

"We wish you to be clean and comfortable. Please." Kebba waved Slap to enter. A servant standing by a tub of steaming water bowed. "We shall leave you to be ministered to." He and his companions bowed and backed out the door.

Slap couldn't argue; he needed to wash. The small basin hadn't allowed much, and after...however much time since he'd been captured and tortured, he even offended himself. Oh, he'd been hosed down of waste and blood from time to time in between Nadi's 'attentions,' but that didn't count as being washed.

A servant stepped forward and pulled on Slap's tunic.

"Oh no, no, friend," Slap said, shaking his head. "I can do it myself." He drew a screen forward and shooed the servants away. He didn't know what to do about the bandages, just take them off, he guessed. Despite various wounds stinging worse than bees, the bath felt like heaven. The scented water reminded him of when he first met Tristan, and the scam they pulled to get off the planet. He paused while washing. Where was Tristan? He blinked and shrugged. His friend would likely soon find him.

When he got out, a servant stepped around the screen and draped him in a robe before he knew what was happening. He rewrapped Slap's wrists in fresh bandages, solving that dilemma. Afterwards two more servants came over with beautiful silk garments in bright colors. Waving them away with his hands, he dressed himself. The pants and tunic were easy, but the sash... A servant timidly approached as he got snagged winding the seemingly endless piece of material and helped him tie it correctly. Over all he shrugged on the long robe

More leading and gesturing and bowing—did these folks ever stop bowing?—and soon Slap found himself in a gilded hall slightly reminiscent of the palace's audience chamber, except this place was monstrous in size. Pillars and statues lined the length of room, and it reeked of incense. His stomach shuddered slightly as the odor brought the nightmarish memories vividly back.

Men dressed in attire similar to Kebba and his companions lined the huge hall. They must all be priests. Kebba and another man flanked Slap and walked him to the other end. There they turned him about, and several priests came forward. One opened a small box as he began speaking to the assembly. Inside lay a gold medallion on a heavy chain. In the midst of his lecture—sermon—whatever, the doors at the far end of the hall opened, and a loud, angry voice called out.

A richly dressed man with a sullen expression strode forward, protected by a dozen well-armed, muscular guards. The priests turned.

"What is this nonsense, Kebba?" the man asked, his lip curling very much like Istvan's. "You would make a god of this barbarian?"

"Huh?" Slap frowned at the mutilated priest and took a step backward. "What's going on here?"

Kebba waved his hand at Slap in a shushing manner. "I saw what he did. He pulled the ceiling down. He crushed your cousin's face."

"Now, wait-a-minute! I broke his nose, sure, but—" Slap stopped and stared at the newcomer with unease. "Cousin?" Oh yes, the dark, taunting eyes were the same.

"And new emperor." The man jerked up his chin.

"It is not confirmed, Abbra. Our fate is in the lap of the gods, not men."

"The gods! Ha! You pretentious charlatan! I am the chosen of the gods, and I will take my place as emperor. And as a god!" He sneered at Slap. "And I will not be usurped by some false god of a barbarian."

"Now, wait—" Slap began, but Kebba cut him off: "It is for the gods to decide! Can you ride the emperor's own mount? No one may approach him. You know yourself he is a demon who can be tamed only by a god." Kebba pointed at Slap. "I saw him ride the creature. We all did! The gods have chosen!"

"Then I declare war on you, the gods, and this barbarian!" Abbra pulled a needlegun from under his robe and aimed it at Slap.

In the Lap of the Gods, *part five*

Sand filled his nose and mouth, gagging him. Tristan spat—and again. He pushed up, blinking, confused. He shook his head and winced as pain shot through his skull. His memory returned with a rush—his leg injured by falling stone, managing to get free, hobbling through the level, trying to find Slap despite the palace self-destructing around him.

Chamber after chamber of prisoners, swiping the guard's card to free one after another while searching for the cowboy. Finding a bolt hole in a crumbled wall and, finally realizing he had no choice and no Slap, escaping. Being knocked down and almost trampled as both servants and those he freed rushed past him to get out.

Tristan spat again, and rested his head on his arms. At least studying the palace architect's design methods had shown him the man loved secret passages—that bolt hole was just the sort of thing he'd expected, but he hadn't known one would save his life. Although the final explosion had partially collapsed the end of the tunnel. He had spend hours digging past the fallen rocks and sand, wondering if the passage would completely give way and bury him.

He touched the back of his head. The wound had crusted over; he must have been asleep for some time. He squinted up at the sun. Perhaps a day?

A distant rumbling made him push up again, looking around. The palace lay in smoking ruins—the sound wasn't coming from it but from farther away. More rumblings, and booms—sonic grenades? What—? More sounds began to register in his mind—drop ships and fighter craft.

The shrill whine of a small ship caught his attention. A square barge with nacelles on each side flew over his head—a Type 1HA Shuttle with Confed markings. It pitched, forward engines roaring to slow for landing. A drop shuttle—holding twenty troops, if he remembered correctly.

The Confederation invasion! *Merde!* Tristan rolled to a more concealed position behind some rocks as the ship landed, rear bay door opening. Troops in heavy Confed-armored suits double-timed out. The shuttle, now empty, rose.

Would the invading soldiers ignore a 'dead' man on the ground? Tristan dare not chance it, but how could he fight heavy armor, only dressed in slave rags, and injured on top of it? No— not only rags! He still had the shock baton he'd taken from the guard, the strap around his wrist, and the key card he'd lifted as well. But what use were they against an armored trooper?

While dragging himself behind some boulders, Tristan gave the matter thought. He propped against a rock, took out the baton, and slid open the casing. Standard power pack. A small smile flicked for a second. Possible. He took the card from where it was hidden inside his waistband and pulled the metal tag free. Letting the card drop, he strained to straighten the bit of metal, ignoring the pain biting into his fingers and thumbs.

He pried the pack out of the baton. The metal was too long. Wonderful. He put the thin strip of metal on a rock and used the baton to hold it. He bent the strip, turned it, and bent the other way, gashing his finger in the process. After several more folds, the metal weakened, heated, and eventually broke. He used the card to nudge the metal across the contacts and set the pack back into the slot and pushed down. The power pack was now in place, but not touching yet.

Next came the tricky part. He'd only have one shot. Timing would be the key; the pack shouldn't take long to overload—eight to ten seconds at best, and the radius of the blast would only be maybe five feet.

The baton would burst like a frag grenade and have a shock-pulse of electricity besides, but a heavily armed Confed trooper would most likely only be concussed. So he needed to be close enough, fast enough, yet not be impacted himself.

The sounds of running feet crunching against the gravel, sand, and stone made Tristan tense. A trooper rounded the rocks and stopped with a slight jump—likely not expecting to find anyone in this forlorn spot while sweeping the area.

"You! What are you doing here?"

Tristan stared up and said in Eridani, "I don't understand."

The trooper cussed rather unimaginatively and added in a mutter, "Stupid backwater planet." He pointed with his particle beam rifle toward Tristan's hands and shouted, "What...you...have...there?"

133

Tristan didn't react, but inside he laughed; *oh, certainly, speak slowly and loudly enough, and a person can understand a foreign language.*

However, this created the perfect opportunity. Tristan pressed the power pack firmly into the baton—but it stuck. Blast it! He gestured with the baton and again answered in Eridani, "What? This?"

The trooper held out his gloved hand, curling his fingers in a 'give it to me' gesture.

Tristan gripped the baton tightly to his chest, and used the heel of his hand to smack at the pack. It clicked into place. He looked up at the soldier's outstretched hand, got to his knees, and with feigned reluctance set the baton into it.

The Confed lifted the baton, looking it over, no doubt. Through his thick gauntlets he wouldn't feel the growing heat. Time was about out. Tristan threw himself into a backwards roll—not a moment too soon; the explosion knocked him out of the roll and onto his back.

Stifling a groan, Tristan crawled as fast as he could to the downed trooper. He grabbed the PB rifle, aimed at the helmet, and fired. One Confed down, an army to go.

He sighed at his own hindsight; getting the bandoliers of plasma grenades off the body was going to be a bloody process.

The bandoliers appropriated, and the extra power packs for the PBR as well, he slowly returned to the boulders. He leaned against the rock, and listened for other troopers, wishing he knew what was going on. If only he hadn't shot the trooper in the head, he could listen in with the comm helmet. More hindsight.

He needed to get away from this spot before the Confeds came looking for their missing buddy. And clear out of here, since they were obviously securing this area before moving on to their next target.

His gaze on the downed soldier, an idea formed. He crept back toward the man and—with the greatest of care—set several plasma grenades and placed them under him. *Gives new meaning to dead man's switch.*

He hurried south as fast as he could crawl, using rocks and boulders as cover whenever possible. Even if he dared, walking was painful and slow with his leg injury. His chances of getting clean away weren't good, but what other choice did he have?

An explosion ripped the air, and Tristan ground his teeth. Too soon. They'd now be looking for whoever set the booby-trap. He scrambled toward a large outcropping on the side of a hill. On the far side he discovered a small niche between several boulders. Not a very good hiding place, but the best he could do.

He wedged in and reached for two plasma grenades.

The whine of capacitors charging made him look up. Five PB rifles stared him in the face.

The Confeds stood on or behind the rocks sheltering Tristan, their weapons trained on him. He looked into the masks of the troopers, wishing he could see their faces. He held up the plasma grenades, showing they were set; only his thumbs kept them from going off. The soldiers froze for a moment.

"Back away or die," he yelled in Eridani, hoping they were all as illiterate of the language as their late comrade; Tristan's knowledge of imperatives was sketchy. He circled his arms wildly, to give the impression he was agitated and desperate, while repeating the phrase.

Instinct is a great thing. The troopers all reacted as he anticipated, jumping back off the rocks and running. He lifted his arms, feigning throwing the grenades, and they all dove for the ground. *Now!* He lobbed the grenades as hard and long as he could—one left and one right. Holding his breath, he ducked back down between the boulders and hunkered in as tight a ball as he could—

Tristan woke, blinked, and shook his head. That was a mistake; his head throbbed worse than with a hangover. The ringing in his ears didn't help. He lifted the PB rifle and stared at the swaying, fuzzy barrel. Dare he stand? Could he stand?

Slowly he rose and leaned against the rock. He couldn't wait; more Confeds would converge soon. He stumbled from cover and swayed, assessing the damage. Two craters marred the landscape on each side of the outcropping of boulders he had hid in. The bodies had been incinerated.

He squinted at a smudge at the far side of the one crater. Not quite. He picked his way over rocks and around the huge depression. The trooper must have been a runner to get so far. But not far enough. Tristan squatted by the body and pulled the helmet off. He examined it and found it in working order. With a grim smile he put it on.

The helmet used an optical interface. That would take a few minutes to adjust to...there—communications. The voices all crowded upon each other and he closed his eyes to concentrate:

Valkyries inbound—ETA on drop one minute
All troops, evac temple perimeter
Razors deployed
This is Squad Theta, palace ruins west secure, awaiting orders
Sir, we're encountering resistance south of spaceport market—
requesting support
MBT Company 45, base perimeter secure—moving to support
MRCV Lance one-three Shuttle Galileo inbound to sector 23
Squad Lambda encountering heavy resistance east of palace
ruins—request support
Razor pilots, beginning temple bombing run
This is AMRCV Lance oh-six, enemy neutralized at sector 28

Tristan wasn't sure if he was the 'heavy resistance east of palace ruins,' but wasn't taking chances. He ran south as best as his injuries would let him. He found another outcropping and stopped to work on finding the squad frequency but didn't have any luck. He could only hear the command channels.

Gritting his teeth, he continued to run.

= = =

Slap didn't wait for Abbra to finish speaking or aiming the gun. He slapped the sneering man's arm aside with his hand and backfisted him in the face on return. The would-be new emperor's guards burst into action, bringing up their weapons and firing at the priests, but a distant *boom* along with an earthquake-type rumbling stopped everyone cold. The lights and music blinked out, leaving them all in the dark. The shriek of fighters flying overhead broke the shocked silence. A wall blasted inward—shards of stone flying everywhere. Slap lost his footing and fell—

= = =

Tristan's sight seemed to be clearing. The ringing in his ears had abated somewhat, too. His limp worsened as he struggled south through the edges of the palace rubble. He wasn't certain his course was wise, considering the Confeds were all over the city, but staying where he was hadn't been possible. He knew where some of the attacks were taking place, but without knowing the location of the "sectors" the Confeds had divided the area into, he was limited.

But one command he heard over the helmet's comm system burned in his brain:

All inhabitants considered hostile—neutralize

Cowards! Battle armor and hi-tech weapons against skin; slaughtering civilians wantonly, giving them no chance.

Moving blurs ahead coalesced into natives, armed with clubs, rocks, and even just barehanded, attacking—or attempting to attack—Confed troops. Tristan didn't care for the Eridani government, this planet's culture, lifestyle, or attitudes, but he had to give them points for guts, if not brains.

Tristan moved a little closer, but had to be careful; if he was seen first, he'd be targeted, instead of doing the targeting. He ducked behind what was left of a stone wall and adjusted the rifle for narrow beam. After kneeling, he propped the barrel on a large hunk of rubble and sighted through the scope. He rubbed his eyes, blinked, and aimed...

Two troopers fell before the rest realized they were dealing with a sniper. They ran for cover or hit the ground. The locals, either not understanding or not caring, ran after them, still trying to beat them with ersatz weapons. Idiots.

Tristan picked off one more.

Hot rock splattered, making him duck and wince. He dove for the cover of another section of wall, rolling into a kneeling position. As he began shooting again, he wondered in passing why he didn't feel anything. *Adrenaline—I'll rue it later.*

The natives picked up the PBRs from the fallen Confeds and began shooting at their enemies. The troops found themselves trapped between Tristan and their 'hostiles,' and soon the fight ended. Tristan rose from his hiding place, took off the helmet, and walked with hesitation toward the Eridani. They waited, grinning.

As he approached one jabbered too fast for Tristan to understand, and he shook his head. "Speak slowly, please," he said in their tongue.

"You are not Eridani?" one asked.

"No. I came looking for a friend. But I think he is dead now," Tristan said, or hoped he was saying. He wished he'd had more time to study their language. "Take all...this," he added, pointing to the dead soldiers' gear. "All of it."

He began stripping the bodies of the bandoliers and other weapons. The men crouched to help, talking among themselves as they divided the spoils.

One stood, pointed to Tristan's helmet, and asked, "You speak the language of these barbarians, yes?"

"Yes."

"Will you come with us to—" the man continued speaking, and Tristan held up his hand.

"I am sorry. I only speak a little of your tongue."

"Come with us, please," the man said then. "You can help us."

Tristan snagged a second rifle and nodded.

They hadn't gone twenty steps when a drop shuttle whined above them. They scurried into the nearby half-blasted building. The ship pitched to set down not far from their location. Tristan played with a notion for a moment, fingering a plasma grenade in the bandolier. Decision made, he pulled it out and limped into the open. Wind blasted at him as the shuttle passed right over his head, whipping sand in a fine, hot spray. He choked and blinked, covering his face with one arm. The vehicle set down fifty or sixty feet from him. As the rear bay hatch began to part, he prayed his aim was good, threw as hard as he could toward the opening, and tore back toward the cover of the building.

He dove over a low section of wall as the grenade exploded. The sound echoed, magnified, as the ship blew up. The natives cheered and ran to Tristan, picking him up. He groaned and bent over, feeling lightheaded. His right calf throbbed worse than before, and he could feel blood trickling down his face.

"What is wrong?" one of them asked.

"I...I think it's because I haven't eaten or had anything to drink in over a day. Plus I am..." *What was the word for wounded?* "...hurt."

"We will take you to—" the man gibbered words unknown to Tristan.

Hoping they meant a place to eat or rest, Tristan nodded, and let them support him as they went underground, into the bowels of the main part of the city.

= = =

Dust and debris settled over Slap. Hot fire lanced through gashes received from sharp edges of marble. *I really don't like this planet.* A boom echoed, and more detritus fell on him. He dropped his head, not even trying to cover it with his arms. *I don't care anymore. Let the building fall on me. Let it all end.*

Many hands grabbed his arms and torso and hauled him to his feet. Kebba stood before him, a huge wound near his temple running freely with blood. He bowed.

Slap scowled. "Do you people ever stop killing yourselves?"

"No, no–it is the Confederation. They are attacking. We must get you to safety."

"Why? Cuz I'm a god? Brago's Bands, if I were a god, I'd zap 'em all, wouldn't I, and not have to worry about myself?"

"The gods have chosen you to join them, but that doesn't mean your body isn't...weak. You haven't reached immortality yet."

Slap growled and rolled his eyes, but let himself be led out through a side door leading to steps. The rumbling continued, but the stairwell stayed intact.

"Was the emperor immortal then?" Slap asked, as they entered an underground passage.

"That happens when your body dies. You are in a...a state between the two. Do your people not teach this?"

"Most of my people believe there is only one deity. Humans are just humans, not gods." Slap paused and added, "The Zendians believe in one god, too. They claim to see and live on both sides of the"—what was an equivalent of the Zendian word?—"curtain between the mortal and spiritual world."

"Who are the Zendians?" Kebba asked, glancing up with a frown.

"Aliens who are the original inhabitants of the world I'm from. They...can do some strange things. Makes me wonder if there isn't some truth to their claim."

Kebba grinned. "They have technology you don't understand. I am a priest. I know. The people must see to believe, so we..." he hesitated, his face twisting in thought, probably trying to recall vocabulary in a language he wasn't used to using much. "We...we *give* them something to see."

Slap shook his head and said no more. Too bad Kebba couldn't meet a Zendian; he'd change his tune.

The maze of tunnels went on. Finally they came to well-lit grotto, filled with armed men, and not all of them looked friendly. Several lifted their weapons, but Kebba and the other priests held up their arms and called out—likely passing word about Slap's 'god status.'

Slap was offered a seat and drink of water. The men conferred, with glances tossed Slap's way. More natives began crowding the archway. New arrivals to their underground headquarters. They listened as Kebba and the priests talked.

After awhile, Kebba approached, bowing. "They would like to know what help you will give us to throw off our enemies."

Slap's mouth fell open.

= = =

They arrived in a cavern, well-lit and well-stocked with supplies. His companions ran in different directions, handing out the collected weapons, while two helped Tristan to a stool by a table.

They set water and a plate of some sliced fried...something in front of him. He'd almost think it was plantain by taste, but this seemed more like a yam by look and size. He drank slowly and ate, relishing the strength that flowed into him. If only he could rest, but the Confeds weren't resting, and if he planned on surviving, he needed to help these people. He put on the helmet, and listened for a while. What he heard clenched his stomach, and he broke out in a cold sweat; in a matter of hours the Confeds were going to destroy all 'hostiles' by dropping the horrific yrallite gas into every crevice and cavern they could find. *Damn the bastards!* Gas masks did no good; that stuff entered pores, burned skin, and caused muscles to slough off bones. Even the Eridani had signed the treaty banning its use. Only the Confeds...

Tristan tore off the helmet and dropped his head into his hands. How could he stop the entire Confederation military machine?

In the Lap of the Gods, *part six*

Tristan had never felt so helpless. Even if he could reach *Giselle* in time, he couldn't leave, not without knowing for certain Slap was dead. He knew the odds; the tall cowboy was likely buried under the tons of rubble that used to be the emperor's palace.

He scrubbed his face with his hands. Slap dead. He had failed his life debt. What tortures had the kid endured before the end? Had he waited for Tristan, wondering why he didn't come? No more of the galoot following him around the ship, asking questions, finding ways to tease and irritate...

His gut knotted, and he found himself shaking. He rose and paced in lieu of finding something to hit or throw. But he wouldn't leave or give up on Slap until he had seen his body—Tristan owed him that much. Perhaps he'd take the body back to Zenos and bury him with his wife and son.

Who knew how long until the locals began excavating to find the dead. He wouldn't wait; he didn't care about the cost to hire workers for the job, he would stay until he had moved every stone, every piece of marble. He must see that body, must be certain.

But first, the Confeds had to go. He couldn't stop their plan to drop yrallite gas, but he could warn the people to evacuate. And he would fight, somehow. But he needed to get to the top of the chain of command. He glanced around at the men in the cavern. "With the emperor dead, who's in charge? His cousin Abbra?"

The one who had spoken to him before stepped forward. "No. He is dead. All the royal family is dead. The high priest rules now."

Tristan was certain he would find his reply amusing at some later time, but he was too concerned with speed and action to pause and appreciate the irony. With a perfectly straight face he said, "All right. Take me to your leader."

= = =

Tristan and his guide pushed through the press into the cave where the head priest was supposed to be. One voice stood out amidst the cacophony. Not just because it wasn't speaking in

Eridani, but because it had lousy grammar, the odd accent of the Three Systems Separatists, and was slightly a nasal, youthful tenor.

Incredible amazement and relief flooded through Tristan's body like a dousing of refreshing cold water, and his priorities settled into a new alignment. He took a deep breath and prepared to make his entrance.

= = =

Slap stared at the crowd staring at him, then looked at Kebba. "What?"

"They want to know how you will help us fight these invaders."

"Help? I keep telling you I ain't no god. Sure as shootin' I'll do what I can, cuz I don't like the Confeds method of 'expansion'—"

"It does tend to be fatal to those in the expanding area."

Slap jumped at the familiar, quiet, bass voice. Tristan? Yes! He gaped as his friend strode forward from among the newcomers and shoved a rifle into Slap's hands.

"Tristan!" Slap stood, a wide grin spreading.

"So you're a god now, are you?"

"I keep telling them—"

"You need a shave."

"So do you," Slap shot back, eyeing the uncharacteristic stubble on his friend's face. And the bruises and cuts, some still oozing blood. And the limp. "Bad day?"

"Not my best."

Kebba, eyes wide, looked from one to another, but before he could say a word, Tristan stepped up, face to face with the priest, and said, "You have a problem. The Confeds are planning on dropping yrallite gas into every cavern they can find in the capital to exterminate your people. I've given you warning—get your people out while you can." His dark eyes bored into Slap's. "Now, let's get out of here."

"What?" Slap's mouth fell open. "You gonna leave, just like that?"

"I came here to find you. I found you. Time to go."

"But these people need help!"

"That's not my concern."

"Well, I ain't going. This isn't just about two armies fighting or something. You said they were dropping some gas—"

"Yrallite gas. It's worse than vile."

"And it'll kill women and kids. *Babies*, Tristan! Brago's Bands, I ain't gonna just leave when innocent little ones will be murdered."

"Staying won't save them. Nothing will. They have to evacuate. And we can't do much to help with that."

"We can too—somehow." Slap spun to Kebba. "How can we help evacuate?"

Kebba spread his hands. "Their fate is in the lap of the gods. We will not stand in the way."

Slap stared at the priest, his mind numbed by the casual, callous expression on Kebba's face. Finally he managed to whisper, "You can't mean it."

Tristan snorted. "In other words, they will sacrifice the people of this city—use their deaths to show the evil of the enemy. And, at the same time, it will destroy the base of any opposition that might exist, since most of those who might have the education and position to oppose them are all here in the capital. Controlling the ignorant populace will be even more facile then."

Kebba's eyes glinted as he gazed at Tristan. "You are too wise."

Bile rose in Slap's throat. "You rotten lizard!" He gestured around the cave at the gathered men. "What do they think of this? They all know now."

"Only some of the priests have learned your barbarian tongue." Kebba smirked. "No one else knows what we are saying."

Slap turned to the other priests. Their faces showed unconcern. He whirled back to Tristan. "We have to *do* something!"

"Their own priests don't want to stop it. Let the Confeds and Eridani wipe each other out."

Slap grabbed a handful of cloth and hauled Tristan close, his teeth clenched. "I ain't walkin' away from women and kids being killed."

Tristan glared at him, his eyes black embers. His lips thinned, and he struck Slap's upper arms. The unexpected jolt loosened Slap's grip, and Tristan stepped back. Slap met his friend's snarl with one of his own while rubbing his arms.

Tristan sighed. He gazed around the cave and spoke to the people in halting Eridani.

Kebba shouted, "No! Tell them nothing!" He then switched to his own language, babbling almost in a panic, but Tristan brought his weapon up with a black expression that wilted the priest. Several other priests stepped forward as if to intervene, but Slap raised his rifle, pointed it at them, and shook his head.

Tristan continued to talk, and the people began to stir. A few asked questions, and he answered. As he made himself understood, their faces began to show horror or fear. Tristan became more insistent, and before long, the men started to disperse, talking decisively among themselves, with confused backward glances at the priests.

Tristan approached Kebba. "You can lead the efforts to evacuate and put yourself in good graces as a leader who cares about his people, or let them see the truth. We're done."

Kebba's gaze darted between the two and finally settled on Slap. "You cannot go. You need to stay. To—"

Slap stabbed the priest's chest with his finger. "I might be a dumb cowboy, but I'm no fool. I could see what you wanted me to be. I ain't no figurehead to prop up your...your rule, or government, or whatever you call it. I'll help get people outta here, but then I'm gone with my friend."

Slap nodded at Tristan and followed him out, leaving Kebba stuttering to himself.

= = =

Slap hunkered behind a demolished wall, gripping his rifle, while Tristan listened on the comm helmet. He was dog tired already, and by the sun, it was only mid-afternoon. His buddy looked like the walking dead, but never stopped. He listened for the Confed plans and informed the Eridani of any updates.

The locals had been surprisingly efficient in moving their people out of the city. The caverns below the surface connected to others farther away with a lattice-like network of tunnels. No wonder the Confeds were stymied enough to resort to such extremes to secure the capital. Well, not that it gave them the right to use something as nasty as yrallite gas. Shoot, what gave them the right to try to conquer other worlds? Ah well, he wasn't going to waste time trying to figure out the Confeds.

Or the Eridani for that matter.

He gazed over at Tristan. "So is there a way to stop the Confeds on their own ground?"

"What do you mean?"

"I know you. Couldn't you find a way to sneak aboard their mother ship and do something...*sneaky*?"

Tristan sighed. "They don't have a mother ship. There are three carriers in orbit, and no, I don't have the time or resources to do any 'sneaking.'"

Slap slumped a little, then nodded at the helmet. "Any updates?"

"No. The Confeds are having some comm trouble. Trying to trace it has diverted them and pushed back the timetable for the gas to be shuttled down. We need to help keep the troops here occupied to give the evacuees more time."

"Gladly." Slap had already downed some stragglers. They were heading toward the spaceport where much of the activity was. "Let's get moving!"

Tristan winced as he stood, which worried Slap. His buddy must really be hurting; he didn't like to show pain.

As they worked through the rubble, Slap saw a pile of rope under some debris and stopped. Perhaps it was the cowboy in him, but he couldn't resist. He began pulling the rope out and coiling it.

"What are you doing?" Tristan asked.

"This is good, sturdy rope. Never know when you'll need a good rope."

"All right, 'Sam.'"

"Huh?"

"Never mind." Tristan shook his head and walked on.

Slap slipped the coil over his head and through one arm like a bandolier and ran to catch up. A rumble stopped him—Tristan too. It happened again.

"What is that?"

"I'm not sure." Tristan pointed to the remains of a nearby building. "Let's wait and see."

146

Slap followed Tristan inside and gazed over the stone while Tristan crouched and listened on the helmet. The earthquake-like rumble boomed and boomed again, getting closer.

"MRCVs," Tristan hissed after a minute. "They're on their way to the spaceport to reconnoiter. So that's where we're going too."

"What are they?"

"Mechanized Robotic Combat Vehicles. MRCVs."

Slap frowned, still not sure what Tristan was talking about. His friend pointed outside. A huge monster 'robot' was walking down the street—what was left of the street anyway.

"Brago's Bands! How do we stop that?"

"A rocket launcher would come in handy. Unfortunately, the troopers I've seen so far were light-armor. If I remember correctly, only the heavy-armor troops carry rocket launchers."

"So what do we do about the robots?"

"'Robotic vehicles.' Avoid them."

"I'll agree with that."

After the 'robotic vehicle' walked past, Slap stood. "How far to the spaceport?"

"About a klick, I'd guess."

"Too bad we don't have rides." Slap straightened with a gasp. *Ride!* "Aw, shoot. Príncipe!"

"What?"

"I gotta find Príncipe! I don't know if he's still alive, but if he is..." Slap darted outside and looked around at the desolate city, wondering where that compound was. "I have to find someone to tell me where he is!"

"Where who is?"

"Príncipe."

"As you like to say, 'chew it fine.' Who is Príncipe?"

"A horse."

Tristan blinked. "We have more important things to worry about than a horse."

"I ain't gonna try to explain. You wouldn't get it. But I have to find Príncipe."

Tristan ran a hand through his hair and shook his head. "Go, then. Try to rendezvous at the spaceport when you can. If all else

147

fails, ask for the way to the forbidden holy cavern west of the city. That's where *Giselle* is hidden. But don't tell anyone she's there."

"Gotcha!" Slap ran off, looking desperately for anyone who could tell him where the emperor's horse was.

$$= = =$$

All he'd gone through to find Slap, and the cowboy runs off to find a horse. A *horse.* Tristan rubbed his eyes. Slap or no Slap, he had to get to the spaceport.

Several more MRCVs passed. Tristan ducked into a building or behind rubble each time. A hover bike buzzed by, shooting; Tristan rolled to avoid fire and shot back, hitting the bike on his third try and spinning it into wall. He rose with a groan, using the butt of the rifle against the earth to lever himself up. His leg throbbed mercilessly.

Limping along, fighting, hiding, Tristan finally neared the spaceport. The journey had seemed like hours, but by the westerly sun hadn't taken very long at all. He supposed it was because he was so exhausted. The helmet didn't help, weighing him down and making him sweat. But he needed the updates.

He knelt behind the remains of a watch tower and regarded the activity through the fence. The Confeds were regrouping, all right.

Static roared through the helmet—and stopped. Confused voices shouted and hollered on various channels, overlapping, conflicting. Finally, he made sense of the chatter. One of the three carriers in orbit had blown up. No one knew why.

Before Tristan could even speculate to himself what could have caused it, the chatter turned into...nonsense. At least to the Confeds.

Various Confed voices could be heard amid the steady 'nonsense' chattering across the channels:

What the hell is that?
Someone is broadcasting across all channels—shut it off. Whoever is responsible, shut it off! We need clear lines!
No one knows where it's coming from!
Trace it, trace it!
We're trying, Sir, but—

What the hell is a Snark anyway?
Boojum? What's a Boojum?

Tristan sat down and leaned back against the base of the tower, laughing long and low.

= = =

Confed communications had almost totally broken down. A few channels worked sporadically, but not for long, and automated systems had begun to break down or react unpredictably. Someone had infiltrated the Confeds renowned, secured system and trashed it. Tristan had his own ideas of who was behind that one.

From broken bits of transmissions, Tristan surmised the second carrier had been disabled by Eridani ships, which had apparently evaded or survived Confederation battles in other areas of their domain. The carrier hobbled away from the planet for repairs. The third carrier sent out a recall signal. That message was not blocked.

Amid the chaos, one thing was clear; the invasion was all but over except for the troops stranded on the surface. They were rushing to get to the last shuttles before the one remaining carrier broke orbit. Tristan—and the Eridani—wouldn't mind that, but the soldiers still seemed determined to kill and destroy in their effort to reach the spaceport.

The Eridani were no warriors, but they quickly learned tactics with little instruction. Tristan worked rogue, darting from area to area, picking off strays, updating the natives on what little he could find out from the helmet, and trying to keep track of the movement of the stragglers converging on the spaceport. The sun sat on the horizon now; they'd soon be at a disadvantage, fighting in the dark against troops equipped with night vision capability.

And creeping into Tristan's thoughts was the constant question: *where is Slap?*

Earlier, Tristan managed to down a heavy-armor trooper and confiscate his rocket-launcher. Several MRCVs now lumbered through the area, heading for a transport ship, firing their weapons. That launcher was about to come in handy.

Propping the launcher onto rubble, Tristan calculated the best place to aim to take out the vehicles. The 'knee' joint would seem ideal, but on second thought, the 'hip' looked to be less armored. But it would take a more precise hit to do damage. He aimed and fired. Torso hit—only surface damage. He had sighted too high. The body swiveled in his direction. He fired again.

Direct hit on the hip. The vehicle crashed to the ground. Another MRCV swerved to face his position. *Uh oh.* Tristan forced himself to concentrate as the arm lifted to fire at him. He launched a rocket. It impacted the leg, just below the hip. The vehicle stepped toward him, and he got ready to fire again, hoping he shot before it did. But the huge robotic vehicle took another step—onto its 'injured' leg, and a creaking of stressed metal filled the air. Tristan watched in fascination as the goliath slowly toppled to the ground.

He had no chance to appreciate his luck—the whine of hover bikes grew behind him. He spun. Three of them. He grabbed a plasma grenade and lobbed it. One bike took the hit, but the other two swerved, flanking him. He dove to the ground, firing left, rolling, and firing right. He missed.

The bikes circled to make another run. But Tristan had more time to aim. Hot sand sprayed in his face as he fired. He rolled again, coughing and blinking, and fired toward the sounds of a bike.

He held still in the ensuing, relative quiet, listening for a bike as the dust settled. He raised his head, and found himself staring up at the bike's rider, a laser pistol leveled at him.

A wild cowboy whoop echoed just then, and the biker whirled. A large copper-colored horse thundered up, Slap on its back, a rope circling above the cowboy's head. He threw the rope, snagged the gun, and snatched it from the biker. Tristan fired, and the soldier crumpled.

Slap caught the gun in mid-air from the noose that held it as he drew the horse to a stop near Tristan, grinning. "Want a ride?"

Tristan eyed the huge beast as it pawed the ground and tossed its head. "You're not kidding, are you?"

"Just tell me where you want to go."

Tristan glanced around the spaceport. The Eridani had the upper hand. "Let's go to *Giselle.*"

"In the desert?" Slap gazed at the setting sun. "At night?"

"I can see in the dark with this helmet."

Slap shook his head. "I know the desert. It's treacherous at night. We need to find a place to rest till morning."

"Staying in the city isn't an option. There are still Confeds about, and who knows if they still won't try dropping the gas as retaliation before they pull out altogether."

Slap hesitated, looking thoughtful. Finally, he shrugged and held out his hand. Tristan took it and let Slap haul him up to sit behind him.

"Hold on tight. Now, which way to ol' Bertha?"

"Go north, away from the spaceport—too dangerous. Then head west. With the Confeds retreating, we can probably leave the planet without becoming a target. If the ship can fly. She was in bad shape when I left to find you. I hope Carter's gotten her functional."

"Carter?"

"The engineer who had been working on the ship. He came with me."

"He came here with you? To Eridani?"

"Yes."

"Is he stupid or insane?"

Tristan didn't hesitate a beat. "Insane."

= = =

Horses, Tristan decided, were not the best method of transportation he'd ever used. The hide was slippery, the ride uneven, and Slap's back not the most comfortable to lean against. And the creature jumped several times at some nocturnal desert inhabitant. Twice Slap used the laser pistol, muttering about lizards and vipers.

Tristan's leg was hurting worse than ever, if that was possible, yet he had a hard time staying awake as they searched for the cavern—a difficult job without any point of reference, as the area had many caverns in it.

"Is this it?" Slap asked as they approached another one.

"No, the shape is all wrong. And there's no rocky hill, just the smooth plain surrounding it. Besides, it's inhabited. I can see heat signatures rising from the crevice, probably smoke."

"Well, regardless, we need to find a place to rest Príncipe. And find water."

"Natives aren't likely to be friendly to 'barbarians.'"

"At least they don't shoot first like the Confeds."

They drew closer, and Tristan could see carved, stone steps leading down along the wall of the cavern. "We *are* taking a chance."

"Yeah, but Príncipe needs water and rest."

"Can he make it down those steps?"

"If I lead him."

Tristan slid off, and Slap swung a leg over the neck and hopped down. They headed toward the edge. The horse's ears flicked back, and he resisted Slap. The cowboy made a clicking sound with his tongue, and tugged lightly on the rope he used to guide the beast. He talked softly to the horse, and with an unease that even Tristan could sense, Príncipe began descending behind Slap.

As Tristan followed, he was glad he didn't fear heights. He did, however, have some vertigo, from lack of food and rest, and his injuries. He removed the helmet, took deep breaths, and blinked to try to keep his mind and sight clear.

About halfway down, in the light of fires and many torches, Tristan could see people gathering below. He kept his hands still at his sides, although he itched to grip the rifle hanging over his shoulder. The people began to bow as they neared the bottom. Tristan couldn't make out anything the natives said. His head reeled, and the world went dark.

= = =

Tristan awoke to the sun streaming in at an angle, hitting the opposite wall. He lay on a pallet set in a niche in the stone. A plate covered with a cloth and a jug with a cup next to it waited on a stone ledge across from him. He tossed back the colorful blanket and swung his legs over the side of the of the bed. His old clothes were gone, and he wore only the loose pants of the typical peasant. His wounds were wrapped, and his leg only throbbed dully.

Since no one else was in the chamber, Tristan figured the food and water must be for him. He sat and ate.

"You do pretty good without a napkin or fork," came Slap's voice.

Tristan twisted to see Slap leaning in the doorway, grinning.

"So how did you get us this treatment? Still a god?"

Slap pushed up from the frame and walked over. "I don't think so. It's hard to tell, since they don't speak our language. But they were impressed because I have Príncipe. He'd been the emperor's horse, you know. I guess there's some local custom or superstition or something like that. Anyway, since I have him, they're treating us like royalty. When you're up to it, I'd like you to palaver with them, and see if they can tell us where the forbidden cavern is."

"Gladly."

= = =

The natives not only showed them where the forbidden cavern was, but went with them for a distance, although they wouldn't venture even into the shadow of the overhanging tor. They also left them with bundles of hay and several large sacks of something that Slap had asked for with signs and gestures. Tristan was afraid he knew what it was, but didn't inquire; he was sure he'd find out soon enough.

Tristan thanked the people, and they bowed and hurriedly left. He went into the opening in the rocky face that led to the cavern below. *Giselle* waited where she'd been left. She didn't look flight-worthy. He hoped that was only surface appearance.

He called Carter as he neared the ramp. Carter appeared and grinned. "I hoped you'd lived through all this mess. Did you find Slap?"

"Yes. He's coming. Is she able to fly?"

"Not for long. But enough to get us off this rock and to a space station where we can get parts for repairs."

Tristan nodded, swallowing his worry about how to pay for those parts and repairs. His money was almost gone. He still had his cargo to sell, but he wasn't sure how far that would go, given *Giselle's* extensive damage.

He narrowed his eyes. "Snarks and Boojums, hein?"

Carter grinned.

"So, who are you to the Confeds to have a backdoor into their secured comm system?"

"No one, now."

Tristan gave him a withering glare and Carter licked his lips. "Uh, Lieutenant Commander Donegal of the Confederation Armed Forces. Or I was before I 'died.' They...don't know I escaped."

Tristan nodded. Now it made sense. And he now knew the real hold Carter's boss had had over him.

Carter's eyes widened and his mouth dropped open as he looked at the cave entrance. Tristan turned. Slap was leading Príncipe toward them.

"I'm bringing him along," the cowboy said.

"And what will you do with a horse aboard a ship?"

"I'm taking him to Zenos." Slap petted the horse's neck, his expression reflective and sad. "I...I want to go home."

Full Circle

"Príncipe is settled in," Slap said from the doorway of the bridge. Tristan nodded without looking up as he checked systems for take-off.

Slap greeted Carter, then asked, "Do you really think Príncipe will be safe?"

"Our cargo bay isn't meant to hold horses," Tristan said, "but as long as we have artificial gravity and inertial dampers, he should be fine. You have him tied up?"

"Tethered, yeah."

After a silence, Carter cleared his throat. "Sir, I know we're going to need repairs, and they're going to be expensive. If you don't mind a detour, I know a way you could pick up a little money on the black market."

Tristan's eyebrows rose. "Oh?"

"That first carrier that blew up? Its computer core is out there. I, uh, disrupted efforts to salvage it, and to my knowledge it's still floating around up there."

"Disrupted efforts, hein?" Tristan turned to regard Carter. "Communications again?"

"Among other things." Carter grinned and looked over at Slap. The cowboy smiled absently, but his preoccupied frown quickly returned.

"And you know this core is still intact?"

"Yes, Sir. Er, well, most likely. I mean, it should have survived because they're hardwired to eject. The beacon is working anyway."

Tristan eyed the displays, his mind calculating the thought of the several million stellars the core was worth against the chance of getting it out of a debris field and escaping intact.

"With their communications screwed," Carter said, "they can't pick up the core's beacon. We could slip in and grab it and get out."

"While ducking fire from how many ships?"

"I'm...not certain. There are ships still in orbit to escort the carrier."

"And where is this core in relation to the surviving carrier?"

Carter pulled up a display and pointed. "The carrier is here. The core is over on the other side of the planet, with probably only shuttles near it, if any of them are still trying to salvage the core—which they'd be doing blind."

Tristan scratched his head, smoothed his hair, and then rubbed his temple. "We could force shield the cargo bay into sections and open the fore hatch..."

"My thought exactly!" Carter's eyes glinted. "I could rig up some of the cargo nets and straps into a catcher net. We'd open the fore cargo hatch, carefully fly over the core, giving the impression that *Giselle* is 'eating' it. The net catches and pads the core while the hatch closes. We recompress the cargo bay and take off."

"Now, wait, Príncipe is in the cargo bay," Slap said, leaning closer.

"Put him aft," Tristan said.

"He is aft."

"Then what's the problem?"

"If something goes wrong—"

"If that force shield fails, it'll decompress the whole ship."

"Except the bridge and crew quarters," Carter put in. "And galley, and—"

Tristan glared at the engineer who squeaked to a halt.

"The point is," Tristan said, looking Slap in the eye, "that force shield is safe. Your horse will be fine unless the ship is blown up. In which case you won't be worrying about him anyway."

Slap frowned but didn't say anything more.

"How long will it take to rig a net?" Tristan asked.

Carter pursed his lips. "Not long. If Slap helps, it won't take any time at all."

Tristan gazed at Slap. The cowboy shrugged.

"Go to it, then. Let me know when you're ready."

= = =

Slap leaned over Tristan's shoulder as they prepared to take off.

"Strap in."

156

The cowboy shook his head. "I'm going to stay with Príncipe and try to keep him calm."

Tristan hesitated. "There's no place to strap in down there."

"If it's safe enough for him, it's safe enough for me." Slap strode out.

Tristan sighed and checked the instruments one last time. He hit the comm. "Ready, Carter?" The engineer was suited up and secured to a strap-down point in the fore cargo bay.

"Yes, Sir."

"Are you in the cargo bay, Slap?"

"Yeah," came the cowboy's voice after a moment. "We're ready. Take it easy. He's flighty."

By all means, I must consider the sensibilities of a horse. Tristan took a deep breath and lifted off.

With Carter's help, he had a map of where the Confeds were. Hopefully, they could get into orbit and near the core without intercepting any ships. The salvage shuttles had limited weapons and range and were no match for *Giselle*.

The beacon was still active. Tristan set a course for it, frowning at *Giselle's* sluggish response. Maneuvering in the debris field was going to be difficult, not to mention lining up to retrieve the core.

His expectations weren't off. But fortunately, the core wasn't in too difficult a position. But before he could align with the core, blips appeared on his screen. "Carter, we have company."

"What are they? Shuttles?"

"Interceptors. Looks like Boomerangs."

"Whoops. Four?"

"Yes."

"Wedge formation?"

"Got it in one."

"Then they don't know what you are. They'd use a starburst attack or claw strike formation if they had any idea of your armament. How close are we to the core?"

"Close."

"Then go for it. If they're carrying torpedoes, our turrets should take care of them."

"I know that. But if they have missiles loaded instead?"

"Uh....then we might have trouble."

"You have a propensity for understatement." *Giselle's* armor was in tatters from that re-entry. One missile and they would be merely more scattered debris around Eridani.

"Don't forget about Príncipe," Slap's voice interrupted. "He's—"

"Keep quiet—this will likely get sticky," Tristan snapped. He slowed more, using both instruments and sight to align to the core. "Carter, you're secured?"

"Affirmative, Sir."

"Force shield is in place," Tristan said for the cowboy's sake. "Decompressing..." He watched the read-out, waiting, then said, "Opening fore hatch door."

Tristan nudged *Giselle* ahead with a tap on the thrusters. The core disappeared under the ship. It was all instruments now. Several *chooms* echoed through the hull—another sign of *Giselle's* damage; they wouldn't normally hear anything—and the subsequent whine from the capacitors told Tristan the turrets were firing at the same time he saw it on the panel. "We're under attack."

"Almost got it, Captain."

"Get a move on, Carter."

"Almost there..."

The ships were spiraling around *Giselle* like vultures. A new blip appeared on his screen. Tristan looked out to see another interceptor approaching, arcing to a position in front of the cargo ship. It began to maneuver to face the cargo ship for a nose-to-nose confrontation. Its pilot was no fool; he was in the ship's centerline—the one small dead spot for the turrets. Tristan could see the pilot grin malevolently through the clear canopy of the cockpit. Intimidation? Some sort of psychological warfare?

These interceptors carried their weapons externally—this one was not carrying mere torpedoes! Tristan's insides turned to jelly. The pilot lifted a gloved, splayed hand and pulled in his thumb... *What was he doing?* First finger... *Counting down!*

Tristan activated the controls for the newly installed particle beams and his breath caught as a red light blinked—disabled. *Why are the particle beams offline?*

Second finger.

—No time! Tristan hit the switches to raise a force shield across the open bay access and close the hatch at the same time. Third finger... *Six seconds to close the door!*

"Carter—we're leaving *now!*"

Fourth finger.

Ignoring Carter's questioning voice, he activated the jump drive.

As the jump whirled in his brain and body, Tristan closed his eyes in horror. Had the force shield held against the negative energy field of the jump, or did he just kill Slap and Carter?

Jump completed, Tristan checked the status of the cargo bay. Intact—hatch and all. He lowered the force shields and bolted out of the bridge like hell's fury. He grabbed the side rail of the ladder and slid down it like a pole, surprising Slap who stood at the horse's head, talking to the stupid creature. Tristan's leg throbbed from the landing, but he was too enraged to care. He stormed forward, teeth clenched, and grabbed Carter by the neck. "Why aren't the particle beams working?"

"I had to use the power taps on the jump capacitor chargers," the engineer squeaked. "It was the only way to get one working."

"One?"

"We've only got the one capacitor right now."

"You should have told me. I nearly killed us trying to face off an interceptor carrying missiles!"

Carter's face blanched. "That's why you jumped with the door barely shut! I—I'm sorry."

Tristan released Carter with a shove and walked away.

= = =

Slap murmured to Príncipe to reassure him as Tristan climbed the ladder. When the stallion's ears quit flicking back, he ambled over to Carter. "Don't let his bark bother you."

Carter gave him a small, edged smile. "I screwed up." He jerked a thumb over his shoulder at the computer core. "Maybe I can make it up to him with this. I better get to work."

Slap nodded and returned to Príncipe. He couldn't just keep him tethered; he had to corral him somehow. He didn't think Tristan would like it if the horse decided to walk all over his exercise equipment, or worse, leave a present. He thought a moment—the cargo nets and straps; they could serve as fencing. But he'd also need something to use as a trough. And to put the feed in. He scratched his head.

= = =

Tristan closed the access panel and sighed. What a mess. Was there one system on the ship not affected by his insane rescue flight? He rubbed his forehead. What he needed was a drink. A hot tisane would be perfect. And, surely, if any place on the ship was intact, it was the galley.

He started across the cargo bay and stopped dead. That horse was drinking water out of—a piece of protective casing for one of the particle beam cannons! With a growl, he scrambled up the ladder. He hit the chime on Slap's door and heard a muffled, "Yeah?"

He entered and halted as he heard Slap mumbling in a drone. The cowboy was reading something from his console, but Tristan could only make out bits and pieces of it. The slump of Slap's shoulders drained his ire over the casing. Whatever happened to Slap on Eridani had defeated him. He was withdrawn, barely talking, and then, mostly to the horse. Tristan had failed him. He should have gotten there sooner, found him sooner...

He took a breath to chase away his guilt and stepped closer to listen.

"...livestock cannot enter Three Systems without a Permit to Import....Guild & Merchant Ordinance #453A requires...health standards necessitate....vaccinations and veterinary certification...subject to quarantine for a minimum of...valid certificates issued by the exporting planet's government declaring..." Slap dropped his head into his hands and groaned.

"What is it?" Tristan asked.

"I'm trying to make sure Príncipe is safe to take to Zenos, for his sake, and the planet's."

Tristan nodded. The Separatists were sticklers for environmental safety. He should have realized Slap wouldn't just take the horse home without going through the precautions necessary. Diseases, parasites—who knew what pathogens the

160

horse might bring to the planet, or what on Zenos might affect the stallion either.

"I take it the bureaucracy is overwhelming?"

"Even normally it's hard. The Guilds'n'Merchants try to make it hard on us. Several of us went in together to import a bull. I paid half, and two others paid a fourth each of the costs. I got to keep him, but they had rights to him every year. Plus we made money hiring him out." Slap grinned briefly. "Petty was a busy bull."

The cowboy leaned back in the chair and shook his head. "But I don't have the proper documentation from the 'exporting planet.' I'm roped and tied tighter'n a calf at brandin' time."

Tristan sat on the edge of the desk. "Do you have any options?"

"Nope. I don't have a bill of sale, even." Slap spun and looked up at Tristan plaintively. "I didn't steal him! The priests who were supposed to take care of him couldn't get close. They'd moved him once to a safer place, but he'd gotten so riled by the noise and fighting nearby they couldn't catch him to move him again. Things were getting so dangerous, and they asked me to take him. The one said, the emperor is dead, a god should have him. I didn't argue."

Tristan nodded. "We'll find a way to get him home for you. But—" he glared at Slap. "You cannot use the protective casing of the particle beam cannons for the horse's food and water."

Slap's mouth fell open. "Er, oh. Is that what that is?"

Tristan had the urge to slap his forehead. "Just find something else. Ask Carter or me if you aren't sure." He let the door close and crossed to the galley. Tisane—he'd had a small supply left. Hopefully Carter didn't like herbal infusions.

He set the kettle on the induction hob and hit the switch. Tisane must be made the old-fashioned way. He measured the herbs into a pot and glanced at the hob. Frowning, he gingerly touched the kettle. Cold. What—?

A quick examination found the problem. Carter had purloined power taps again. This was the end—if a man couldn't even have a hot drink! He strode out of the galley in search of the engineer, but slowed. No, Carter was only doing what was necessary; several non-essential systems or equipment were out of commission for now. He would find out from Carter what power taps could be borrowed temporarily. He would have his tisane!

= = =

Slap kicked the covers off, draped an arm across his eyes, and tried again to fall asleep. Eridani was past; Nadi was dead. He was safely back on ol' Bertha, and he had Príncipe. He was going home soon. So why couldn't he sleep?

Yeah, he'd had a bad time, but not as bad as losing Shallah and Evan and Ol' Pa. Except...memories flooded his mind, and shame rose. He fought down the bile, but it won. He made it to the head just in time, and despite the facilities not being created to handle vomit as such, they did an adequate job.

When his stomach finally stopped heaving, he stayed still for a long time, shivering.

He longed for a wet cloth to wipe his face. He stumbled to the galley, thankfully not running into either Tristan or Carter, and washed his face with cool water.

Slap then descended to the cargo bay and made sure Príncipe was all right. He rubbed between the stallion's eyes with his knuckles. "We're going home soon, boy," he murmured. "You'll like it. We'll be better then."

He leaned into Príncipe, pressing his face into the horse's neck, and inhaling deeply. The smell of horse. The smell of home.

= = =

Tristan brought his steaming cup into the lounge and sat with Slap and Carter. Slap's eyes still seemed haunted. He wasn't eating, just pushing the food around the plate with his fork. Tristan fought down his sense of guilt and asked, "So, Carter, where do you suggest we go for repairs?"

The engineer tapped a finger on the table absently. "The Aries Station is a good one. It's not far from Three Systems, and it's out of bounds of both the Xanthus Commonwealth and the Eridani Sovereign Union." He stopped and grinned. "Think they'll change the name again, now that they no longer have an emperor?"

Tristan snorted. "Oh, they'll soon have a new emperor, if he hasn't proclaimed himself to be one yet. Or a god directly. That priest Kebba knows what he's doing."

Slap scratched his ear. "But I don't get why the people wouldn't understand what the priests are up to. They know now their emperor was no god. Why would they just accept another man who says he's a god? Don't they want the truth?"

"But that system of belief is all they know," Carter said, shaking his head. "Most of them are very ignorant."

"That wouldn't matter anyway. Most people aren't interested in truth." Tristan paused and sipped his tisane, then added, "Unless it's convenient or advantageous."

Carter opened his mouth but stopped and closed it again, looking pensive.

Slap shook his head. "I'd think folks would want the truth."

Tristan set his cup down into a retaining slot and flipped the cap shut. Drink bulbs would be easier; he'd have to pick up some. He met Slap's eyes. "Pardon me for repeating a famous—or infamous—quote, but 'what is truth?'"

The cowboy stared at Tristan. Finally, he said, "What do you believe?"

"What do I believe about what?"

"About...about God, I guess."

Carter sat back, the weathered skin around his eyes crinkling slightly, but he didn't deign to smile.

Tristan felt his spine straighten and his mouth tighten but reminded himself Slap was really only a kid. *Tread lightly.* "Belief doesn't validate a claim of truth. However, in my experience, whatever the truth is, men have twisted it until it's unrecognizable." Tristan thought of the competing religions within his childhood subculture. *What is truth?* He swallowed. *Other than the fact I have a black, damned soul, I don't know.*

"So you don't believe there's a God?"

Tristan inhaled sharply. "I *believe* we need to get this ship to a facility for repairs." He turned his attention to Carter, dismissing Slap and his topic. "Aries, you said?"

"Yes, Sir. For the necessary repairs, anyway. A refit would take too long with Príncipe to consider. He's going to get restless in such a confined space."

Tristan sipped the tisane and said nothing—back to the horse and its sensibilities again.

"But you could get the hull and armor done, plus that landing strut, and uh," Carter cleared his throat with a nervous glance at Tristan's cup, "get the parts to get the power grid working."

"By all means, let's get the grid up to one hundred percent," Tristan said dryly. "However, she doesn't need a complete refit."

"Pretty close to it, Sir. But, for what you need right now, Aries fits the bill."

"Fine. Their black market is excellent. I should be able to pick up a good price for that core."

"Aries also has veterinarian quarantine," Slap put in. "That's usually where Three Systems' livestock comes through."

"Granted," Carter said, gazing at Slap with a frown, "you want to be careful—that's your upbringing, and I respect that. But aren't animals illegally brought to Zenos all the time? I mean, what stops a ship from landing just anywhere?"

"The patrol tries to stop any illegal landings, like anywhere else, but it's done." Slap scowled, tapping his fork on the plate. "And we've had some plagues from it. But that's why I want to be careful. It's not just for Príncipe's sake."

"Then, Aries it is." Tristan peered at Carter. "Now, what about you? With your engineer skills, why are you worried about that tag?"

Carter smiled. "Well, I'm no doctor. But I can find one to remove the tag now that I'm off Dulesh."

"And change your identity again, no doubt. What if Kane puts out a legal screamer on you?"

"I already have to avoid any identity scans—my retina, DNA, everything is on file and might still be screamered by the Confeds, despite my 'death.'"

"The real reason you couldn't just leave." Tristan nodded as Carter's smile grew. "Well, I'm going to contact Kane, once we sell the core, and pay him off. If he doesn't want to legally release you, I'll remind him that Confederation agents aren't smiled upon in the Xanthus Commonwealth."

"He's not an agent, but he does pass them information."

"Only for a price, I'm sure." Tristan replied dryly. "But do you think the Xanthian government cares for semantics?"

Carter's lopsided grin widened. "Captain, remind me to never get on your bad side. But thank you for your help."

"Without yours, I don't know if I could have gotten onto Eridani Prime—at least, not in anything near a timely manner." Tristan cut his eyes to Slap, who seemed preoccupied. "Although still not timely enough."

Tristan stood. "I will need a list of parts from you, Carter, and one from you, Slap, for supplies. As well as any information I might need to facilitate getting your horse back to Zenos in good health. Get to work, gentlemen."

= = =

Aries Station was, as usual, lucrative. His cargo from Dulesh—both hidden and official—had sold, as had the core.

However, the space station, as usual, gave him the feeling he needed to watch his back. And Slap was getting more and more agitated. He knew they had to depart soon.

By ship's time, his two companions should be in bed, but as he suspected, they were in the lounge. Carter was eating, but Slap merely stared into space.

"How go the repairs?" Tristan asked from the doorway.

"Good," Carter replied, smiling. "The crews should be finished with armor repairs by tomorrow. And I should be done in a day or two."

"Good," Tristan echoed. "We'll be leaving as soon as everything is completed." With a flourish, he tossed a chit at Carter, who managed to make a clumsy catch—hand against chest, and set the other one on the table in front of Slap.

"I sold the core. This is the cut for each of you. I took out the costs of repairs first, so it's not as much as it could have been."

Carter slid his through the reader of the console on a nearby table and whistled. "Captain, this is too much!"

"A pirate captain shares equally with his crew or there will be mutiny," Tristan replied, eyeing Slap. He hadn't picked up the chit.

Carter grinned. "You consider us freebooters?"

"Not really. We don't raid ships—or commit any of the subsequent atrocities. But we're on the dark side of legal."

"So are some of the galactic governments. But back to this," Carter held up the chit. "The sharing equally is a crock." He paused and grinned. "Sir."

165

"Depends on the captain. This is my way of doing things."
Carter shrugged.

Tristan cut his eyes to Slap. "And I have to disagree. The galactic governments are all strictly legal—from their own standpoint."

"Well, then, their morality is questionable."

Slap snorted. Tristan and Carter both looked at him and exchanged glances.

Tristan changed the subject. "I also have the veterinary certificates you need, Slap. Apparently, the priests did a good job keeping that beast of yours as healthy as possible. He passed the health examination, so he's safe to be taken to Zenos, and he's had all his inoculations, so Zenos is safe for him."

Slap perked up a bit. The cowboy had all but wrung his hands when the veterinarian had come aboard to examine the animal, and hung over the man incessantly until Tristan dragged him away.

"Of course, he won't pass the legal requirements for importation," Tristan continued, "but I can land you wherever you want."

"The patrol will be on your tail, but I know you and Bertha can handle it. Thanks." The cowboy actually essayed a small smile.

Tristan pushed the chit at him. "And don't forget this. It's yours—and no argument!" He finished as Slap opened his mouth. He turned back to Carter. "Are you going with us to Zenos?"

Carter hesitated. "Do you foresee you'll need me?"

Tristan narrowed his eyes. "That sounds like a tactful way of intimating you are saying good-bye."

Carter chuckled. "Yeah, I guess it is. I enjoy traveling with you, and maybe we'll meet again one day, but this is the closest I've been to really being free in many years. I'd like to try it out. So I'll be staying here on Aries. I can catch a ship, or"—he held up the chit—"buy one."

Tristan nodded.

= = =

Slap patted Príncipe's neck, murmuring to him, telling him—again—about his new home. "Soon, boy, you'll get to see it. Wide

166

open skies, and ground with grass on it. You'll like that. Not sand everywhere you look. Real soon, now..."

Carter sauntered over, wiping his hands on a cloth. "Hey, Slap. I officially just got the last of the repairs done. We need to celebrate. Let's all go to a restaurant. Be a change from the packaged rations we've been eating. There are a few good restaurants on Aries."

"I dunno." Slap dropped his gaze, while his fingers played through the hair of the stallion's mane. "I think I druther stay here."

"You've been cooped up here since we arrived. Come on."

Slap shook his head.

Carter stared at him for a few moments before saying, "I know you had some rough times on Eridani, and you've wanted to be left alone to sort through things. But sometimes being alone ends up being in a rut, and you sink into it, rather than work your way out of it. Just one hour."

"But—"

"As a good-bye meal, since you'll be leaving tomorrow. I'm packed and have a hostel room already. This is the last you'll see of my homely face."

Slap smiled at Carter's attempt at humor. "All right."

= = =

Slap took in the sight of Aries Station with wide eyes. In design, it looked like Perseus Station, that first space station where Tristan had tried to dump Slap. But this place bore little resemblance once in the civilian ring, other than the crush of people—human and alien.

Perseus had been pristine, like it was brand new, although Slap knew all the stations had been around between half to a standard century. Aries seemed seedy by comparison. The structure appeared sound, but it lacked the attention to detail. Perseus had fancy wall tiles and bright paints. Aries was a dull metal, almost unfinished-looking.

Kiosks littered the concourse in a hodge-podge fashion, and the inner wall that had contained neat shops, restaurants, and hostels on Perseus was filled with bars and—Slap blushed— brothels with girls in windows, displaying their...wares.

The restaurant Tristan took them to was on an upper level with one curved, clear wall displaying the space kept safely at bay. Slap was glad Tristan wasn't one to chatter on, and—although Carter usually was, he made surprisingly little small talk. Slap managed to eat and did admit—to himself—that Carter was right. Getting out had helped. A little.

The three left the restaurant, and Carter said good-bye, wishing them both well. With a nod, he sauntered off.

Slap sighed and followed Tristan. Once back on the main concourse, they encountered the crowds of passengers, tourists, and hawkers. Slap wove with Tristan through the press. A girl barely more dressed than those in the brothel windows bumped into him. She looked up and smiled—a feral smile reminding him of Nadi. His stomach turned, and he shuddered and broke out in a cold sweat. With a convulsive gulp, he pushed her away and rushed ahead. *I won't throw up! I won't throw up!*

He broke into a run, his stomach still threatening to upheave, and didn't stop until he was aboard Bertha. He hurried to Príncipe, taking deep breaths, and buried his face in the horse's neck.

He heard his friend come up behind him. Without turning, he said, "Take me home, Tristan. Please!"

= = =

Tristan watched the forlorn-looking figure holding the stallion's mane and waving as he took off. The cowboy was back at the mouth of the valley where his home had been. He wished he could have done more, but what else was there to do?

Giselle rose and banked west, and he set course for Zanti City where he and Slap first met. He'd refuel and see if he could get cargo. And find out what was left of the Mordas; perhaps he could give them another punch in the stomach before he left. And then— he would head into space and be by himself again.

That was, after all, what he had wanted.

Strange Bedfellows, *part one*

It was the planet; it had to be. Tristan didn't know what Zenos meant, or even if it was from a human language or some native tongue, but it had to mean 'bad luck.'

He'd wanted to discover the status of the Mordas, and who was in charge now—at least it seemed that was forthcoming. However, he hadn't wanted to find out with his hands bound and at the wrong end of a dozen weapons.

At any rate, he knew that one merchant was in the Mordas' pocket to allow an ambush in his store. Or perhaps duress had forced his cooperation. Either way, it was an indication the Mordas were still powerful.

With a nudge from the muzzle of a particle beam rifle, he was encouraged to enter the office of the new leader of the Mordas.

The odor of cheap perfume hit him at the same time he noticed the frilly feminine décor. Irony twitched his lips as he saw the person sitting at the large desk dominating the room: Betts, the brothel owner who had helped them escape the Mordas last year.

She stood with a smirk. A good-looking woman, but she was past her prime despite trying valiantly to hide it with makeup. Her taste in clothes was still what it was last year, with an emphasis on displaying wares that were—or had been—for sale. Ample wares, he admitted, his gaze flicking to her tempting cleavage.

One of her minions released the electronic cuffs.

Tristan rubbed his wrists as he met her eyes, wondering what she wanted with him. "Congratulations," he said evenly. "I see you have overcome your worries about who might fill the power vacuum."

She laughed, showing white teeth against her red lips. "A perfect solution." She waved at her men, who all lowered their weapons and left.

As the door shut, he said, "If you wanted to see me, why not merely send an invitation."

She walked toward him, swinging her hips, her eyes alight with whatever game she was playing. He had to get a handle on it—fast.

"MacCay—yes, I know your name now. And I know your reputation." An eyebrow quirked, and her smile became sly. "I thought this would save ever so much time."

"So, I'm here. What is it you want?"

Betts pursed her lips in a faux pout. "That's not too friendly. We were friends before. I thought that might continue."

Tristan tipped his head slightly, frowning. "We were allies, not friends."

She straightened slightly, her expression becoming rigid, which also emphasized the lines in her face. "Are you trying to make an enemy?"

"Merely clarifying the past." *What does this woman want? Men I can play, but women...* To find out what she wanted, he had to play her game, at least, to a point. Tristan took a breath. "It doesn't necessarily forestall friendship in the future."

Betts' resultant smile gave Tristan chills.

= = =

Slap slid off Príncipe's back and surveyed the mountains looming over him. His insides knotted. He was tired of the pain, of the horrible remembering, and guilt. He'd seen the wary look in Tristan's eyes, wondering if he'd end his life. He'd thought about it, but didn't want that choice. The Zendians could help him—if he could bring himself to let them.

The stallion nudged his side. "I don't think the Zendians would mind you, boy, but you don't have to come with me."

Príncipe nudged him again and snorted. Slap patted his neck and, with a sigh, started toward the pass. Príncipe followed.

Before long, shapes appeared in the distance and slowly melded into the bipedal forms of Zendians. The long, serene faces, covered with short hair, all gave him knowing looks. Could they know what happened? His face burned as shame filled him anew.

One approached, her body hair brown with black mottling. Slap recognized her. She was the one who nursed him when they'd brought him here after the Mordas had destroyed his home and left him for dead. Her name, as close as he could pronounce it, was Leefah.

Welcome home, Young One, she said softly.

The affection in her expression and voice broke Slap. He fell to his knees, his head bowed, as he sobbed uncontrollably.

= = =

Betts filled the goblets and gave one to Tristan as she sat on the sofa—a bit too close to him for his comfort. "Drink up. It's very good."

He sipped the wine and managed to swallow. Her taste in wine was as refined as her taste in clothes and perfume. He set the glass down on the table in front of them. "So, I take it you wish to do business?"

Betts looked up from under her lashes. "Most men aren't usually so dispassionate with me."

Tristan hesitated, suppressing a shudder, then leaned forward and picked up the goblet; it might be a useful shield. Time to dodge and beguile. He essayed a smile. "I'm more astute than most men. They might merely see the very delightful surface. I see a"— *shark*—"very intelligent, resourceful woman." He lifted the goblet in a salute.

Betts seemed gratified and leaned back. "So where is your quaint, backcountry friend?"

Did she know who Slap was? Tristan wasn't sure what her direction was for the Mordas, but in the event she wanted the Separatists' land, as her predecessor had, Slap might be in danger. The Mordas, by reputation, didn't like leaving anyone alive who had crossed them.

Tristan posed no threat, being from off planet, but Slap—he had resisted the Mordas, fought them. And would again. "We parted company some time ago."

"A pity. He blushed so prettily."

Tristan's eyebrows rose, and he pretended to take another sip of the horse urine—er, wine. "I would like to know about my ship, and any claims you might have on it."

"I have no interest in it as former property of my organization. After all, I did help you get inside the port to steal it. Whatever problem you had with the Mordas is over. You needn't be worried about that."

"My problem wasn't with the Mordas," Tristan lied smoothly, "but with their buyers."

"That's why you stole those shipments? To get at the buyers?"

"Exactly."

"And who were these buyers?"

Tristan narrowed his eyes and flashed a smile. "Oh, come now. You're too intelligent to make me believe you don't know."

"Myers' Mercs?"

He inclined his head.

"Nasty." She gave a delicate, helpless-little-girl shiver. "And they have a reputation for double-crosses. Lyssel was a fool to deal with them. If you hadn't killed him, it's likely they would have."

"I take it you aren't interested in being one of their suppliers then."

"No, although they've contacted me three times about it." She leaned forward, her low-cut top displaying her enticing wares to good advantage. "I'm afraid of them, and I need someone who isn't."

Ah. This was the heart of it. Good. Now he had solid footing. He raised the goblet and smiled.

= = =

Stepping out of the doorway and into the sunshine, Tristan reexamined his interview. Betts' offer of friendship had some positives, but Tristan knew he had to watch for the inevitable knife in the back. Nevertheless, for now, it served his purposes to play along. He had freedom to conduct his own business; take care of the final ship repairs needed on *Giselle* and replace the rest of his specialty items, confiscated by the Confeds and not easily obtained in more...legitimate territories.

He wasn't sure how he felt about being put in the position of fending off Myers' outfit. He liked choosing his own battles, but on the other hand, irritating Myers was on his list of favorite pastimes.

He paused, waiting for a flivver to pass, glancing at the shadows and niches out of habit, then crossed the wide boulevard. The merchant buildings lined each side, their awnings flapping in the breeze. Several guild buildings were nestled in among them. This upscale part of town allowed no mendicants or kiosks to litter the street. A skiff scurried by, piloted by a sun-bronzed slave in a loincloth, his master sitting under a canopy behind him.

A movement in a side street—a motion, as of a weapon steadied on a shoulder—caught his eye, and before he could think, he dove into a shoulder roll. An explosion sounded in his ears, and debris rained down. Screams rent the air from nearby shoppers.

Tristan uncovered his head and peered into the alley—empty. He gazed around the street. A crater now graced the spot he had been walking moments before. He rose, dusting his clothes, his injured leg aching again. Could Myers already know Tristan had been hired by Betts? Or was Betts double-dealing? Or—did yet someone else on this backwater planet want him dead?

Two of Betts' men ran toward him, their faces white.

He swung around and headed back to see Betts, trying not to limp.

= = =

"I don't need bodyguards."

"But look what almost happened." Betts' eyes were round. "You can't protect my interests if you're dead, you know."

"Look what didn't happen. Whoever was behind that was haphazard—and cheap. That weapon didn't even have auto-targeting. If that's indicative of their work, I'm in no real danger. I'm more inclined to believe it was a warning."

"From who?"

Whom. Never mind—think assassination not grammar. "I'll leave that to you. Unless he has spies—and don't count that out—Myers shouldn't know of our association yet. You want me alive, find out who that was."

Tristan spun on his heel and stalked out. Set her defensive, yes, but he wouldn't rely on her to find out who his assailant was.

= = =

The *tink-tink* from an incoming message interrupted Tristan's work. He slid himself out from under the bridge panel and hit the comm button. "Yes?"

Betts' voice filtered through, faux-demure as usual. "I've just had a call from Ben Myers. He is being very insistent. I need you to come by right away. I'm sending a rover for you."

Tristan stifled a sigh. "I understand."

As he stepped into the craft a few minutes later, he wondered if it was the same rover he and Slap stole escaping from the Mordas last year. But he didn't think it would be polite to ask to examine the undersides for weapons' fire.

Betts was alone in her office. She stood by her desk, her ringed fingers twisted together. "I told him it was an inconvenient time to talk. He should be calling again soon." She lifted a hand to indicate a tray filled with pastries on the table in front of the sofa. A wine bottle stood next to it. "Please, make yourself comfortable while we wait."

If not for her agitation, Tristan would wonder if Myers had called at all. He had the distinct feeling of being stalked. Some men might not mind, but his standards balked at her offering.

"Thank you, but I'd rather not get too comfortable. I have work to do on my ship, and too many distractions"—he flashed her a brilliant smile—"lovely though they be, will set me behind schedule."

Betts' face grew lined with displeasure, but the comm chirped, making her jump. She gave Tristan a wide-eyed helpless female look. Did she play these feminine games with all her minions? If so, he wondered how long until she undermined her authority fatally.

He strode over and gestured toward her chair with his open hand, asking permission. She took a step away, and he sat, hitting the comm key.

Myers face appeared, and Tristan gave him a cool smile, waiting—due to time lag—for a reaction. He counted the seconds.

Finally, his old adversary blinked. "MacCay. I thought you were dead. You must have the lives of a cat."

"I always land on my feet. You should have realized that by now."

Another pause, then Myers sniffed. "What are you doing on Zenos?"

"Disrupting your business. Just as I did last year." Glee filled Tristan when, after the delay, Myers' mouth dropped open.

174

"So it was you," Myers' spluttered. "I should have known. But—" He frowned. "If you were behind Lyssel's death, and the downfall of the Mordas, what are you doing there now?" His face grew enlightened. "Ah. In bed with them now, are you? Or, shall I say, with her?"

Ugh. Never. "Let's just say...I have interests here. And neither I, nor the Mordas, want your business. Consider Zenos off limits."

He sat still during the time lag, keeping his face cold and challenging.

"And if I insist?" Myers asked after a few moments, his tone deadly.

Tristan let his icy-black gaze grow intense. "Then you deal with me. Not the Mordas. Me." He paused for effect, his stare not wavering. "You know I don't bluff. Do you call—or fold?"

Tristan had to fight the urge to fidget as he waited for this so-important reply.

At last, Myers face contorted. "I'll bury you under your arrogance. I'm coming for you." He began a recital of his opinion of Tristan's birth, ancestry, and habits, which, although vile, were so unimaginative that Tristan nearly yawned. With a bored flick of his finger, he disconnected.

He turned to see Betts shaking, her face red with fury. "You've just brought him down on us!"

"No, I brought him down on me. You wanted me to deal with him, you'd better be disposed to help." He rose and bowed. "Now, excuse me, but I have some preparations to make."

He departed, leaving her spluttering.

= = =

Slap sat on a low rock, staring into the fire. Leefah and two others sat with him. They hadn't talked to him much at first, letting him grieve. But now they had begun again, as the last time. Telling him he could heal, if he would only do the one thing he couldn't do.

It is the only way to begin healing, Young One, Leefah said.

But I don't want to! How can you, when they killed Ol' Pa?

*Ohl'pah is missed. We are grieved. But it is not our place to seek vengeance. Bitterness only destroys oneself. You must

175

forgive those who have wronged you, or you will eat away your own soul. Look at the Avenger. His soul is dark, and he has done it to himself.*

Slap straightened with a frown. *What Avenger? You said last year I should go into the city to meet with this avenging angel sent by your god. Well, I went, but I didn't meet any angel.*

You did. He began his work, and you left with him. But now he returns, as was foreseen.

Tristan? Did they mean Tristan? An angel? He threw back his head and laughed aloud. Oh, if only he could tell his friend he was seen as an angel by the Zendians!

I don't think my friend sees himself as an angel, he said with a chuckle.

Those chosen often do not. He has much pain, and has nurtured it into black hate for many. If you do not wish to eat your soul into an empty shell, you must learn to forgive. And then, perhaps, you can teach him, as well.

Dang, they never let him sidetrack a conversation. Leefah and the other two stared at Slap. He dropped his gaze and sighed. Forgive Lyssel? Forgive Nadi? He didn't want to, but...he couldn't go on this way, either. He slumped. *I...I don't even know how.*

Leefah touched his arm. *That is a start.*

= = =

Tristan ate his meal, his back against the wall, as usual. This was the same courtyard restaurant he had come to last year with Slap the day they met. He stared at the seat across from him, imagining the cowboy sitting there, talking with his mouth full. *How is Slap doing now?*

Well, emotionally wounded though he was, Slap was alive and away from Tristan—away from the line of fire.

And thinking of line of fire, Tristan hadn't had any luck in finding out who had been behind that attack last week. Neither had the Mordas.

He would have attributed their lack of success on either incompetence, or on knowing already who was behind it. But given the fact he had been unsuccessful as well, that argument was nil.

But who was it? How could the attack be so ineffective, yet the cover up be so efficient? A paradox. Tristan didn't like paradoxes. He frowned, sipping his coffee. This puzzle clouded his mind—and he had to concentrate on the upcoming standoff; Myers was on his way.

He wouldn't put it past Myers to cause mass destruction just to get to Tristan; an image of a person with a particle beam rifle blasting a house to bits while trying to shoot a scurrying mouse flitted through his mind. But Myers, although not afraid to kill innocents, or shoot someone in the back, would not strike without first letting Tristan know he was there. He'd want to be face to face.

What Tristan had to do was make Myers focus on him and not on any standers-by.

= = =

Betts mouth dropped open. "You want me to what?"
"Betray me."
Betts stepped around a chair, one long, painted nail tapping her chin. "It seems your plan relies on the Mordas quite a bit."
"You asked for my help. Quite forcefully. Don't tell me you don't intend to do your part."
Betts pursed her lips and continued walking around the room—stalking was more like it. "I had hoped you would merely emphasize to Myers that we weren't interested in any deals with him."
Tristan glared at her. "As head of the Mordas, 'emphasizing' is your job." He took a breath to bring his anger to a more manageable level. "My job—as defined by you—is to make sure Myers backs off. I know him; he doesn't back off."
"I know *of* him, which is why I didn't want to have anything to do *with* him." Betts sat and crossed her legs. "You probably don't believe it, but I *can* be ruthless. Myers, however—"
"You'd better worry about the Mordas, not Myers. You said you could be ruthless, but all you've shown me is a woman playing games. If your people hesitate in following you, it's my neck on the line. Wake up!"
Betts stood, her eyes snapping. "How dare you—"

"How dare you! Playing the helpless female might have been a ploy you could afford as a brothel madam, but it won't work now."

She lifted a hand to slap his face, but he grabbed her arm. She fought for a second then went limp, leaning against him—still playing games. "I'm not like that with them." She looked up, her eyes pleading. "Only with you."

Oh, please! "Save it. We don't have time. You say you can be ruthless. Show me ruthless." *Let's try a reversal of her gambit on her.* Tristan lowered his head slightly, letting his cheek brush hers as he whispered in her ear, "I find that much more attractive."

Her eyebrow arched, and a smile slowly grew. "Tell me how you want me to betray you."

= = =

"You seem to have this all worked out," Betts said later, leaning back on the sofa. "But what about your ship? Don't you think it might get blown up, like last time?"

Tristan wished he could maneuver her to a table or desk. But the best he'd managed so far was being at the opposite end of this piece of furniture. He'd never danced around a woman so much in his life.

"No, I sold it." Not strictly true, but close enough. And hopefully that information would keep all eyes away from *Giselle*.

Her eyebrows rose. "Why?"

He gave a soft chuckle. "It really doesn't fit me. When this is all over, I'll be in the market for a small yacht."

"Who did you sell it to?"

"Some Separatists who wished to do their own cargo runs and avoid Merchant fees."

Betts laughed. "I now control the Merchants, and the Guilds too. You're pitting the Separatists against me?"

Also not strictly true. Some of the Merchants were opposing the Mordas. Tristan had been busy and knew all about the links and ties of the local mob. But Betts didn't need to know what he knew about the local balance—or unbalance—of power. He shrugged. "I merely sold the ship. What happens from this point on isn't my concern. But, at the moment, I'd say you have more important concerns than one old freighter."

"True. Between you and Myers I have my hands full." Her lips twitched, fighting a smile.

Tristan wasn't going to acknowledge the double-entendre—or anything that might stray toward the inevitable hints of more than a business relationship. So far he'd deflected her advances with a business-first/play-later response.

But he'd better redirect the conversation. "Back to our plans. Myers will likely contact you when he—"

Fwoom! The door blasted into flaming pieces. Tristan dove over the coffee table and toward a side room. He shut the door and looked around. No exit but the window, covered with iron bars.

Strange Bedfellows, *part two*

"There's no way out, MacCay," Myers shouted while Betts shrieked wordlessly.

Tristan stood to one side, as far from any line of fire as possible, in case Myers decided to blow the wall in. His right leg ached again from his acrobatic dive into this side room.

He eyed the ventilation shaft near the floor. He'd checked out this building one previous night, and as he'd discovered on his first visit to this planet, the older buildings on this planet all had commodious ductwork. He could pry the cover loose; he only needed about ten seconds to get inside and escape, if he had the chance. Would Myers shoot first or talk?

"Myers, you do tend to make a splashy entrance."

His adversary gave a wicked chuckle. "Thank you. But do you come out, or do we further demolish this lady's place of business?"

"I'll thank you to not do further damage," Betts yelled. "And you'll pay for what you did do!"

"Ah," Tristan called, his leg twinging as he squatted by the shaft's grille cover. "Take note of that response, please. I think we have something to talk about before you try again to kill me."

"And what might that be?"

He's talking. Now we're on my turf. "You want to deal with the Mordas, yes?"

"They're in a perfect set up to smuggle weapons—on the edge of two major powers—three if you include Pegasus, with no real opposition."

"Then what you need is a person running the Mordas who knows how to play the cards," Tristan said. "Lyssel was sloppy. This ex-madam doesn't understand the rules. She can't see further than worrying about the destruction of a mere door."

Betts let out a string of blue language, and Myers yelled at her to shut up, probably backed up with a weapon's aim. Tristan grinned while carefully, quietly working on the vent's cover. His smile congealed as the grille stuck.

In the sullen silence that followed, Myers asked, "What are you suggesting?"

"I've been studying the dynamics of the Mordas," Tristan said, trying to get a firmer grip on the cover; it was rusty and didn't want to give. "The intricacies of their power structure, how the rich leech off them in a semi-symbiotic relationship, and the control they wield over the Guilds and Merchants. I know the smuggling racket, as you well know. I think we could work together."

"You...and me? We've had a feud for years."

"Merely a misalignment of our goals at the time. We have talents which compliment each other. Think about it." *Take the bait...take it...give me time...* Tristan held his breath as he tried to ease the grille off without making any sounds.

"You have a point. Come on out, and we'll talk."

"I don't mean to throw cold water on the beginning of a new business relationship, but just a minute ago you were intent on killing me. Walking back through that door does cause me some trepidation."

A slight scrape—he held his breath—and the cover came off.

"Another point. How do you propose we solve the problem?"

"I'll leave that to you."

His heart thudded in the silence as he listened for any movements in the next room. He could hear murmured discussion still going on as he slid into the shaft.

"All right, MacCay. One of my men will open the door to the room, and..." the voice faded as Tristan made his escape.

= = =

Slap slowed Príncipe and stared at the homestead in the valley below. How could he face Shallah's father after letting her die? But he had to do this. He took a breath before descending.

The house grew closer, and before long, one of the children playing in the yard saw him and ran to the barn. Ewan came out followed by two others, all carrying weapons—one had a pitchfork, two old-fashioned rifles.

As he drew near, the older man's mouth dropped open, and he gave the rifle to the young man to his right. It took Slap a moment to realize the young man wasn't a hired hand but Ewan's son Sean. He'd grown a foot since last year! The almost-grown youth on the left was Aillil.

Slap felt his stomach shudder as he slid off the stallion to face his father-in-law.

Ewan stepped forward, breaking into a grin. He threw his arms around Slap. "We thought you were dead!" His accent was thick with emotion.

"No, I—"

Sean ran up and pounded on Slap, whooping for joy. Children swarmed out of the house along with Shallah's mother Brìghde. The whole family backed up a step as she rushed into his arms, weeping.

"Awww, shh, Bree. Don't. You'll get me crying," Slap murmured, holding her tightly, tears stinging his eyes.

When she finally let him go, Ewan said, "Come inside, Son."

Slap nodded back toward his horse. The stallion was flicking his ears back unhappily, stamping his feet, and sidling around. "I have to see to Príncipe first. He's not used to people."

Ewan's eyes lit up. "A beautiful beast! Where did you get him?"

Slap hesitated. "He was...a gift. I'll tell you about it later. Can I use your corral for him?"

"Aye. Let's see to him. Then we'll talk."

$$= = =$$

Tristan brushed himself off and sauntered around to the front of the building. Two guards stood by the limo alight at the curb. He walked up to one and held out a data card. "Give this to your boss when he comes out."

The guard took it with a frown, and Tristan continued down the sidewalk. He ducked into an alley and began winding his way through the maze of streets.

He wished he could see Myers face when the guard gave him the card.

Now the fun began...

$$= = =$$

Slap drank the strong tea as he told how the Mordas had beaten him, broke his back, and forced him to watch as they burned his home—his family inside. Then left him for dead. He brushed away tears and continued, telling how the Zendians had taken him away and nursed him to health. How he had gone to Zanti City, met Tristan, and left the planet with him. He didn't tell much of what happened with Tristan, just how he had wanted to come home. He mentioned nothing of Eridani.

His gaze kept drifting to Shallah's younger sister Aylish. She was growing up fast and looked so much like her oldest sister. His heart ached to look at her, yet he couldn't stop.

He wound down the story and concluded, "I was afraid to come here. I thought you'd blame me for what happened."

"Why would you think that?" Aillil asked.

"If I'd just taken them and left..."

"You were fighting for your home." Ewan lifted his chin. "I wouldn't have done different."

Slap's throat tightened up, and he couldn't answer.

"We're glad you're back home now, Son," Brighde said softly, breaking the silence.

"Aye. Will you be rebuilding your place?" asked Sean.

Slap gaped at his brother-in-law. "Rebuild? On Shallah and Evan's ashes? How can I?"

Brighde stepped close and put a hand on his shoulder. "We buried them on the hill with your family," she whispered. "We...we didn't know what to think when we didn't find you. We thought the Mordas had taken you away and left you dead somewhere else."

"Your return is incredible timing," Ewan said, leaning forward, his elbows on his knees. "The Mordas have started sending their men around again, like they did before Lyssel died. Last week they were at Chandler's place. They burned his barn down. We used to think we could just go about our business, that they wouldn't really do anything. But last year..." His father-in-law stopped, pain in his eyes. Slap felt the tears welling up again in his own.

Ewan inhaled roughly and continued. "We know now we have to fight. You are a symbol of what we are fighting for. You will help us, Son?"

"Fight the Mordas?" Slap felt his heart speed up. Now he had something to live for. "Yeah. Yeah, I'll help."

= = =

Slap gathered with his fellow ranchers and homesteaders around a fire in Chandler's yard, a plate piled high in one hand. The women had brought food enough for two barn-raisings. It had been a long day, but one filled with purpose. Now, with the task done, it was time to talk.

The men all regarded Slap with grave respect. Granted, his people looked more at achievement than age, but he wasn't used to being treated as if he were one of the elders. He ate, listening to the discussion of how to fight the Mordas.

Finally, he swallowed the last of his meat pie and said, "This won't work. You can't go against the Mordas without some plan, and without weapons to at least match theirs. Not to mention, you need someone to lead, who knows what he's doing."

"That's where you come in, boy," old man Russell said. "You've fought them. You know them. We want you to be our Chefe."

"I was nearly killed by them," Slap yelled, banging a fist on his knee. "My family murdered! If anything, that shows just how much I don't know about how to fight them."

"That was last year. You've been around some since then, and with a man who, from what all the gossip says, knows how to fight. You had to learn something from him."

Slap shook his head. If only Tristan were here, but he had long gone by now.

"You're the best we've got, Son," Ewan said. "We're not trained fighters, but we're strong. We're not all very educated, but we aren't stupid, either. Give us some direction. That's all we ask."

Slap stared at the fire. He couldn't begin to guess what Tristan would do. That man's mind could think in twenty directions, and not one of them expected.

He sighed. He'd fought mercenaries, Confeds, Eridani; perhaps it was all to get him ready to tackle the Mordas. He looked around. Would his people—quiet, living off the land, law-abiding—be able to do whatever needed to be done? "All right. But you understand, this can't be a fair fight. Not against them. Not if you want to win."

His neighbors exchanged looks. A few wagged their heads.

"Look," Slap stood, glaring around. "I've seen what the enemy can do. They don't play by rules, and they don't care who they hurt or kill. Women." He stared at one man and on to another, his young son's face wavering in overlay. "*Babies*. You have to be as dirty as they are. And you can't back away once you've committed. That would be suicide."

Ewan stood. "Aye. He's right. It goes down hard, but we have to be as ruthless as they are. I don't want more of my children killed by those ruffyans."

"It was only my barn burned this time. They told me it was a warning, that next time it would be my home." Chandler nodded at Slap. "I thought of you." He straightened. "I don't want it to happen again. Not to anyone."

Russell came forward, his weathered face alight as he met Slap's eyes. "I'm with him." He turned to face the crowd. "Are you with us?"

Chandler stood, his chin high. Several others jumped up quickly. Slowly, the rest got to their feet.

Ewan grinned. "Some of the Merchants, and Guild members too, want the Mordas' stranglehold broken."

"Yes, and since they've found *you're* back"—Chandler nodded at Slap—"they've been cooperative. Willing to pass on information, and—" he paused, his brown eyes sparkling. "This morning, hidden in a wagonload of supplies was a crate of weapons. All we need now, is a plan."

Movement in the shadows caused everyone to freeze for a moment. But they resolved into—of all things—Zendians. They came forward; the Separatists stepped back, confusion on most of their faces. Slap was just as confused.

We have listened, one of the Zendians—Slap couldn't begin to pronounce his name and just called him Kohn—said. *The Evil must be driven from our world. The Avenger is not enough.*

Slap translated, and Kohn stared at him saying, *You will lead, Young One. We will help.*

Slap scratched his chin for a few moments. "All right...all right..."

= = =

The rooftop opposite had a steep slope and more height. Tristan couldn't successfully make that leap.

But he had to get across this alley without being seen. He wondered how long until Myers figured out he wasn't the cat in this cat and mouse game. He'd baited the mercenary before, but never had he gotten the man to personally come after him. This was finally the time.

The building across and farther along the alley had a lower roof. He sprinted to the end and gauged the distance. Acceptable. He took a breath and leaped—his right leg collapsed on landing. He rolled, grit grinding into his clothes.

Tristan sat, rubbing his leg for a moment. He refused to even think he was getting too old for this sort of thing anymore. It was just not being recovered from the wounds he received on Eridani— his leg especially. He flexed his foot to stretch the impaired calf muscle and slowly got to his feet.

Time was running out; he had to hurry. He had to get to the meeting place unseen—and before Myers' minions. He knew the merc would have his men surround the meeting place the moment he received the next message from Tristan.

He peered over the edge and saw pipes running down the side of the wall. He stretched his fingers inside the gloves before swinging over the side and shimmying down.

He landed in a squat, watching and listening: clear. He kept moving.

The block of old, brick buildings stood empty, near the edge of Zanti City in the warehouse district. Tristan had chosen and prepared the area as soon as he left Betts after Myers' call.

He scanned the dead-end street and the windows above as he maneuvered into his hidden vantage point, in a narrow, shadowed ledge above a ground story window, and set his camo-net in place. From here, near the center, he could see the entire cul-de-sac.

Much rested on whether he truly understood how Myers thought. He'd seen him in action before, several times; he was a creature of habit. Tristan let his breath trickle out slowly and prepared to wait.

Before long, the mercenaries arrived and fanned out in groups of threes, crouching and leapfrogging each other as they searched for him and attempted to secure the area. More were on the rooftops.

He waited, assured they couldn't find him.

Soon, movement at the open end of the street caught his eye. Myers. But—Tristan's stomach sank into his feet. Myers held a small child against his chest, a handgun pointed at her head. Her eyes were large with terror, but she was silent, her face, framed by dark curls, pale. Vile, just vile. But that was Myers all over. Tristan had done his best to keep this conflict away from innocent victims; it hadn't been enough.

His mind's eye filled with the image of another child from years ago, when he had thought himself hardened to everything. But despite his black soul, he still hadn't been able to kill that little one—even for his own survival. Dray called that being weak. Perhaps he was right.

"Come on out, MacCay, if you don't want to see this sweet little girl killed." Myers voice echoed slightly. "I know you're here somewhere, even if my men haven't flushed you out."

"You are assuming I care if you kill the kid," Tristan called. "If you do, then you have nothing to keep me from taking you down."

"I mean it, MacCay. Come out now and drop your weapons. Or she dies."

Rage boiled in Tristan, making his whole body shake. No choice. Myers did not bluff. *Damn, damn, damn!* He turned off the camo-net, stood, and jumped down to the street.

Myers laughed. "I sorta figured you'd have a trick like a 'net up your sleeve. In your effort to keep me from being able to ambush you, you chose a place where you couldn't hide either. Now," his voice lowered, "drop your weapons. All of them."

Tristan lifted one hand, and Myers made a show of re-gripping the handgun. "Easy. Thumb and forefinger."

He splayed his hand, and made a pincer as ordered, reaching carefully into his vest. The PBG came out, dangling from his fingers.

"Toss it—carefully."

It wasn't Tristan who'd die if he tried anything, it would be that girl. He did as he was told.

"Next?"

Tristan lifted his eyebrows, and Myers grinned. "I know you have more weapons. Don't play games."

One by one, Tristan emptied his inventory.

"Stim-blade too."

Damn. Tristan slid the blade out from its hidden sheath within his vest, and tossed it down.

"Good boy. Now, you walk—slowly—to the middle of the street. Don't forget, my men have you covered from all angles." To prove the point, two men stepped forward, PBRs trained on him.

Why didn't Myers just kill him? He wasn't about to ask and give his adversary any ideas. Delay meant Myers might make a mistake. He obeyed the mercenary, gauging distance to his weapons and to his opponent with every step.

"That's close enough," Myers said when Tristan was about twenty-five feet from him. "I wanted to clearly see your face when you die."

Tristan didn't answer. The child was likely only spared from death for the amount of time it took to kill Tristan. But perhaps, perhaps Myers would—no, the child had no chance. This world had no chance. Tristan's failure condemned them all. Condemned Slap and his people. Myers would take over now, either keeping Betts as a puppet, or installing one of his own, thus guaranteeing his power in this sector.

He was letting one child condemn a world. Yet he could not make himself act and bring about her death. *Weak,* he could hear Dray sneer at him out of his distant past.

"You coward," Tristan said. "You unmitigated coward."

"Referring to the kid?" Myers snarled.

"To her, to your men. You haven't the guts to face me alone. That's why I knew I had to find a place to keep you from ambushing me."

"Quite right. An army isn't safe attacking you head on. This isn't cowardice—it's survival. Doesn't feel good being the target, does it?"

"What doesn't feel good is losing to a lesser man. One who hides behind children. And weapons. I'll take you with my bare hands, if you have the guts."

Myers laughed. "Oh, no! I won't fall for one of your tricks. Not this time. You've been a thorn in my side for years." Myers aimed the handgun at Tristan. "This is going to be a pleasure."

In the next fraction of a second, Tristan would die, standing still or attacking. The gun wasn't aimed at the child in this moment. He dove for the ground, a moving target.

An explosion ripped up the ground where Tristan had been standing. Tristan rolled to protect his face from the rubble raining down. He had no time to run back to his weapons; he jumped up and raced toward Myers through the cloud of dust.

Screams came from the little girl crumpled onto the street, and Myers staggered up, stunned. Tristan dove at the mercenary, knocking him back and flipping the gun away, out of reach. Myers grabbed Tristan and pulled into a roll, landing on top of him. Hands grasped and tightened around Tristan's throat. Myers' sweaty face grinned into his, his weight pinning Tristan down.

The gloating face and beady eyes were too much. Tristan wove his arm around the mercenary's and twisted, breaking the hold. He wormed out from under his opponent, striking him in the jaw. Myers grabbed for him, but Tristan rolled away and up to his feet.

The merc rose, his head swiveling as he looked around the ground. Tristan wasn't going to give him the chance to look for the gun. He leaped up and spun—his foot connected with Myers' face. The man went down with a groan. Tristan landed next to him and drove his fist into the mercenary's throat. He felt the crunch and knew the blow was fatal—but not fast. Myers clawed at him, trying to breathe.

The ground around him began to spit and pit with weapons' fire. He dove at the girl and covered her with his body. It was only a matter of time before he was hit, but perhaps his body could save her.

Another explosion battered his ears. He turned his head to see part of a building collapsing. Some of the mercs were firing up at a roof, while more ran past Tristan, trying to get away. He saw Myers' handgun just within reach and grabbed it. He rolled and aimed at the fleeing men and dropped several. The rest kept running.

Who was up there? Who had fired at him, and had blown up that building?

Tristan had no place to put the little girl to keep her out of harm's way. He had to trust she would be safe near Myers' corpse if he ran to get his weapons. He knelt by the child and said, "Stay here. Do you understand? Stay here and don't move."

Boom! Another wall crumbled onto the street. More men appeared, running toward the exit of the cul-de-sac, but they stopped as they saw him and raised their guns.

No time to run for his arsenal. Cowards. Murderers. Lending themselves to the evils Myers perpetrated.

He rose and took a step forward, aware that only his presence protected the little girl behind him. His heart icy, he raised the handgun and picked off a man. And another one. They would get him in one of the next shots, but he had the satisfaction of taking as many with him as he could.

But as their companions fell, the remaining mercenaries threw down their weapons and lifted their hands. "Don't shoot us!" one called, while another shouted, "We surrender!"

"Take ten steps backwards and kneel," Tristan ordered. "Hands on your head."

The irony of seven men on their knees, held at bay by a mere handgun, wasn't lost on Tristan. He felt a tiny hand grasp his left leg. He didn't dare look down, but his free hand found the top of her head and stroked her curly hair.

One of the men looked at the girl and up at Tristan. He gazed over his shoulder. "Your friend up there won't kill us, will he?"

Tristan spared a quick glance at the buildings. Who *was* up there? Would Betts have sent someone to help? No, this seemed to be the same weapon that had been fired at him before. He wasn't even sure if the person's aim had improved. He hadn't been hit— again, but neither had Myers. Who was the target? What did he want?

"Well, now, I can't say for certain," Tristan said. "Perhaps if you don't want to become another hole in the pavement, you'll be very still."

They stared at him, eyes huge. He stared back as he slowly stepped forward. Among the armament they'd dropped was a stunner. Perfect. He picked it and thumbed it for wide dispersal. Without a word, he fanned them and watched them fall.

He looked up at the rooftops again.

Silence. He waited, looking for any movement.

Nothing happened.

He picked up the little girl. "You're safe now," he murmured. He heard the sounds of sirens. "You'll be going home soon."

She wrapped her arms around his neck. It had been years since he'd held a child, any child. The last one he'd carried in his arms— he pushed that memory away. At least this one was alive. Anger rose inside, churning up until it nearly choked him. Myers was as bad as Dray, as bad as the Mordas. This place needed to be made safe for little ones. The Mordas needed to be destroyed. But how? The hydra had too many heads to fight from the outside. He had to look deeper...

A thought occurred to him as the police arrived en masse, brandishing their weapons. This time, he'd fight from the *inside.*

= = =

Slap grinned as the fires roared through the warehouse, the heat on his face mirroring the heat in his heart. This was the third Mordas target they'd hit in two days. They were drawing closer to Zanti City with each one. But the Mordas, for all their fancy means of transportation, would find it hard to flush the warring Separatists from their hiding places in the hills.

Especially with the Zendians' help.

After the second attack, a small group of Mordas tried to enter Zendi Valley, but the Zendians met them. Slap didn't know what they did to them, but no one was hurt on either side. However, the Zendians sent the men, naked, back across the desert to Zanti City.

Not necessarily a death sentence, but close. It did send a clear message to the Mordas. Slap hoped he was prepared.

= = =

"So you still don't know who the unknown person was on the rooftop?" Tristan asked as he accepted the glass. He eyed Betts as she poured herself a drink.

"No." Her red lips pursed tightly. "I take it you haven't found out either?"

"I searched the area, and found evidence of where the person had been. I am of the feeling this is the same one who shot at me in the street last week. It's the same weapon. I'm as stumped as you."

Which has me on edge; why can't I get a handle on this attacker? He tries to drop me, then stops Myers and his men on the next go round. What is his angle? What does he want?

Betts sat on the sofa and crossed her legs. "We'll keep searching and asking questions. But for now, I have a new proposition for you." She patted the cushion next to her.

The word and gesture made Tristan's hackles rise. He crossed and seated himself on a chair opposite her. He wanted to worm into the organization, but—ugh, no!—not through her bed.

Betts eyes narrowed. "Are you completely immune to feminine...blandishments?" she asked in exasperation.

Tristan stared at her with a stoic expression. "My body or my heart?"

Betts fingered the goblet in her hand. "You once said you had no heart."

"You remembered." He lifted his drink in a salute, took a sip, and set it on the table.

She sighed and shook her head. "If I didn't need you right now, I'd be deeply offended. But business first." She leaned forward. "We hear the Separatists have a new, strong chefe, or leader, now. We'd offer a lucrative deal to anyone who would get rid of him for us."

"You have the Guilds and Merchants sewn up." Tristan crossed his arms. "The rich who reside here are all in bed with you—"

"Nice way of putting it," she said with a laugh.

"So," Tristan continued, "I don't see how the Separatists can possibly cause you much trouble; they have no money. They have no voice, no say."

"They have *land*." Betts sat up straight, her eyes glittering. "Most of the good land—all that green, lush land across the desert by the Zendi Mountains. And one other thing that gives them clout. The Zendians have come out of their holes in the mountains. When we've tried to move against those backwater dirt grubbers, the Zendians actually protected them. It seems they listen to Chefe."

"I think you have Lyssel to blame for that. He attacked one family and, in the process, killed one of those aliens. I think that got their attention."

"Yes, and that brings us back to their leader." Betts gazed over at Tristan. "Are you willing to take the job?"

"I usually don't commit assassinations." *And this isn't how I imagined myself allying with the Mordas.*

"Any price." Her smile became seductive. "I'll make it worth your while."

I doubt it, he thought but kept his face bland. "Assume, hypothetically, I decide to take the commission. What's the leader's name?"

"William McCarty."

Tristan's stomach flipped, but he remained impassive. *They want to kill Slap!*

Strange Bedfellows, *part three*

Tristan took a sip of his drink to gather his thoughts, his gaze on Betts' smug face. "Let's assume for a minute that McCarty is out of the picture. What are your plans?"

"To drive the Separatists out, of course. This planet doesn't have an abundance of green land. And they have most of it."

"I wasn't referring to your objectives. What exactly are you planning to do? Will you continue as Lyssel did? Burning them out and killing them?"

Betts' eyes glowed. "You've thought me weak. I know you have. But I'm not." She leaned forward. "Yes. I'll do whatever I need to in order to get that land."

"Even killing innocents? Children? Babies?"

Her mouth drew tight, showing the lines around her mouth. "Is this a trick question? You did save that child from Myers."

Tristan's back stiffened; those first on the scene—and the little girl's parents as well—had called him a hero. It still rankled. "I told you—don't attribute virtue to that. Letting that kid die would have been a net win for Myers, that's all."

"She would have just been collateral damage."

"No, he turned her into a target, an objective in his game." He lowered his voice, and spoke through gritted teeth. "I don't like to lose."

Her chin lifted, she met his gaze with determination. "Neither do I. I'll do whatever it takes."

She thought he was looking for affirmation of her resolve, Tristan realized, and was trying to show how strong she was. Whether she truly had the stomach for it or not, she just put herself in the same league as Dray and Myers. He was right to want to take the Mordas down.

"First things first." Tristan picked up his glass and took a sip. "If I'm going to work for you, I have certain conditions."

Betts frowned. "What do you want? I told you I'd pay any price."

Tristan shook his head. "I want in."

"In?" The ex-madam sat up straight, her eyes narrowed. "What are you really after?"

Tristan waved his glass in a dismissive gesture. "Not to take over, if you're thinking of that line of muck I told Myers. But," he smiled, a difficult task with his stomach turning over, "I think we could...make a good team. Cover each other's weaknesses."

Slowly, with deliberation, Betts leaned back, eyeing Tristan warily. "This *does* sound like the same line you tried to sell Myers."

"Are you buying?"

"You want to be my partner." It wasn't a question.

Tristan snorted. "That would be hubris at this point in time. Let's say, I want to earn your trust. Work my way up."

"I'll...have to think about it, but..." She paused, her stare becoming more calculating. "If you take this contract and kill McCarty, I'll give it serious thought."

Tristan raised his drink in a conciliatory salute. *So, I'm on the inside—if I kill Slap.*

= = =

Tristan snagged a basket and slowly walked around the kiosk, testing and choosing various vegetables and fruits. He pretended not to notice that the vendor kept flicking his gaze to Tristan. Finally, he asked the man, "You're a member of the Merchants' League?"

"If I weren't, they'd run me out."

Tristan gave the vendor the basket. "What percentage do you pay?"

"Same as the rest."

"And that is?"

The vendor told him.

"And that includes the cut the Mordas take?"

The vendor licked his lips, his eyes darting nervously up and down the street. "The Merchants' dues are separate from the Mordas's."

"And what do you pay them?"

When the vendor answered, Tristan whistled through his teeth. "Seems like the Guilds and Merchants both cut their own throats when they got in bed with the Mordas."

The vendor didn't answer, but instead told Tristan the cost for his purchases. Tristan paid for his produce.

"Do you wish us to deliver, Sir?" the vendor asked.

"No. I'll carry them."

Bag in one hand, Tristan wound his way through the marketplace, watchful and alert, shopping and asking questions.

Finally, he started toward his rented house, eager to be out of the hot sun and dry desert air. A large dog ran past him, tongue lolling. Space was much better; invariable temperatures, cleaner, and—he sidestepped the dog's generous deposit on the road—no animals.

He keyed himself past the security safeguards and entered the house, shivering in the cool, climate-controlled air. He put his groceries on the table with a sigh, wishing he were on *Giselle*, but the sleight of hand of seeming to sell her to the Separatists was likely safer for her.

While the herbs steeped for his tisane, he began chopping mushrooms and onions, his mind wandering to the last time he'd worked in a kitchen. It was on *Giselle*, with Slap. He drove the knife into the cutting board with a *thunk* and ground his teeth. This was not the time to get sentimental. With a see-saw motion, he worked the blade out of the board and concentrated on cooking the omelet.

After his meal, he poured another cup of tisane, sipping it as he paced, mentally reviewing his plans. Juggling all the pieces of this game at all times was going to be a difficult act. A stronger drink would suit him about now, but he needed his wits about him.

What he should be doing was sitting at the comdesk, working, but he was fatigued, mentally as well as physically. A shower was what he needed. He set the tisane on the end table by one of the chairs and went to the bedroom.

= = =

As hot needles of water attacked his body, he felt himself reviving slightly. One advantage of being downside; water instead of sonic showers. He scrubbed the planet's grime and sweat from his body, then just stood under the jets, trying not to think, eyes closed.

A light rumble and tremor made his eyes fly open. He jumped out of the shower, dashing water from his face, and listened. A sound from his security board in the foyer indicated a matter requiring his attention. Water still dripping from his hands, he keyed the display. Someone had just tried to blow up the house. From the configuration of the blast, it was probably the same weapon that had previously been used against him. Whoever was after him must be an idiot to try to attack a force-shielded house.

He pulled on a pair of pants, snatched up his PBG, and headed for the door. The perimeter scan showed clear. He hit the latch, and the door slid open. From here, he was still inside the shielding, but could see the street. Two of Betts' men stood outside, PBRs drawn.

"She was on the roof, Mr. MacCay," came the one man's voice through the wall comm by the door. "We saw her jump from one building to another. Three of our men are chasing her."

Her? Tristan's mind skidded to a halt. What *her* could want him dead? Not Betts, and he'd met no other women on this planet.

Tristan wanted to join the chase, but by now they were too far away, and besides, he was barely dressed. He nodded at the men through the shield as he keyed the comm. "Let me know when you catch her."

He closed the door and stood motionless, his thoughts in a muddled whirl. *Her?*

Some moments later, the chime sounded, interrupting his train of thought. He checked the security vid. A woman, blonde, tall, not really a beauty, but with sparkling, blue eyes and a wide, full mouth waited between the two guards. This couldn't possibly be *her.*

"Yes?" he asked through the comm.

"Mr. MacCay? My name is Tanya Daniels, and I represent a guild which wishes to discuss matters with you."

"Which guild?"

"The Courtesan Guild."

Tristan bit his lip. They even had a guild for *that?* "Betts didn't send you."

"She...probably won't like that I've come to see you. No, she has nothing to do with our guild anymore."

This could be interesting. Tristan lifted a finger to key her entry, realized he only wore pants, and instead said, "Give me a few minutes."

After getting dressed, he allowed her entry and watched as she passed through the scanner. No hidden weapons.

She gave him a blinding smile. This woman had natural grace and style, and impeccable taste in clothes. He waved her to the living room and watched as she settled herself into a chair. He sat on the arm of another chair and let her scrutinize him.

"Aren't you going to ask me what I want?" she finally asked.

"I'm sure you'll tell me."

Tanya laughed. "I like you." She leaned forward. "I want in, Mr. MacCay. Whatever you're up to, I want in."

"I'm not 'up to' anything except what Betts has hired me to do."

"And what is that?"

"That's between her and me."

"Which brings up a question: what *is* between her and you?"

"That's none of your business."

"Hmm." Her eyes teased him. "I might want it to be my business. I saw you in the doorway earlier. A shame you got dressed before letting me in."

"I'm not in the mood for flirting, and I have work to do."

"Score one for me. You went from being willing to wait for me to start the conversation to urging me to get to business."

"Which is?"

"There are a few places where secrets are most likely to be leaked. One of them is the bedroom."

"Go on."

"My girls are trained to pay attention and pass on anything that might be of interest." She paused, obviously waiting for an expression of curiosity. Tristan kept his face bland. Her eyes twinkled. "You *are* good."

She rose and began to wander about the room talking, her fingers touching a lamp, an objet d'art, trailing the back of a chair. "Now, my girls probably wouldn't see much, only getting bits and pieces of the jigsaw puzzle, but I'm seeing a pattern. A very *interesting* pattern. And I think you're definitely 'up to' something—much more than whatever you're doing for Betts."

Tristan had barely begun his assault; he didn't even have his big guns assembled yet. What had she gleaned already? Without a doubt, this woman was dangerous. But, for whom?

She approached, and he had the feeling of being stalked. He didn't allow himself to move, keeping his eyes on her face, not the cleavage that was conveniently at eye level from his perch on the chair arm. This woman had naturally what Betts strove for desperately yet failed to achieve.

Steady on—don't let her know she's gotten under your skin so easily. "And whatever it is you think I'm 'up to,' you don't think Betts would have her own sources handy to pass on the puzzle pieces?"

"She might get a few, but not enough." Tanya's dazzling smile lit her face. "I'll pass on anything I hear. You just remember that when whatever it is you're 'up to' is going down."

She stepped back with a knowing look. "I'd better go before Betts is told I'm here. She'll likely have words for both of us. But I can honestly say I wasn't here long enough to do anything but tease." She headed for the door with a soft laugh.

Tristan rose to key her out. As the door slid shut, he let his breath out in a slow exhale, running his hands through his hair. He needed another shower now. Cold, this time.

= = =

A little later, Tristan sat at the comdesk with a cup of steaming tisane and attempted to push the *her*, Tanya, and Betts all to the back of his mind. He must force his thoughts on the now. After checking the installation of all his own custom software, he opened one of the applications.

Eyes narrowed, he opened a second program and began making notes. He understood the basic power structure of this hierarchy but needed to know details, specifically strengths and weaknesses of each tier. Most especially, the rich. Striking against them felt like a mosquito attacking an elephant—a herd of elephants.

A call interrupted his research. He didn't bother with the ear comm, just hit receive. "Yes?"

"We couldn't get her, Mr. MacCay. She was like a...ghost. She just vanished. We've been searching, but it's no use."

Tristan wasn't surprised. He'd had no luck tracking her, and he was the best. Whoever *she* was, she was a mixture of inexperience and experience. His curiosity was piqued.

"Thanks. Keep on it." He broke the connection with a frown, closed his eyes, and shook his head. Two women invaded his world on the same day. He had to set both Tanya and *her* aside. With a sharp sigh, he focused his mind on the display.

Finally, a pattern emerged; weak points easily exploited. He cupped his chin in his hand. *If you can get just one elephant going in the direction you want, the others will follow.*

He opened an interlink window and began working...

The chair creaked as he leaned back with a sigh. He reached for his tisane, took a sip, grimaced, and set it down. Cold. How long had he been sitting here? He rose, tossed the drink, and busied himself brewing a fresh pot. As he turned toward the living room, he stopped, arrested, as a lingering whiff of perfume hit him.

This woman wasn't going to blindside him a second time. Sipping the tisane, he reseated himself and opened a new interlink...

= = =

Tristan was in his element, and doing one of the things he could do best: wait. The restaurant was one of the finest; only the most elite dined here. And Tanya had made a reservation—for one, as usual. Telling.

The table was in a dim corner, allowing a modicum of privacy. It would be enough.

Soon, the waiter approached, a tall blonde in his wake. She was as alluring as he remembered.

She pulled up short, her mouth dropping open. "What are you doing here?"

He stood, seated her, then reseated himself. "I thought it only right to repay your visit." He poured the chilled champagne. "I ordered the meal already. Here. Enjoy."

She took the stemmed glass with a disconcerted frown. "You're very presumptuous."

"It's your favorite vintage." He lifted his glass. "You have good taste." A sip. He set it down and leaned back. Waiting. Predator stalking his prey.

"My fav— What are you up to?"

"You asked me that once already." Tristan lifted his glass and sipped again. "You've come a long way from the abandoned child you were. Your drive has taken you from the streets to being the president of your Guild. You've let nothing and no one stand in your way." He named several incidents from her past, enough to let her know he had dug deep.

She took a long gulp of champagne and licked her lips. "How did you find my past? I've been very careful to keep it quiet."

The waiter arrived with their meal, and Tristan set the napkin in his lap, waiting for privacy.

As the waiter withdrew, she stared at her plate and murmured, "My favorite food."

"When I research, I do a thorough job."

She bit her lower lip, making her seem vulnerable—and even more sultry. When she looked up, the discomposure was gone. Her assurance, her intelligence shone in her eyes. "Would you, by chance, consider a partnership?"

"What did you have in mind?"

A finger traced the rim of the goblet. "I think partnerships are best when they combine personal and professional interests."

Tristan hesitated, to quiet the thudding in his chest and steady his voice. "I think...I might be interested."

= = =

The door slid shut behind Tristan. Betts sat at her desk, talking into her ear comm, and she didn't look happy. She indicated the sofa with an outstretched hand. Keeping to habit, he sat instead in the chair opposite and waited. His mind wandered to Tanya, and inevitably he compared her to the woman in the room with him, making Betts seem seedier than usual.

"Would you, by chance, consider a partnership?"

His thoughts whirled as he realized how he had changed from a year ago. He'd come here to harass Myers and, inadvertently, the Mordas. He didn't care about mobsters, or the people they controlled and terrorized. People were marks, no more, no less. *What am I doing? This isn't me... Taking down a mob, helping people—how did this happen?*

Somehow, in hooking up with Slap, he'd changed. And he wasn't sure he liked it. And...did he need to destroy the Mordas? He could seize control and—a vision of Tanya swam in front of him—run it with a partner.

He yanked his mind off Tanya and her proposal and listened to Betts' conversation.

"I don't care about your bank's troubles. You owe me that money, and I want it paid now." Her fingernails tapped against the desktop as she listened. "I've held up my end, but you haven't. If you wish, I'll withdraw all my men, and you can provide your own... No. No! Payment now, or the deal's off!" Her fingernail flicked the ear comm, and she swiveled toward Tristan.

Would Tanya look so pitiful when she aged, he thought, while aloud he asked lightly, "Problems?"

She waved her fingers, trying to be nonchalant, but her make-up had set in ridges along her worry lines. It must have been a long day.

"How can those rich slugs have no money? Three of them now have not paid me and blamed their banks. Something about electronic robbery. But I know it's a lie—it's not possible to hack into a bank and steal the money. Their systems are foolproof. Besides, they all have money in more than one bank. They'd still have access to funds."

"Nothing is completely foolproof," Tristan said, "but I agree, the banks are very secure. Especially the out-systems banks." Where various criminal factions hid their money, as did most of the rich in the Three Systems—as it was ill-gotten and, therefore, tax free. Those banks existed to serve those who skirted or shunned the law of the galactic governments.

"Precisely. I imagine you have money in one of them yourself?"

Tristan inclined his head.

"And your bank hasn't been 'robbed,' has it?"

"Not as of this morning. Yours?"

She shook her head. "No. It's a ludicrous claim."

The comm buzzed, and she ticked at the ear piece. "Yes?"

Her eyes widened as she listened, and she shot to her feet. "What?"

Tristan kept his expression one of polite interest, wondering which news she was hearing.

"No one hijacks my shipments! You find who did it. And get our merchandise back. Do you understand me?"

Tristan wished he had a drink to raise in a toast. Cheers to the new leader of what had been Myers' Mercenaries. Their mystery employer had paid them well, but they'd be losing that when their bank was hit. They could, however, resell the wares eventually and make a profit.

Betts tossed the ear comm on the desk. "That's the second shipment I've lost! The first was bungled through—they claim—a clerical error, and this one was stolen!" She glared at Tristan. "And you—I want to know what you're doing." She stood and walked around the desk. "What did Tanya want with you? And you with her?" Her eyes narrowed, and she hissed, "I found out you had dinner with her last night."

And with Betts' spies, if they'd done more than dinner, she'd know it, and he'd have likely gotten a raving visit from her before the night had been over. "She seemed to think I was discriminating against her guild by overlooking it. I assured her I wasn't. I've been examining all the guilds. Fascinating system."

"That's another thing! You've been seen all over the city this week, talking to the merchants, to various leaders of the Guilds— what's going on?"

Very good. Mentioning the guilds diverted her from ranting about Tanya. One crisis averted. "Look, you want me to fight the Separatists. I need certain knowledge for the job. Some of those in the Guilds and Merchants are sympathetic to them."

"I *want* you to kill McCarty!"

"His death alone won't stop the Separatists now. They've found a backbone."

"They never fought before now! Not until he arrived." Betts glared, leaning forward, her hands on the back of the sofa. "Not until you brought him back."

Tristan leaned back with a smile. "Took you long enough to find out."

"Why didn't you tell me he was your friend when I told you I wanted him dead? You've been stringing me along, all this time—"

"Hold on!" Tristan rose and strode to Betts. She flinched, her expression a gratifying one of fear. "He's not my friend. Get that clear. He did me a favor, and I returned it. I was glad to get rid of the hick."

He grabbed her arm, teeth clenched. "*You* renewed the war Lyssel started. And the real leader of the Separatists isn't McCarty, but his father-in-law—Lyssel murdered his daughter and grandson."

Tristan let go and paced, not only to give the impression he was talking out his plan of attack, but to distance himself from her. "Killing my former passenger isn't enough. Ewan Campbell must die too, and a few other key players. McCarty learned a few tricks in his time with me, and I have no doubt he'll be teaching them to the rest."

"So, what are you planning?"

"I'm trying to plot where this...resistance might be attacking next. With a good strike force, we might be able to take out all the leaders in one fell swoop."

"I already have a team working on that." Betts' calculating gaze told Tristan she wasn't totally buying his story. "Perhaps you could join them."

He lifted his eyebrows and smiled. "Perfect."

= = =

Tristan went through the building to where Betts' team was gathered, his mind racing. He got off the lift and leaned against a wall, feeling light-headed. *Run the Mordas with Tanya...*

Slap would never understand or agree with it. He'd fight. To become the new leader of the Mordas, he'd have to sacrifice the cowboy.

"Would you, by chance, consider a partnership?"

Oh, he was. He most certainly was...

The door slid open. Betts' men nodded and murmured greetings. Tristan's mind spun as they brought him to the table. He shook himself; he must concentrate.

"They've been hitting targets closer and closer to Zanti City," Leddy, Betts' minion said. "We've tried to guess where they might hit next. These are the most likely spots."

Tristan peered at the map. Slap was being too predictable, and that made finding him and his allies easy. He sighed. *At least make this a challenge, cowboy!*

"So are you setting up an ambush?"

"Yes, Sir. On all three sites."

Tristan nodded. "Good. Show me the details."

Leddy and his cohorts did, and Tristan had to admit, the plan was solid. "Good job. Nice to know the Mordas isn't all frills and lace nowadays."

One of Leddy's men turned a laugh into a cough. A second said, "Betts might not like such talk."

Tristan swung around to meet the man's eyes. "Was the Mordas run the same under Lyssel?" He let his gaze grow intense. "And do you think you should worry more about Betts—or me?"

The men shifted stances and glanced at each other, but no one answered.

However, Leddy's eyes glinted as he met Tristan's gaze.

= = =

"Mr. McCarty! Mr. McCarty!" The boy rushed into the house where the men were seated, poring over a map.

Slap turned. "Call me Slap, kid. Everyone else does." Except his father-in-law, who always just called him "Son."

"Er, yes, Sir," the boy said, bobbing his head. "I was told to give you this." He held out an ear comm.

If they had been in Zendi Valley or the mountains, the comm wouldn't work, but here in the desert they could use the most modern technology available.

Slap took the tiny device and twisted it into position in his ear. The familiar motion made him almost homesick for ol' Bertha; he'd taken care of most of the communications traffic while with Tristan.

"Yes?" Slap asked.

"The Mordas are planning an ambush on wherever you hit next," whispered a voice he recognized as their spy.

"And how do they know where we'll be attacking?"

"They're guessing, based on your previous raids. They have three places staked out." The spy told him the areas, and Slap muttered an earthy word under his breath; all three were on his list of future targets, the next scheduled for tonight.

"And that's not all."

"Oh?"

"You ever hear of a man named MacCay?"

Slap snorted out loud. One of Tristan's aliases—the one he was known by here, obviously. "Yeah."

"He's working with the Mordas and is helping plan the ambush. I was told to tell you to be very careful. He's extremely dangerous."

A chill swept over Slap. Tristan—working with the Mordas? "Are you sure?"

"Oh, yes. Word is, he's lovers with Betts. He's already killed a mercenary who was threatening her. We think he'll end up being the real power behind the Mordas before it's done."

Slap thanked the spy and took the comm from his ear. He set it on the table, frowning blankly into space. Was Tristan up to something or really now on the other side? Tristan had never really ever indicated Slap was his friend, only someone he owed his life to. And they'd settled that up when he dropped Slap off and left.

He knew what Tristan meant to *him*, but what did Slap mean to Tristan...now?

Slap set his jaw. He didn't dare trust his...*former* friend. But how could he possibly out-think him? Outfight him? Somehow, though, he had to.

He turned to his fellow Separatists. "We have to make new plans..."

Strange Bedfellows, *part four*

"You're sure this place is safe?"

"I'm relying on that inside tip," Slap muttered back. In truth, he wasn't sure. It wouldn't be beyond Tristan to falsify information to draw someone into a trap. Which was why Slap was going to do this one himself; he wouldn't put another life on the line—this was between him and Tristan now.

He ran forward in a crouch, trying to stay in shadows to avoid being seen even in the moonlight.

Hitting the main Security Guild office in the city was bold and totally broke their pattern. One of his men had gone inside with the intent of filing a complaint in order to plant a smoke bomb. It should go off—he glanced at his chrono—about now. That should clear the building of night personnel. Slap had few misgivings about any security men who might be killed; the Security Guild had long ago been eaten up by the Mordas. But he wasn't going to just slaughter them wholesale if he could help it.

In a few minutes, folks began pouring out of the building. *Good job, Jake!* He raised the rocket launcher, and as soon as the flow of people trickled to nothing, he fired.

And again. The building really was on fire now. He ran off before the men could pinpoint his location—he hoped.

Once back with his companions, he grinned. "Let's go."

= = =

Tristan flexed his calf muscle to ease the ache and took a deep breath before hitting the key to enter Betts' office, the feeling of being stalked descending on him.

He found himself comparing that feeling with what he felt with Tanya. Big mistake—he needed to concentrate on the moment, and adding Tanya to his thoughts only further muddled his brain, already overloaded from the night's work. He'd been waiting at the most likely attack site when he'd been informed of the hit on the Security Guild building. This summons dragged him away from a group of men sifting through the debris. Dawn was still an hour away.

"What happened out there? How did those stupid hicks get away with another attack?"

Tristan rubbed his eyes. "They're obviously much smarter than we've given them credit for."

She began raving, and her voice hit a pitch that made something in him snap. He held up a hand. "I need to re-think my plans. Defensive isn't going to work." He turned and hit the pad. The door slid open.

"I'm not finished—" she shrieked.

He kept walking.

= = =

"So, what's going on?" Sean asked.

Slap grinned at his brother-in-law as he took the comm from his ear. "Word is, Betts hasn't stopped screaming since she found out, and MacCay walked out on her. They're making bets on whether she kicks him out before he gets rid of her. They're in chaos, not knowing which way to jump." Sean laughed with him, then Slap added, "And, get this—there's been some sort of bank problems. Some say a collapse, some say embezzlement, some say an electronic bank robbery. But it's frozen the rich, and they're scrambling to recover." *And why does that situation have such a familiar ring to it?* Slap would bet Tristan was behind it...

"Wow. So, what now?"

With a sigh, Slap shook his head. "I'm not sure. If I knew what MacCay was really up to, it would be easy."

"You got to know him pretty well, didn't you? Were you friends?"

Only Shallah's family knew MacCay's name was really Tristan, although everyone knew he was Slap's companion from his jaunt in space. "We...helped each other out of a few scrapes, and yeah, I considered him a friend. But I can't say where his loyalties are." *I wish I could! Tristan, what's going on?*

"Must be hard to wonder if you can still trust a friend..."

Before Slap could answer, Sean's younger brother Aillil ran in, breathless, and handed Slap a data crystal. "This just arrived for you."

Slap plugged it into the reader and his mouth dropped open. He finished and looked up with a smile. "Oh, yeah. Yeah—now I know what to do."

= = =

A soft, insistent sound soaked through the fog. And repeated. And again. Tristan forced his eyes open, realizing someone was at his door. A glance at the chrono told him he'd gotten about an hour's sleep. He tossed back the covers with a sigh.

He tugged on pants, then shuffled unevenly to the door, riffling his fingers through his hair. He squinted at the security vid and groaned aloud. Tanya. Not now—he didn't have the strength to spar or match wits.

He thumbed the comm. "Yes?"

"It's Tanya. May I come in?"

"I've been up all night. Come back in a few hours."

"It's important. I have to see you now."

"I'm really not up to it."

"Please. I have information you need to know."

I'm going to regret this. He keyed her in and slipped into the kitchen. Hot tea would help a little. No, he'd better get coffee. He placed the cup in the dispenser and dialed his preference, sending mental daggers at the machine to hurry it along.

"Oh my," her voice said from behind him. "You weren't kidding. You look like the morning after. And without a night before. What a shame."

"I'm not in the mood." The dispenser light came on, and he picked up the cup, taking a sip before turning around. She was gorgeous, as usual, and looking ready to feast. He sipped again. "What do you need?"

One eyebrow quirked up. "Hm, loaded question. But I'll take pity. I was informed a little while ago that Betts is going paranoid about you. She's making plans and has no intention of letting you in on them." She leaned against the counter and crossed her arms. "I think you're in big trouble."

"That's my concern."

"Not if we're planning a partnership." She eyed him, frowning. "Are we?"

Tristan took another swig before saying, "I think we should discuss what our goals are. We can't be at cross-purposes."

A slow smile spread and she said, "I tell you what—you sit, and I'll fix breakfast. Then we can talk."

= = =

Tristan was impressed with her culinary prowess. He'd returned, dressed and shaved, to find a full meal waiting.

He set down the fork and wiped his mouth. "Somehow, cooking wasn't one of the things I imagined you doing."

Lacquered fingernails tapped the edge of a cup. She smiled across the table. "Don't assume that domesticity is one of the skills I offer in partnership. You looked ready to fall over, so I did you a favor."

"Thank you. Equality is best in a partnership. I would do the same for you."

"Smooth words."

"I only say what I mean."

Her eyes held his for a long moment. "I believe you. You're very direct."

"And you appreciate that."

"In my business, all a woman hears is sweet talk."

"Then let's be frank. What do you want?"

Her laugh rang out, a soft, golden tone. "You do leave yourself open, don't you?"

"We can assume that's a personal want for both of us. Let's keep it to business for now." *By all means.*

"You know my past. I clawed to the top so no one could have control over me. But there's a higher step to reach for. I want it."

"Control of the Mordas."

"What else?"

"So I am a means to an end?"

"You were. At first." She hesitated, settling back in the chair. "But you fascinate me. You...you don't look at me as if I were a woman."

Tristan snorted. "Oh, believe me, I do."

She laughed again. "Good to know, since you hide it so well. But you know what I mean. Intellectually."

210

"I would be a fool to underestimate you."

The door chime sounded. Tristan rose, excusing himself, and checked the security vid. *Oh, great.* He called into the kitchen, "We have company."

"Betts?"

"Astute."

"Expected."

A smile escaped Tristan—he did like this woman. "You ready for this?"

"I've been ready since the first time I heard of you," came her voice. "It's going to be fun seeing what you're made of when caught between two fighting cats."

"Who's direct?"

More laughter.

He keyed Betts in and waited in the foyer.

The leader of the Mordas stormed in, glared at him, looked around, and swept past. Searching for her competition, no doubt. She stopped in the archway to the kitchen. "You! You brassy, street-walking—" Betts' diatribe degraded into cheap vulgarity.

To her credit, Tanya didn't seem affected. She picked up her cup, but before she could take a drink, Betts swatted it from her hand. Coffee splashed on Tanya, and the cup crashed to the floor.

"That's the only way you know how to deal with everything, isn't it?" Tanya's voice was cool, but her eyes glittered. "Blundering in like the cow you are."

Betts' face flushed with rage. She raised a fist, but Tristan grabbed her arm. "You will show no violence to another guest in my home."

She whirled, spat in his face, and contested his parentage. "You've led me on all this time! You're out—d'you hear? Out!"

"So are you." Tristan twisted her wrist and led her to the foyer against her will. When the door slid open, he shoved her outside. The door shut, cutting off her wild raving.

He let out a quick breath, wiped his face, and returned to the kitchen. Tanya was standing at the counter, blotting coffee from her blouse and skirt. She appeared calm until he got close; her hands were shaking ever so slightly.

"Are you all right?"

"The coffee wasn't hot enough to burn."

"I know." He stepped closer, but realized his mistake when she lifted her head and gazed into his eyes. Then she was in his arms, his mouth on hers, and all thoughts fled his mind—

No! He broke the kiss with a gasp. "No," he repeated aloud.

"What? Why? What's the matter?" she whispered.

"Not the right time," he muttered, trying to control his voice—and reactions.

"Why?"

"This...this isn't about fleeting pleasure." It took every bit of will power, but he took her by the shoulders and set her back. "This is about a partnership. It should start slow, earning trust. No short cuts."

"Partnership? She just cut you out. Your 'in' to the Mordas is gone."

"It makes no difference to my plans."

She froze, her blue eyes riveted to his. "How? What *is* it you're scheming?"

"Let's just say, Betts doesn't hold the cards she thinks she does. And mine are better than she could imagine."

"Mm." Her hands traveled up his arms. "Sounds...intriguing. Won't you share any of it with your future partner?"

"As I've been trying to tell you, I don't trust easily. You shouldn't either. We have to earn it. That takes time."

"For a business partnership, yes, I can see your point. But..." Her hands kneaded his shoulders and neck. "...in our personal lives?"

He brushed strands of blonde hair from her face, striving with everything in him to hold back. "To me, they're intertwined. I don't expect you to understand."

"Perhaps I do. But we have to start somewhere, don't we? Can't you consider this an...earnest on my part."

Her lips met his before he could reply.

= = =

Slap's fingers drummed on the table. "This day is getting stranger and stranger..." First the spy's information, then the data crystal, now this...

"What is it, Son?" Ewan asked.

212

"I just got a note from Betts. She says she wants to parlay." Slap chewed his lip. "I don't trust her." *And why no mention of MacCay? Tristan should be in the middle of this. Maybe he's pulling her strings...*

"What are you going to do?"

"I'm going to meet her."

"Just like that?"

Slap shook his head. "Nope. We have to prepare for some kinda trap."

$$= = =$$

"Don't answer it," Tanya murmured as the comm chirped.

"I have to." He unwound her arms from his neck and strode to the security board where he'd left the ear piece. "Yes?"

"I don't know what happened inside your house," Leddy's voice whispered, "but she flew out, taking her guards with her. She's planning something big. I don't know what yet, but she's moving fast, giving orders left and right."

"Keep me informed."

"Will do."

Tristan left the comm in his ear; he was going to need it with him. He turned to Tanya, who was smoothing her blouse.

"Trouble?"

"Betts is up to something. I daresay she started it before she got here. She probably intended on creating a scene, and your presence gave her the perfect excuse. She's been suspicious of my sincerity." He stopped at her amused expression. "For some reason."

"What are we going to do then?"

"You are going back home, and see if you can find out anything through your unique grapevine. I'm going to try other methods of discovering her plans."

"I'd like to be with you."

"Wherever I go, things tend to get lethal. I'd rather have you at a safe distance."

She opened her mouth, but the comm chirped in his ear again. He held up a finger telling her to wait. "Yes?"

"She's sent a truce message to McCarty," Leddy hissed, "saying she wants to talk. But it's an ambush."

"Where and when?"

Leddy told him then closed the connection.

Tristan shrugged on his vest and picked up his PBG. "It's going to get hot. You go home—and watch your back."

She ran to him, hands on his chest, blue eyes wide. "Be careful."

He kissed her long and hard before racing out the door.

= = =

Slap rubbed his hands on the sides of his jeans as he scanned the lot from behind a pile of rusted machinery. The burned-out factory dominated the center of the property, and the blown-up outbuilding littered the far side, but several outbuildings remained. This was where Tristan had killed Lyssel; it wasn't a coincidence that Betts chose it for their meeting.

His men had fanned out around the perimeter, looking for hidden Mordas. He only hoped he'd brought enough. And was Tristan here? How did he fit into this?

A rover approached from the south. Slap squinted upward, a hand covering his eyes against the sun. The vehicle landed, and four Security Guild goons climbed out. He could see movement inside the opaque dome, but no one else exited.

"McCarty, come into the open, alone, then I'll come out," a woman's voice said through a speaker.

"As long as you have guards," Slap called, "I'll keep my men with me."

No answer came from the rover, but the sound of whining engines grew—reminding him of the landing troop shuttles on Eridani. Their men and weapons couldn't compete with armored aircraft—they didn't have the training. Shoot, *Slap* didn't have the training to know where to hit to take one down.

"A trap," he called into his ear comm as he turned and ran. Jake Chandler and Sean flanked him, PBRs up and ready to fire. "It's a trap. Get out!"

Sure enough, three Guard assault vehicles were converging on the area. The ground spatted with weapons' fire, and Slap wove as he raced toward their waiting rover.

No—it could be too easily targeted! He was stuck; this was it. He had to stand and fight, even though it was useless. Good enough; he'd soon be with Shallah and Evan. He spun and whipped out his PBR and fired at the aircraft hovering not far away.

The vehicle exploded. Slap ducked, not only to protect his eyes, but from the falling debris. But—what blew up the craft? Not his PBR.

"Slap, get down," Jake called. A body tackled him, taking him to the ground. He rolled away from whichever of his buddies had knocked him out of harm's way and tried to figure out what was going on.

The sounds of various weapons filled the air as the two remaining craft strafed the ground while jockeying to land. The western-most one landed, and the hatch opened.

Slap needed leverage, something to even the ground. If he could get to the rover, get to Betts, he'd have a hostage.

The one to the south exploded while still in the air. Had to be a rocket launcher. Had to be. But who? Tristan?

Slap rose and ran toward the rover, firing. The guards abandoned their positions. The third craft was hit—a fireball that splattered along the ground. Slap reached the rover—empty. He whirled, looking around in frantic dismay. The retreating guards had turned, their guns trained on him.

"Drop your weapons," one guard called, his voice amplified through the rover's speaker. "Or McCarty dies." He repeated his command, louder.

Slowly, the sounds of fighting ceased. In the ensuing silence, Slap's heart hammered, shame filling him. He'd failed, failed in everything. As a rancher, a husband, a father, a fighter. He didn't mind dying; it was living that was so hard. But to go knowing the Separatists had lost their homes, their lands, their lives—that grieved him.

"Stand down," a familiar voice broadcasted from the rover. "McCarty dies, you all die."

The guard who had spoken spun, looking around. "Who's there?"

215

"We took out your assault vehicles—you're next. Put down your weapons."

"Who—" the guard began, but held his rifle out at arm's length in a gesture of truce.

"I don't know," hissed a guard, "but how'd they get the rover's frequency?"

Another vented an earthy word and tossed his rifle down. Some followed suit, but several of the guards from the Guilder ship didn't move.

"This war is over," Tristan's voice said. "You go tell your leader—any move against the Separatists will have similar results. We repeat, this is *over*: put down your weapons."

Slap grinned as the rest of the guards complied, and he began collecting their guns.

= = =

"What's going on?" Sean asked as the men gathered.

"I don't know, except that MacCay let them think we were behind their aircraft getting blown up and them surrendering. He's trying to get the Mordas to leave us alone. I wish he would have stayed and talked." Slap squinted into the distance in the direction the guards had gone on foot; it wasn't far to Zanti City from here. "I guess he thought we shouldn't be seen together."

"So what do we do now?" Jake asked.

Slap scowled in thought. "I'd say give 'em room. See if they stop or not. MacCay has to be putting pressure on them from the inside. If they come after us again, we pick up where we left off."

A holler to his left made Slap turn, his PBR swinging up. But it was a group of Separatists, and one of them had a young woman with a mop of curly hair by the arm. She twisted and fought like a wildcat, but couldn't get loose. Ewan held up a rocket launcher. "Look what we discovered. She was the one who destroyed their aircraft—with this."

She seemed familiar, and Slap frowned, trying to place her.

"She'd been using a camo-net, but when she turned it off to move, we found her."

Her defiant face changed to one of recognition. "You! You let him leave me there! You—"

216

Oh! The stowaway. "Hey, you're alive, aren't you? Glad you found your way home. And why'd you fire on your own vehicles?"

"*My* vehicles? You think I'm Mordas?"

"Aren't you? I suppose you're not an engineer like you claimed either."

He cut off her scathing reply with a raised hand. "Now, that ain't very ladylike." He put his fists on his hips. "So, you're not Mordas. What are you then? Assuming you'll tell us the truth this time."

"I'm from a Merchant family. We've been driven into the ground by the Mordas. I was trying to sabotage that cargo ship last year when you two stole her. It took me all this time to get back home from that planet you deserted me on."

Slap wanted to grin but having experience with a mother and a wife, didn't think it was safe. He bit his lip. "Well, glad you made it. Sorry we couldn't do better, but we were in a bit of a hurry ourselves."

"Yeah, well..." She shook off the hand of the man who had been holding her. "At least you kept him from spacing me." She whipped a curly lock off her forehead with a grimace. "Thanks. I guess."

Now he did grin. "Welcome. So"—he nodded at the launcher his father-in-law had taken from her—"you're pretty handy with that thing."

"I've learned. I'll get MacCay with it yet."

Slap barely kept his mouth from dropping open. "If you were aiming at him, I'd say your aim is slightly off."

Her hot glare burned all the way from her soul. "I hate them more than him. So I had to make a choice. Besides, I couldn't find where he was hiding. He must have had a camo-net too."

"Y'know," Slap said, taking the rocket launcher from Ewan, "there's better ways of dealing with things than trying to blow people up."

She laughed aloud. "This coming from you?" She grabbed for the weapon, but Slap held it out of reach—easy considering how short she was.

"Give it back!"

"Aw, no. I don't think so. You'll have to find another way to blow up MacCay. But you might want to put it off for a while till he's through messing with the Mordas. I'm not sure what he's up to, but I'd bet it ain't good for them."

"He's working with them."

"Naw, he ain't. No matter what it seems like." Slap scratched his chin. "Look, I did you a favor last year, so will you do me one? Leave him alone for now. All right? Give him time to do whatever he's doing. If you want to kill him afterwards, then, by all means, try."

She crossed her arms, her mouth set.

Slap sighed. "Come on with me. Let's talk."

"You can't make me go anywhere."

Her defiant chin and eyes made Slap chuckle. "How do you figure that? I'm bigger'n you, and I somehow doubt you know enough fancy fighting to take me down. I carried you over my shoulder knocked out, I'll do it while your awake. If that's the way you want this to go."

Her lower lip stuck out, reminding him all over again of last year. "Tears won't work either—grow up. Now, come on."

Two Separatists took her arms and helped her keep pace as they went to their rovers. Slap wished he had a gag—that gal had a mouth. He pulled a little ahead to think.

"Where are we heading to, Son?" Ewan asked, coming up to walk next to Slap. "Back to the valley?"

Slap shook his head. "No. As much as I'd like to, I'd be in a communications blackout there." *Besides, if I go back, I'll see Aylish and be reminded of Shallah that much more.* "I only need one team with me for now though, I think. The rest of you can go back home. There's so much work to do, and it's nearing harvest."

"The boys and I will stay."

"You're needed home, Ewan, so are the boys. I can send word if things heat up again."

His father-in-law's face clouded with worry. "Are you sure, Son?"

"Yeah. I gotta feeling Tristan's got things under control in the city now."

= = =

"It's chaos," the voice on the comm said. "The city has turned into a war zone. There's twenty rumors flying as to who's fighting who and why it started. But the fighting began about the time news came through that the Separatists defeated an attack by the Mordas—good job, by the way. Things have been tight lately, and that news seemed to spark something."

Slap glanced around the room at his men—and the girl, who had quit snarling, finally—as their spy continued.

"The top gossip is that Betts killed MacCay, and his faction is fighting back; MacCay killed Betts, and her men are fighting back; that the rich pulled their money from the Mordas, and the Mordas are fighting *them*; that the Guilds and Merchants are fighting the Mordas—it just goes on and on. I'll let you know anything more I find out."

"Are you all right?" Slap asked.

"Yeah, I got out in all the confusion, but I'm still trying sort out what happened, so I'm not too far away. The city is a mess though: buildings blown up, people shooting at each other in the street. I've never seen anything like it. No one has heard from Betts or MacCay, probably why the rumors of them killing each other are going around. Look, I have to go." The connection ended.

Slap scratched his chin. Tristan was all right; he *had* to be.

Strange Bedfellows, *part five*

Once he saw Slap had things in hand, Tristan headed back toward the city. His comm chirped; it was Leddy.

"Glad you're alive. Word is Betts had you killed."

"What?"

"This place is a war zone. The Guilds and Merchants heard of the Separatists winning that fight against the Mordas, and it sparked them. Betts's men are fighting back. Orders?"

"Don't fight the Guilds and Merchants except in self-defense. Have our men try to join them against Betts' people. Where are you?"

"East side, by the Trophy Theatre. The fighting isn't bad here."

"Good. I'll meet you there."

"Uh, Boss?" Leddy's voice sounded strained. "One of the buildings Betts blew up was the Courtesan Guild. She also took out Tanya Daniels' home. I...thought you should know. I'm sorry."

For a moment, Tristan felt frozen, his mind blank.

"Boss?"

With an effort, Tristan swallowed. "Thanks. I'll be there shortly."

As he neared the city, he saw the smoke rising and allowed himself a bitter moment of realization that he'd been foolish to think he could have someone to take away the loneliness, the sense of futile survival. He shook himself, set his face, and landed in the street near the theatre.

Leddy ran forward, almost cringing. Expecting to be blamed as news-bearer?

"Any idea where Betts could be?" Tristan asked.

"Far from the action, if she's alive. One of the rumors is that you killed her."

Tristan set his jaw. "Not yet. Get in and let's search."

= = =

"You think she's hiding out at Lyssel's old mansion?" Leddy asked as they circled the rover, looking for a likely place to land nearby.

"I'd bet on it. It's on the outskirts and protected. She's safe while her minions fight."

"Getting in will be a challenge." Leddy chuckled. "But I get the feeling you enjoy challenges."

Tristan's lips stretched in a grim smile.

As they approached the property, Leddy spoke again. "I would never want to be the one you're going after in revenge."

"This isn't revenge, it's putting an end to the Mor—" Tristan stopped in realization and veered the rover so quickly they strained against the straps. "Revenge or not, going to the mansion is the move she'd expect." *And I don't allow myself to be manipulated.*

But what now? He had to draw Betts out. She wouldn't let him outdo her, so if he wanted her in the open, he had to be in the open. "Where's the action thickest?"

"Most of it is in the market area where the Guild and Merchant buildings are."

"Then that's our target."

= = =

Slap paced. He couldn't get rid of the notion that he had to go help Tristan. He didn't know why, just a feeling. He looked at the girl, leaning against a wall, arms folded. "You've been listening to all this. You understand now why we need MacCay alive?"

She nodded, her curls flopping.

"I'm going to the city to see if I can help him. You seem to enjoy a fight. Wanna go help him bring the Mordas down?"

"What do you think?"

Slap scowled. "I think if you aim at MacCay, I'll rip your arm off, beat you with it, and stomp on what's left. You got that?"

Jake laughed. "Little girl, you better know he means it. He's like a bear when he fights."

"My name is Addie," she spat. "And I said I wouldn't try to kill MacCay." She brushed a curl off her forehead. "For now, anyway."

Slap glanced at the other men in the room. "This isn't about the Separatists now, just me helping a friend. You don't have to go. Likely, the Mordas won't be bothering you again."

"We're with you, Slap." Jake hefted his PBR. "We've got your back."

The others nodded.

"Then let's go."

= = =

With Addie making five, they had to squeeze into the rover. The men opted to give Addie one of the seats, but none of them could fit into the small empty floor space, so Addie huddled on the floor by his feet; it was either that, or sit in one of the men's laps. Her eyes blazed, and Slap tried to keep from grinning.

"So any idea where all this fighting is going on?" Slap asked as Jake took them toward the city.

"Nope, but I expect we'll find it easy enough. Probably in the city center."

Jake was right. As they neared the Zanti City, smoke rising homed them in on where the action was. They flew lower, and he could see ant-sized bodies massing in the streets, with bright flashes flying in all directions. How would they find Tristan?

"Better land fast before we get too close, or someone could take us out," Slap said.

A *ping* on the underside of the rover emphasized his recommendation, and Jake lost altitude at an alarming rate.

"Don't crash us, you idiot," Addie yelled.

The rover eased its descent but wobbled alarmingly.

"Easy, Jake," Slap said, his stomach flipping. His friend was no Tristan as a pilot. Slap got a flash of appreciation of the skill the dark man had. He made everything he did seem so easy.

Now if he could just *find* him...

With a teeth-rattling jolt, the rover hit the ground in an alley. Slap jumped out and ran toward the noise of battle on the main street. Security Guild guards had made a line and were trying to push the mob back, but were losing ground. Screams, furious yells, and the sounds of weapons' fire filled the air.

Addie ran past, PBR in her hands. He held out his arm as Sean jumped forward to chase her. "Let her go. She wanted to fight Mordas, let her."

"What do we do, Slap?" Jake asked.

The line swelled and receded, bodies grappled, fell to the ground, and more bodies pressed forward.

"Use stunners and target the guards—they're Mordas. I think our Separatist clothes will mark us as not-Mordas. We're behind the guards—we can break their line."

"Stunners? You kidding?"

"Look at the way those folks are moving. If we miss, we hit the good guys, and I druther not drop the wrong people."

"But that's not fair! They don't care who dies. You said we had to fight dirty like them."

Slap gave him a hard look. "Not that dirty."

Jake almost got killed not a minute later. Slap dove into him and rolled him behind a vehicle. "See what I mean? You can't stand up in the street and shoot! Find cover."

Shaking, his clothes and skin ripped from grinding into the pavement, Jake nodded. The others looked grim. Perhaps they truly realized how real this was—life and death, not a game.

Slap fired, ducked, moved from location to location, closer and closer to the line. The others watched and followed suit. He targeted guards in one section and saw the line break, but more guards swept in to try to fill the gap.

Amid all the chaos, he kept looking for Tristan. *Was* he here?

Then he saw him—a dark figure with a PBR running behind the line like a madman, not only firing his PBR, but using the butt on guards' heads, and spinning and taking them out with his fancy fighting. A trail of men followed him, dealing even more damage in his wake.

Slap chuckled out loud and ran toward his friend. He had almost closed the distance when Tristan went down like a sack of potatoes. Slap skidded to a halt in shock, then ran faster, yelling like the banshees in Shallah's family's stories. He couldn't see what took Tristan out, but the dark form wasn't moving. His men were rallying around his body. With shock and horror, Slap saw Addie with them—had she taken Tristan down? He'd kill her! He swore he'd—no, she was standing with his men, defending him as the guards tried to get to Tristan's body.

A mob of guards ran across the street heading straight for Tristan, a gaudily dressed woman in their midst. Betts. She brandished a PBG, her smug, hard smile making Slap want to toss *her.*

Slap aimed the PBR at Betts, but it wouldn't work. He roared and swung the rifle at one guard then another, and finally, just began grabbing and tossing bodies, trying to get to the brassy woman.

He had gotten close when a small figure darted past him. Before anyone could stop her, the girl ducked under a guard and stabbed Betts with an old-fashioned steel knife. The older woman's face froze in pain and shock, and she crumpled to the ground.

Addie didn't move, staring down at the body. Betts' men grabbed her, and Slap lifted one by the throat. The guard released Addie, and Slap threw him like a rag doll, then grabbed the other. Jake and Sean pulled Addie between them. Slap continued fighting.

Slowly, he became aware that no gunfire could be heard. Voices had silenced, and he stopped, looking around. Everyone was staring about with open mouths; Slap saw the reason: the Zendians had arrived.

He didn't care about them, only Tristan. He pushed past people and knelt by his friend. Tristan's face was pale, and his scalp was bloody. He felt for a pulse at his neck and sighed. Alive.

One of the Zendians—Kohn—came over to him. *You must tell them what we say, Young One.*

Slap stood, wiping his wet face. *Make it quick. I have to get help for my friend.*

The Avenger has done his job. The Evil is defeated. Your people must not allow it to grow again.

Slap repeated Kohn's words. The crowd looked confused.

We will retreat from this place, but if need be, we will return and abide here. This will cause destruction of your way of life. As you can see, your weapons and your vehicles—none of your equipment works since our arrival. You can choose a better way, or you can live as the Young One's people do, in simplicity.

Again, Slap interpreted.

"What right do they have to tell us what we can do?" yelled someone.

Kohn turned and swept toward the man who had spoken, his long legs moving smoothly. The man backed up.

This is our planet. The Creator made it for us, and us for it. We have allowed you to live here, but it is our domain. We rule it. Kohn turned to Slap. *You make them understand, Young One.*

Slap told them what Kohn had said, then added, "I don't know what I believe about their god, but I do know they mean it. And you see what they can do. Just by being near our stuff, it quits working. You can call it magic, or what you will, but you see it's real. I'd take their warning seriously."

Slap sighed at Kohn. *I guess this is really over then.*

The alien bent over and touched Tristan's head. *Take the Avenger away, Young One.*

The Zendian spread his arms as if to offer a benediction, then they all moved off.

"Who is the Avenger?"

"What do they mean?"

Questions grew into a swell of voices that Slap couldn't even distinguish—and didn't want to. He knelt again by Tristan and gently picked up the limp form.

"You heard what the Zendians said," he called, looking around. "No more Mordas, what they call 'Evil.' Now get outta my way. I need a doctor."

= = =

Tristan became aware of a pounding head and eyes that hurt from the light even while closed. His nose itched—he wasn't breathing filtered air. This place was hot, and the air dry.

He heard a soft voice humming. With an effort, he opened his eyes to see a rough, wooden ceiling. What the—? Where was he? The room was spartan and primitive. A bureau, a small stand with a large basin and pitcher on top, and the bed he was in—granted the bed felt luxuriously soft. Sunlight streamed in the window, and plain white curtains fluttered in the soft breeze. No wonder his nose itched.

He slowly sat up, willing away the dizziness and increased thudding inside his skull, and touched the bandage on his head. He pushed back the covers with the intent to rise and sighed. Where were his clothes?

225

"Well, hello," a feminine voice said. "How are you feeling?"

Tristan squinted at the doorway. An older woman stood there, smiling.

"I'd feel better if I knew where I was—and where my clothes were."

She laughed. "Slap said you were to the point. Your clothes are in the bureau here." She opened a drawer and took out folded garments.

Tristan noted her gnarled hands as she set the clothes on the bed.

"As for where you are, on my homestead. Slap brought you here to recover. You were injured in the fighting. I'm sure you'll want to be up whether you should or not. Stubborn you are, likely. If you can make it to the kitchen, I've got some soup ready."

He watched her hobble out. Who was this old lady?

He gritted his teeth in an effort to keep from falling over as he got dressed. He managed to find his way out the door without weaving much. A chair was pulled out at the table, and he sank into it.

The woman brought over a bowl of soup and then shuffled over a second time with a plate of sliced, brown bread. Her blue eyes bored into his in a way that made him feel she saw to his soul, yet accepted what was there. "Your first meal should be light. We have food cooking in outside ovens and folks will be bringing their own offerings for the gathering tonight. The whole valley will likely be here."

He ate, wondering if the food really was that good, or if he was merely that hungry. He'd never had bread that had such texture and flavor. And the soup—an extraordinary culinary experience. Was it the fresh, home-grown vegetables perhaps? The spices weren't anything unusual. He couldn't actually taste much other than salt and pepper.

The woman bustled about the kitchen, humming to herself. Something about her seemed familiar. A memory flooded him—an old woman who had shown him kindness when he was very young.

"What's your name?" he found himself asking.

"Folks mostly call me Gran. It'll do."

Slap, Gran—did these people use real names at all?

She turned and met his eyes. "And what's your name?"

Tristan saw the knowing twinkle and nearly smiled. He hadn't felt so drawn to a person since...forever. "Most folks here know me as MacCay."

"Yes, and Slap calls you Tristan. But what's your name?"

A burst of honesty tore from his soul. "I don't have one." *What made me admit that?* He put a hand to his head aching head.

She nodded. "Tristan is good. You have much sorrow in your life."

A flash of anger shot through him. "Why didn't you say, 'but everyone has a name'?"

Her maddening, knowing smile fueled his fury.

"I took you at your word. You wish to tell me how you can not have a name?"

Tristan pushed back the chair and stood. He wanted to storm out, but the room swayed.

"Back to bed for you. By tonight, you'll be more yourself."

Hands pushed him toward the bedroom. He found he couldn't resist.

= = =

The sun no longer cast bright streams of light across the room; he must have slept a long time. It wasn't quite dusk, but close. The faint strains of music could be heard outside.

He rose and went to the kitchen. Gran was there, and Slap. And a few others. A sort of old-fashioned fire lamp provided light in the growing dark.

Slap grinned. "You look like you lost a fight with a couple of sand lizards."

"Thanks." Tristan dropped into a chair, unable to dredge up the effort to find a comeback.

"We won." Slap pushed a cup toward him. The pleasant aroma of coffee rose, although he would have preferred a tisane or even just tea. "The Mordas are broken. Betts is dead—Addie killed her."

"Addie?"

"You remember the stowaway we left on the Separatist planet last year?"

How could Tristan forget? She'd been a wildcat, all claws and a big mouth. He nodded, sipping the hot coffee.

227

"Well, she wasn't Mordas—good thing you didn't space her after all. She's from a merchant family and had been trying to sabotage the ship when we stole her." Slap snickered. "She's fairly riled at you for stranding her. My boys caught her with a rocket launcher after that rendezvous with Betts that went sour."

Tristan set the coffee cup down and leaned back in the chair. *She* was the person who'd been trying to kill him? He rubbed his hand over his mouth, chuckling silently. "So Addie killed Betts. Am I next on her list?"

"I don't think so. She's still not happy with you overall, but the fact you worked so hard to bring the Mordas down earned you some points with her. The fact the Zendians seemed to regard you highly made an impression on her too."

"Zendians?"

"Yeah, they showed up just as you got hurt. They said you did your job and warned everyone not to let the Mordas start up again."

"They said—what? I did my job?"

"Yeah. They call you the Avenger. Well, close enough anyway. It's hard to translate. Avenging Angel, the Avenging One—doesn't matter. You did the job."

Tristan stared at Slap in disbelief. "Have you lost your mind?"

Slap threw back his head and laughed. "Yeah. Didn't you know their god chose you to be the Avenging Angel to stop the Evil?"

His deadliest glare didn't faze Slap. He finally dropped his gaze and sipped the coffee. Who cared what some aliens thought? The fight was over, Slap's people were safe. If only...if only Tanya had lived...

"Everyone would like to meet you, and thank you. We've got a celebration going on outside."

Tristan had no desire to go join some hick party, but what was he to do, being their guest, and—he supposed—guest of honor?

He rose and let them lead him outdoors.

"They, uh...I'm sorry, I gave away the name Tristan. I tried hard not to."

"Doesn't matter."

Bonfires and torches lit the grounds, even though it wasn't dark yet. To one side, local musicians played rustic tunes. Table after table filled with food lined one side by a fence. In the middle of the grassy yard, groups of people danced in sets. The setting sun blazed across the scene, casting long, purple shadows, making it all seem surreal.

He sat on a bench at a wooden table, watching the festivities and putting up with having people introduced to him, wanting to shake his hand. He heard several versions of the end of the riot scene when the Zendians arrived. He was perplexed as to their ability to disable all weapons.

As one farmer and his family moved off, a woman slowly approached, hugging her arms. Her sullen look and curly hair made Addie unmistakable. "I, uh, wanted to say sorry for trying to kill you, and to thank you for stopping the Mordas."

"You got home safely—you must be a resourceful young woman."

"It was hard work, and not fun," she spat, her eyes blazing.

"Sounds like life in general."

Gran came over and set a plate of food in front of him and a large mug. "There you are. Leave him alone, Addie. He's still recovering."

The girl moved off, glaring back over her shoulder. Lots of anger in that one; Tristan wondered at the cause of it.

The cider was sweet, and the food, again, excellent, although simple fare.

With a grunt, Slap flopped down on the bench next to him, with a grin. "Good stuff, huh?"

Tristan managed to quirk his lips into a quick smile. But all he really wanted was to finish eating and return to bed. The firelight swam in front of him.

"You know, you had me worried at first, wondering what you were up to."

"You thought I might be truly joining the Mordas?"

"Yeah. Sorry."

Tristan didn't answer. Nice to know he wasn't the only one to not trust implicitly.

"I realized, though, when I got the credchit for that huge account set up for the Separatists, and the notice I'd been made legal owner of ol' Bertha."

"Giselle."

"Ho, no, no," Slap chortled. "She's mine now. I can call her what I want."

Tristan gave a small snort.

"So why'd you give her to me?"

"If you remember, the Mordas blew up my last ship. I thought she'd be safer with a different owner. And I thought you might be able to use her to schedule independent supply runs for your people."

"Yeah. Good idea. And the money—it's what was stolen from those banks, wasn't it? I don't know if I feel right about that."

"It was stolen from those who obtained their wealth illegally, or, well, at least immorally. Call me Robin Hood."

"Who?"

"Never mind."

The music stopped, and the voices faded into silence. Tristan turned to see why. Shapes approached in the dusk, slowing forming into bipeds, too tall to be human. Their long faces had a wise look, despite the hair covering them. Zendians—they had to be. The aliens came straight to him, and one began speaking.

Slap translated.

"They say they welcome the Avenger, and hope you heal quickly."

"Tell them I'm no Avenger."

Slap spoke haltingly in their tongue and gave their answer: "They say the chosen often don't feel worthy, or realize they are called. But it makes them no less a vessel."

Tristan rubbed his eyes. "I won't argue their beliefs with them."

"Good, cuz it doesn't do any good. They talk of their god as if they really see and hear him."

"Thank them for their concern for my health."

Slap did.

The Zendians bowed to him and began to move off, but Tristan called out, "Wait a minute!"

The aliens stopped.

"Ask them how they incapacitate our devices."

The ensuing conversation was long, and Slap's brow was furrowed as if in deep thought or deep pain—or perhaps with him it amounted to the same thing.

230

"I don't get their answer. I'm sorry. I don't know their language that well, and they're talking in terms I just don't understand."

Gran walked up. "Haven't you figured it out? Any of you? It's their bioelectromagnetic field. It's incredibly powerful."

Twisting to see her face, Tristan asked, "And how do you know this?"

"Never know what knowledge might lurk in the mind of old folks. Now, you need to rest. Aliens or no."

Tristan didn't fight her.

He listened to the music and laughter drifting through the open window, mourning Tanya. With a moan, he rolled over, punched the pillow, and finally fell asleep.

= = =

Slap worried about his friend. The others probably couldn't see it, but something was really bothering him, and not the head wound. And knowing Tristan, he wouldn't talk about it if Slap asked either.

He leaned against the fence, arms folded, watching the square dancing, wondering why he didn't feel a part of this.

Aylish walked up with a shy, tentative smile, holding a ribbon in her hand. Slap stiffened and uncrossed his arms. He had hoped Aylish wouldn't do this, but from the way she always looked at him, he'd feared he'd have to face such a moment—and break her heart.

"Don't, Aylish," he whispered. "I can't."

"But Slap, I am much like Shallah. I love you, and you can learn to love me."

"You look so much like Shallah that it breaks my heart, girl. But I still love her, and still feel married to her. I can't handfast you."

"I can wait. I will wait forever."

The look of raw love in her eyes hurt. "Don't wait one day. Find someone who can love you for you, not because you look like your sister. You're worthy of being loved on your own account."

Tears filled her blue eyes, and Slap wanted to cry with her. This place still held too much sorrow on too many levels. No wonder he didn't feel he belonged here anymore.

She stood, motionless, as if turned into a statue. Finally, she spun and ran off, skirts held up and hair trailing like a white-gold ribbon. Slap took off his hat and ruffled his hair, choking back a sob. He headed for the little cabin and the solace of the dark quiet inside.

= = =

Slap landed the rover in the center of the yard, and wiped his sweaty hands on his jeans.

Ewan came from the barn, and he wasn't smiling. Slap's stomach sank.

"I...I didn't want to hurt her," he said as Ewan got close.

"I know, Son. It's not your fault."

"It's just that...looks or not, she's not Shallah. She's really nothing like her. Shallah..." How could he explain it? "Shallah had fire. Aylish...doesn't."

Ewan chuckled. "Aye. I understand, Son. And she will, in time."

Ewan wasn't angry with him? Slap felt some of the tension drain from his back and neck. A snort drew his attention to the corral. Príncipe trotted around the circumference. With a smile, Slap went over and opened the gate. The horse saw him and ran over, ears perked.

"Wanna ride, boy?"

The stallion tossed his head. With a grin, Slap grabbed his mane and swung up. "I just need to be by myself for a bit."

Ewan nodded. "Go, Son."

With a "Heeyah!" Slap took off. For a long time he and Príncipe just rode, enjoying the freedom, the air, the sense of being alone.

But—

He found himself at the edge of his property. He turned the stallion aside but looked back to the hill overlooking the burned out house. Knowing it was a mistake, he slowly walked Príncipe up to the top.

He dismounted and took a shuddering breath, seeing the graves of his wife and child for the first time, their names engraved on a simple stone:

Sheila and Evan McCarty
Beloved Mother and Son

"Sorry I failed you," he murmured. "Sorry I couldn't beat them." His throat tightened, almost choking him, and he dropped to his knees, the names on the stone blurring. "I can't come back. I know you'd want me to. To build again. Live here. To show they can't win, can't force me away."

Tears streamed down his face. "Sorry I can't be strong. Not now. Maybe someday I can, though. I'll...I'll work on it."

He touched the cold stone and rested his head on his hand, wishing he could hear an answer. After awhile, he rose, wiped his face, and took a deep breath.

Her garden, long gone wild, still showed signs of once having been well-tended, and the wheelbarrow, now rusted, lay tipped over at one end, near where she'd had the tomato plants. The clothesline had survived the fire, but one pole leaned in, looking defeated, the line sagging almost to the ground.

Some of the fencing remained in the west pasture, but a large section was gone, where Lyssel's men had busted it down and chased out his stock. Ewan had done what he could to find and keep the cattle and horses.

Enough. He couldn't stand it anymore. He swung back up on Príncipe and galloped away.

He mused over all that had happened since he left Zenos, and despite the Zendians' help, knew it would take a long time to heal from what had happened on Eridani.

Tristan had come for him then. How could he have doubted whose side he was on in fighting the Mordas? If there was one thing he knew for certain, Tristan was truly his friend. He wanted to be with him, regardless of what Tristan might be up to.

And he had an in—he now owned Bertha. He started back to Ewan's and found his father-in-law working in the yard.

The older man walked over, nodding at the stallion. "He's a beauty a'right. Ready to take him home?"

Slap hesitated, winding his fingers in Príncipe's mane, unable to look at his father-in-law. "I'm...not rebuilding the homestead. I'm not staying. I can't, Ewan. I just can't."

"I was afraid you were going to say that."

"I'll be leaving with Tristan, but I'm not going to be away forever. I have a ship now, and thought, maybe I can do some cargo runs for our people. Visit sometimes." *But not too soon. Not till Aylish has lost that look in her eyes...*

"That sounds good. I just wish I could do something more for you."

"You can." Slap took a deep breath. "Will you keep Príncipe for me?"

A hand settled on his shoulder. "Aye, Son. That I can do."

= = =

Tristan had just wiped the last of the strawberry jam off his plate with the final piece of pancake when Gran said, "You have a visitor."

Tanya stood in the doorway, smiling. With that infuriating knowing look, Gran walked outside.

He rose, his mouth gaping. "You're alive?"

She rushed into his arms, and after a long, glorious, breathless moment of time, he broke the kiss. "Don't take this wrong, but how is it you're alive? Betts blew up the Guild and your home."

"You said to watch my back, and I thought, where would it be safer than if I stayed at your place? Glad I did from what I could find out, which wasn't much. The channels were almost all locked out. I couldn't hack into any of them." She was more amused than accusing, her eyes sparkling. "I'm glad you're all right. I was worried."

Tristan didn't answer, just held her, felt her closeness, smelled her perfume. If this were his place, not Gran's... With regret, he let go and said, "We need to talk."

Tristan poured them both a cup of coffee from the old-fashioned percolator warming on the back of the wood stove, then joined her at the table.

Tanya's eyes narrowed. "So what are your plans here now?"

"When the dust settles, these people will have a chance to choose what they want for the first time. I'm hoping they'll want to turn what's left of the Mordas from a mob into a legitimate government."

"You too? That's all everyone in the city is talking about." Tanya set her cup down. "We've never needed a government on Zenos."

"Exactly why the Mordas so easily took over." Tristan sipped his coffee, wishing it were twice as strong. "Not that there's much difference between the two, but a government gives the people some limited say." *Well, sometimes.*

"And how do you think my guild would fit in with a government?"

"As well as it fits in now. It's a lawful guild, recognized by the Guilds and Merchants."

She paused, looking pensive, then asked, "So...you're planning on becoming the...leader of this government? The king or president or whatever you want to be called?"

"Hell, no!" *What a revolting notion!* "I want no part of it."

Tanya sat back, her eyes snapping. "If you weren't offering me a partnership in running the Mordas or whatever ends up controlling the planet, what were you offering, then?"

A sigh escaped Tristan. "The Zendians won't allow anything like the Mordas to start up again. But...I have many interests off planet. With a partner, I would be willing to expand them." He leaned forward. "You thought of merely controlling the Mordas. But there's much more the galaxy has to offer. That I have to offer."

In the ensuing silence, Tanya's expression wavered between anger and deep thought. Weighing options, Tristan guessed, and wondering how much trust she should put in him. That he could understand. She was starting to comprehend what he had meant by earning trust.

"Off planet..." she murmured.

Tristan held still, barely breathing, hoping she'd decide to give him a chance. If she did, he could prove himself to her. If not, his dreams were as dead as when he'd thought she was.

"I'm...going to have to think this over." She tapped her fingernails on the table. "I've never considered leaving the planet, not sure I could. And with all that's going on, I think I need to be here to protect my guild's interests."

The death knell keened, burying his dreams; she was a dirt-sider, not a spacer. He let his breath out slowly, quietly. Some men might plead, cajole, but her decision had to be hers, so he said nothing.

She waited a moment, then rose, kissed him with a lingering sweetness, and left.

Tristan wondered if Gran kept hard liquor anywhere.

A shadow filled the doorway. Slap's face was one of sad contemplation. "You ready to leave?"

Tristan shook his head. "I'd have to find a ship."

"I happen to own one, and have some leads on cargo, but I need a captain."

Despite his sense of loss, Tristan felt a smile tug at his mouth.

= = =

Tristan walked up the ramp.

"What are those?" Slap nodded his head to the two items Tristan carried.

"Books. I'm finally replenishing my library."

"Don't look quite like any books I've ever seen."

"These aren't the old-fashioned pulp-paper books you're used to." Tristan handed one to the cowboy. "Here. Enjoy."

Slap opened the book, riffled through it, and frowned. "What is this stuff? Not paper. And there's nothing on the pages."

"It's e-paper. Choose a title from the inside cover."

"Huh? How?"

Tristan reached over and ticked a title with his finger. "You should enjoy this book."

Slap turned the page and whistled through his teeth. "This looks like real words on a real page."

"It is real words on a real page. And when you're done with that book, you can choose another. Or bookmark that, and go on to a different novel. Each of these volumes contains several hundred works. But try this one. I think you'll find it a pleasant read."

"*Shane*, huh? I'll let you know." Slap walked off, nose stuck in the book.

Tristan grinned.

www.ingramcontent.com/pod-product-compliance
Lightning Source LLC
Chambersburg PA
CBHW071143170626
46809CB00002B/749